This Broken Heart

JORDAN TRYGG

Welcome to Silver Bend

Silver Bend isn't a real place—not exactly. But it's made up of a patch work of *real* Nebraskan memories. This is a place where people slap their knees when they get up, then follow that up with a "welp"…. (this is the signal that they are ready to leave). This is a place where chili and cinnamon rolls go together and everybody is pretty dang nice.

The characters were born on the page, not inspired by real people, but I did try to capture the heart and the heartache you find in rural America. It's a good place with its own share of downsides, but one thing is for sure… you're always welcome around here.

Now, as to the order in which you oughtta read these books… I wrote them the way farmers live—by the season. Out here, we care less about designations like August and November, March and July… and we care more about planting and harvest (and the seasons in between).

Point being—read the books by the season. If it's summer, read *The Best Kind of Bad*. If it's fall, try *Teach Me How*. They're all related, and you're bound to see the same characters show up again in other books—that's just what small towns are like. Small casts and lots of second acts. But each of these books feature a new couple and can be read as a stand-alone.

Author's Note

Dear Reader,

A quick heads up, this book is not intended for young readers. It contains extra steamy scenes.

Our MMC and FMC are both dealing with recent loss. They say *grief is just love with no place to go*. For those who have loved and lost, this story is for you.

This book is part of a series, but can absolutely be read as a stand-alone.

Thank you for reading *This Broken Heart*.

-JT

"God weaves the pattern in your life, and he has purpose in the black threads he uses.

Perhaps because black makes the colors stand out more clearly."

- Florence
  (my grandmother)

THIS BROKEN HEART

By Jordan Trygg

1.

Erin

I've officially reached a new low.

Quite literally.

I've been telling everyone I'm totally, completely, one hundred percent over Matt.

I even started to convince myself.

And yet, here I am, squatting behind an orange stand in the grocery store.

Not my finest moment, but when I saw Matt come, I panicked.

He's with his new girlfriend.

It's been six months. He's allowed to find someone new.

I just wish she wasn't so skinny.

And beautiful.

She's dressed to kill in a cozy little sweater dress and me? I decided to wear my Betty White t-shirt and sweats today.

Who dresses up to run errands, anyway?

"Erin?" This stealthy bastard snuck up behind me.

I squeeze my eyes shut, hoping he'll just disappear.

Climbing to my feet, I turn around with feigned surprise. "Oh my God, Matt." My enthusiasm is so plastic, so brittle, it could crack down the middle. "What are you doing here?"

He's holding a bag of limes. "We're having a few people over."

The word 'we' hangs between us. It's not 'us' anymore, it's Matt and that other girl. Seeing him doesn't hurt as much as it used to, but it's hard to get over the sting of being dumped.

He tilts his head. "Were you hiding behind the oranges?"

"No." My cheeks color. "I dropped my keys."

"Ah." He bites back a fond smile. "You always were a silly little duck."

Silly duck.

It's hard to understand how I went from being his girlfriend of five years, to being a silly duck.

I mean, I know why we broke up.

Matt laid that all out on the table. And it had nothing to do with ducks or silliness.

He told me he wasn't sexually attracted to me anymore.

Admittedly, the spark had gone out for me, too. I just assumed it was because we were so comfortable with each other.

But seeing him in here with that skinnier, cuter girl…

It's salt in a wound I thought had healed.

I struggle to keep a neutral face. "How's your mom?"

Matt smiles. "She's good. Finally got her roof fixed."

"Oh, that's good. I know she was waiting on that." I take a tiny step backwards. "Well, tell her I say hi."

And that her son is a shallow, superficial piece of shit.

Matt turns around, scanning the produce area. "I was going to introduce you to Lily."

"I'm running late. Maybe next time."

Maybe never, asshole.

I spin on heel and stomp out the entrance, going against traffic, but too pissed to care. Once I'm outside, I feel like I can breathe again.

I climb back into my car and peer up at the grocery store, mentally marking off another place I can never go.

I'd rather drive across town for milk and eggs than run into my ex.

Looking down at my sweats, I realize they had a little stain on the knee. I wish I could say looking haggard like this is an isolated event, but the truth is, I've been moping.

My friends, the ones I didn't lose in the breakup, have noticed. My mom has noticed.

I'm the only one who's been denying it.

Maybe the writing was on the wall for a long time. Five years together and we never took the step of moving in together.

It wasn't perfect, but it was comfortable. We went through a lot together. I can't go five blocks without coming across some corner, some street that dredges up old memories.

It's hard to get over him when I can't get away from him.

I glance up at the grocery store and take a deep breath.

What I need is a change of scenery.

A fresh start in a new town.

Excitement, like I haven't felt in months, kindles in my chest.

It just feels right.

My mom likes to say the universe tries to push us in the right direction. This feels like one of those moments when I'm finally going the right way.

2.

Josh

Trace is making sounds of distress, doing his best to wiggle away.

You'd think I was torturing the poor boy.

I'm just trying to brush his teeth.

But for a four-year-old?

Yeah. Straight torture.

It doesn't help that I have Maven hanging on my legs, demanding to be picked up.

I lean down, sweeping her up in one arm, toothbrush in the other, and deposit her on the counter. She immediately snags the toothpaste and pops it in her mouth.

"No, not for eating, Mavey." I gently tug the tube away, but she starts wailing, anyway. She's two and has very clear ideas of what she wants in this world. Someday, she'll be a boss ass lady. But at the moment? Driving me just a tiny bit nutty.

Meanwhile, Trace has slipped out of my clutches and is sprinting down the hallway.

I sigh, looking down at sweet Maven's tear-stained face. She has my thick, dark hair, but Ana's beautiful, sleepy eyes.

Smoothing my hand through her thick hair, it occurs to me that both children have essentially the same hairstyle.

Overgrown.

I should probably do something about that, but I usually just lean on my mom to know when they need their hair cut.

Kissing her salty cheeks, I lift Maven into my arms and chase after Trace.

He's in Maven's room, which sets her off yet again. She wiggles out of my grip, and I just barely set her on her feet before she's diving towards him. "My room!"

They're playing tug-o-war over a Barbie. It was one of Ana's from when she was a little girl.

Her mother dropped off a whole box full of Ana's toys and the two kids treat them like priceless treasure.

"Trace, drop it." I step forward, dislodging his hand from Barbie's hair. "This is Maven's."

"It's mine, too." Trace whines. "Mommy would have let me play with her toy."

That makes my heart squeeze painfully, because yes, Ana would certainly have let him play with it. If she was still here, maybe she would know what to do, because I sure as hell don't.

I kneel beside him. Wrapping my hand around the back of his head, I tug him in and plant a kiss on his forehead. "Why do you need Barbie, anyway? You've got plenty of toys in your room."

"I need a girl doll." His lower lip is wobbling again.

"Why?"

"Because it's bring your mommy to school day and I don't have a mommy."

Oh, shit. My eyes burn and my throat gets hot. I clear it a few times, trying to think of something to say.

Anything. "You do have a mommy, Trace. She's up in heaven right now, looking down."

He looks up at me, a skeptical look in his eye. "She's really there?"

I nod. "Yes. And she loves you very much."

He balls his hands into fists. "Then why doesn't she come down?"

I swallow hard, wrapping my hand around his narrow shoulder.

"She would want to, bud." My voice gets thick, I have to clear my throat again. "She just can't. I'm so sorry."

The front door opens, and my mom calls out. "Where is everyone?"

My mom will know how to handle this.

I put the toothbrush in Trace's hands. "I'm going to talk to gram real quick. You brush your teeth, okay?"

He nods, already recovering. I'm amazed by his resilience sometimes.

He can dig deep and soldier on when most of the time I feel like I'm barely hanging in there.

My mom smiles at me when I round the corner, her warm brown eyes immediately filling with concern. "What's wrong?" She's a tiny little thing. Barely comes up to my shoulder with heels on. But I can always count on her to be in my corner.

"It's bring your mom to school day."

Her face falls. "Oh, Josh." She glances down the hall. "Did the school give you a head's up about it, at least?"

I shake my head. "If they did, I missed it. They send so many damn emails. I can't keep up with it."

"His teacher should have reached out. How could she be so insensitive?" She takes a deep breath. "You know what? I'll take him."

Relief eases some of the tension from my shoulders. It's not the same as a mommy, but at least he won't be on his own.

"Thanks, mom."

"What about Maven, though?"

I shrug. "She can check cattle with me today."

Mom smiles. "She would love that."

"I bet grandpa would love it, too."

Mom shakes her head. "Sometimes, I wonder if I ought to be jealous."

My dad and Maven have a special relationship. He's a crusty old farmer, incapable of emotion, but when it comes to Mavey, he's a fucking teddy bear.

I don't know what I'd do without my parents.

I thought Ana and I had it all planned out. Our future seemed so sure. So good.

But life has a way of throwing curveballs.

I may not have my Ana anymore, but at least I've got a good team behind me.

3.

Erin

I plop down in the seat across from Darla, my temp coordinator.

Fixing my polka-dotted skirt, I try to work up the energy to look at the list she has prepared for me.

She flips a few more pages on top of the pile. "So, Sunshine Academy wasn't a good fit?"

"A good fit?" I huff a sour laugh. "It was a nightmare."

Darla pauses, tilting her head with an ironic twist of her eyebrow. "A nightmare?"

"Okay, you're right. It wasn't a nightmare." I pause. "I think a better word might be purgatory. A sad, sad daycare with no outdoor space and the lingering scent of tater tots."

Darla laughs, sitting back. "They get good reviews."

"From who? Satan? No. Trust me, Darla. It's not a good place. And the pay was terrible."

Darla nods, allowing that last point. "These childcare centers complain they can't find good help, but they just won't raise their wages." She turns back to her computer, clicking around. "And you're sure you don't want to work here in town? It has to be in another city?"

"If I was going to stay in Lincoln, I'd just keep my current job. The pay isn't great, but at least I know what I'm getting into."

"You're a great candidate." She murmurs. "An associate in Childhood Development, a few years of experience… Have you ever thought about nannying?"

I wrinkle my nose. "Like Mary Poppins?"

Darla slowly scans me from head to toe, saying nothing.

I'm wearing a vintage dress, a beret, and a red scarf.

Okay, Darla. Fair point. Sometimes I do dress like modern day Mary Poppins, but in my opinion, that's so much better than being boring. And the kids love it.

Darla sits back, pointing at her computer. "I have some listings here that pay better than Sunshine Academy, *and* include housing."

"Housing?" I put my hands up, warding off the idea. "As in, I'd be a live-in nanny?"

She shrugs. "You said you wanted a change."

"A change of scenery, Darla. I'm not trying to turn into a governess."

"It would be worth considering. All of my daycare listings are basically duplicates of the one you just interviewed with. I have a ton of nannying jobs available, though. From Omaha to North Platte."

"North Platte's too far. I don't want to move too far away from my mom. She counts on me."

"Okay, not North Platte. Would you be willing to move to a small town, though?"

My first impulse is to say no thanks.

I like shopping. And having takeout delivered. And sufficient internet connection.

But there is something compelling about getting out of the city and trying something completely new.

Darla sits back. "You said you wanted something new. How new are we talking?"

"I'd consider it—just so long as it's not too far away from Lincoln."

She nods, getting a second wind. "I've got a few listings from families in Fremont. Tecumseh. And Norris."

I'm sure I've heard of those towns before, but I never really venture past Omaha and Lincoln. There's not a lot out there. Just lots of cornfields. And cows. So many cows.

Darla shoves a handful of listings in my hands and instructs me to go home and think it over.

I go to lunch instead.

My mom and I always get brunch together on Thursdays at a cute little French bistro downtown. My heart flip-flops uncomfortably as we sit at our usual table.

I'm going to miss being so close to my mom.

Can I really give this up?

All over Matt?

She unfolds her napkin, watching me with sharp, blue eyes. "You're making that face."

"I am not."

She tilts her head, her voice sing-songy. "You are."

"I'm just having second thoughts." I look up at her. "Am I being too hasty?"

She pauses, a hand automatically adjusting her hair. My mom has always fretted about her weight, but to me, she's beautiful. She's like a redheaded Marilyn Monroe.

Smoothing her hand over mine, she gives me an earnest look. "I'm glad you're taking steps forward, Erin. You've been stuck. It's good you're moving on."

"Even if that means leaving Lincoln?"

She winces slightly. "I won't pretend I won't miss you. But this will be good for you. You've never lived anywhere else. You need to get out there. Spread your wings a little."

"What about you?"

"What about me?" She waves her hands dismissively. "I've had my turn, Erin. I had my adventures, found romance. Built a family with your dad. It's your time now. Don't miss your chance because of me."

"I'm not missing anything because of you, mom. I'm happy with the way things are."

"You deserve more." She nods at the job listings lying on the table. "I think it's time you took a chance."

4.

Josh

I grew up with three little sisters.

Which means I got a solid education on the emotional and physical habits of teenaged girls in the wild.

I also turned into a protective caveman. Keeping assholes away from three beautiful girls is a full-time job.

I love my sisters equally, but Reese and I always seemed to get each other. She's got a whip-fast sense of humor and isn't afraid to go out there and get her hands dirty.

We pull up to the farm and start walking towards the house.

I grab and handful of her parka and tug her behind me so I can walk ahead.

She squawks indignantly and hurries to catch up to my side. "Dick."

I glance down at her. "Oh. Didn't see you there."

She's short, like my mom, and has her dark hair and eyes.

"We drove together."

"Did we?"

She laughs, shoving me. "You picked me up from the airport."

"I did?"

She rolls her eyes, glancing back at the cattle feedlot. "God, you forget how pungent the smell is."

I take a deep breath and sigh dramatically. "Smells like money."

"Smells like cow shit."

I grin. "Are you ready to graduate?"

She sighs. "Very. If I never see a textbook again, it will be too soon."

"Got any job prospects lined up?"

"No." She shrugs. "Remind me again why I decided to study community planning? I should have gone into nursing like Parker and Charlie."

"Yeah, but you have a weak stomach and hate needles."

She nods. "There is that."

We walk into the house. This is where the four of us grew up. Where my dad grew up.

It's got a lingering scent of chicken noodle soup, as though the thousands of bowls of soup left their impression on the house.

I laugh when I see what mom has on the stove. She watches me pick up a spoon to stir the soup, pulling Reese into a hug. "How was your flight?"

"Good." Reese answers, allowing mom to plant a kiss on her temple.

I find Maven playing quietly in the living room. She's got Reese's old plastic horses. When she sees me, her face lights up and she's on her feet, reaching for me.

Her love is so unconditional. I hope she's always this excited to see me.

But I have survived living in a house with my sisters, so I know changes will come, eventually.

I scoop Maven up and nuzzle her hair, breathing her in. "Don't ever change, Mavey. Okay? Be my sweet little girl forever."

She plants her hands on either side of my face. "Okay, daddy."

We fall into old routines, setting the table while mom dishes up food.

Everyone has their designated seat, the soup pot, the rolls, everything has its place.

I'm helping Maven eat her soup, blowing on the noodles, when dad clears his throat.

I do a double take when I see his face.

Reese puts her spoon down. "Uh-oh. I know that expression. Someone's in trouble."

My dad laughs, expression softening. He's tall and broad-shouldered. Except for the salt and pepper hair, we've been told we almost look like brothers. "Nobody's in trouble, but your mother and I do have some news."

They look at each other, and he places his hand over hers. My stomach does a little twist. What could it be? A tiny voice whispers that someone is sick. The thought grows in my mind, morphing, twining through my chest until it's almost hard to breathe.

"Your mother and I bought a condo in Florida."

I let out a noisy puff of air. "What?"

Mom looks at me with worried eyes. "And we're downsizing."

Reese sits back. "What?"

Dad laughs. "Do you kids know any other words?"

"What..." I sputter, pausing to gather my thoughts. "You're moving out of the house? This house?"

Mom nods. "It's too big for us, honey. And with the stairs… my knees just can't do them anymore."

Dad starts eating his soup again. "We found a ranch-style house in Clark."

"In Clark?" Reese repeats, incredulous. "You're moving into town? You hate town."

Dad shrugs. "But I do like golfing."

Maven knocks her spoon on the ground and I reach to pick it up, slowly processing their words. "You hardly ever have time to golf."

"I'll have time now." He meets my gaze. "We're retiring."

I glance at mom, who's looking even more worried. "What do you mean, you're retiring? Both of you?"

Mom puts her hand over mine. "We'll give you time to find a replacement for Maven."

It feels like the floor is bottoming out. "You aren't going to look after the kids anymore?"

"Josh…" She hesitates. "I just can't keep up. Maven deserves more. She needs someone who can get down on the floor with her. My body just won't let me."

I sit back, realizing I have three pairs of concerned eyes on me. I've always hated pity.

And after Ana's death, I've had more than my share of it.

It makes me feel weak. And maybe I am, because right now, I'm one thread away from a full-blown panic attack.

5.

Erin

My little sedan bumps down the snow-packed drive. I park next to the big, white house and scan the yard.

There's three industrial-sized sheds. Or maybe they're barns? And a big, two-story house. It looks old. And romantic. Like a stately 19th-century mansion.

A mansion that faces a poop-filled feed lot. I haven't even opened my car door and already the smell is curling up my nostrils.

The feed lot is literally on the other side of the lane. Hundreds of cows line up, snow matted to their backs, eating from a trough along the fence.

I had no idea people lived this close to their livestock. Glancing back at the sheds, I see a few pickups and two men standing next to each other.

Everyone is staring at me.

The guys are staring at me. Even the cows are staring at me.

Feeling a familiar burn in my cheeks, I push the car door open and stumble out.

I didn't dress for this madness. I'm wearing a velvet pinafore dress and a blouse with little birds on it. My shoes are matching velvet pumps. The second my foot hits the ground, dingy snow submerges my shoe.

I pick my way across the lot acting like this is a completely normal event for me. The men watch me with open curiosity.

Not friendliness. Not disinterest, either.

Just open, vaguely hostile, curiosity.

The experience is compounded by the fact that they are both drop-dead gorgeous. They're clearly father and son—tall, well over six feet, and broad-shouldered. Like they played football in high school. In fact, it feels a little like I've been transported back to my teen years. The swing choir nerd pathetically picking her way over to the homecoming king.

I stop in front of him, and he finally remembers to offer me a smile.

I almost shrink back. That million-dollar grin is more than I can handle.

I liked it better when he was looking surly. He's got bottomless brown eyes and expressive dark eyebrows. I feel an absurd impulse to run my fingers along his scruff-covered jaw.

He extends a hand. "You must be Erin Hanley. The agency said you'd be coming today."

I marvel at the way his hand swallows mine up. It's warm and callused. "And you're Josh?"

"Yep." He nods, tipping his head towards the older man. "This is my dad, Keith."

Keith offers his hand but doesn't bother to smile.

An awkward pause descends on us, and I grapple for something to say. "I didn't expect all the cows."

"Cattle." Josh and Keith automatically say. Correcting me.

"Cattle." I reply with a tight smile.

Keith nods. "Hope you like beef. We have it at almost every meal."

"Oh."

Keith tilts his head. "You don't like beef?"

My cheeks color again. "I mean… it's fine, I just don't really…"

Keith's eyebrow flicks up. "Don't tell me you're one of those vegetarians?"

I bite my lip, glancing between the two of them. Is this some sort of yokel interview process? "I'm not a strict vegetarian, no. But I don't eat it on a regular basis."

I could mention that my dad died from heart disease and that my mom struggles with heart health, too.

"My dad was a big prime rib guy." I say, hoping my voice sounds light. "Where are the kids?"

I don't miss the way Josh scans my body, head to toe. Judging from his reaction, or lack thereof, he's not impressed. Oh well, I wasn't dressing for him, I was dressing for the kids. He shrugs, shoving his hands deep in his canvas jacket. "My mom's getting Trace from school. She took Maven with her."

I don't miss the way both men instantly soften at the mention of the toddler's name.

So, they do have an Achille's heel, after all.

I shiver, regretting everything about my clothing choices. My pea coat is too thin, my legs are bare, and my feet are both wet and cold.

So far, my fresh start is turning out to be a false start.

I glance back at my car, wondering if it's too late to make a break for it.

Both men turn and I follow their gaze to see an oversized pickup bouncing down the drive. Josh is striding forward before the truck even stops, his dad right behind him. A tiny woman hops down from behind the steering wheel while both men unbuckle their respective children.

Josh pulls a preschooler out with a big bear growl, spinning him in a circle.

He's a big-eyed little thing, with a solemn expression and dark hair just like his daddy.

And dear God, his daddy. He's absolutely transformed in the presence of his kids. If he was standoffish with me, he's practically glowing with his son. He plants a big kiss on the boy's cheek. I can hear his dad making shockingly accurate horse noises for the little girl as he bounces her.

The love they have for these kids is obvious. And powerful.

As far as I'm concerned, it gives them instant redemption.

6.

Josh

I've made a huge mistake.

Where did they find this girl and who wears a dress and high heels to a farm?

And she's a vegetarian, for Christ's sake. Did this girl even look at the job description?

We're ranchers. What was she thinking?

Trace hooks his arm around my neck, leaning in to whisper. "Who's the lady?"

Difficult question.

My instinct is to send her packing. There's no point in her getting to know the kids because she isn't a good fit. But Trace is tugging at my ear, asking to be put down. I let him slip out of my arms and he scampers across the gravel, offering his hand to Erin like a perfect gentleman. She squats down, a bright smile on those lips.

She seems normal enough, I guess. Her hair is bright, coppery red. She's got a round face and even rounder lips. Like a ripe peach. Bare legs. Generous curves.

Not really my type.

Ana was my type. She was a tomboy. Sporty. Quiet.

This girl's very appearance is loud.

Mom sidles up next to me, a grin stretching her face. "She's just perfect."

I look at her, surprised. "She is?"

Mom nods enthusiastically. "The kids are going to love her. Oh, look. Trace is taking her over to meet Betsy."

Betsy is a black and white heifer. She's thirteen years old. My sisters developed a fondness for her back when they were kids, and my dad never had the heart to send Betsy to the slaughterhouse. She just hangs out in the feedlot. My dad swears she's a good influence on the other cattle.

Trace drags Erin over to the fence, pulling her through a good foot of snow. She follows gamely behind him, though I'm sure those pumps are filling with icy muck.

She leans down to listen while Trace points at the cattle. He says something and the two of them burst out laughing.

A tiny fragment of skepticism flakes away from my heart. I need a nanny. Ana was always adamant about the kids being raised at home. So, a daycare is out of the question. And it's not like nannies are falling from the sky around here.

"Maven is going to love her." Mom says.

We watch Maven point with an imperious, tiny finger. Dad relents, obediently taking her over to meet Erin. Maven lunges out of dad's arms and Erin is ready to catch her. She smiles at my daughter, letting Maven grab a handful of red hair.

"This is what they've been missing, honey."

I glance over at her. "What do you mean?"

"They need a woman in their lives."

I frown. "They've got you."

She shrugs. "I'm not like… that."

She means she's not overly feminine. My mom never messed with makeup and almost always wears blue jeans and a work shirt.

"I like you just the way you are."

Mom grins at me. "You're sweet." She sighs. "But I just can't keep up with them anymore, as much as I want to. This girl is young and full of energy. And look how she's ankle deep in the snow, like it's not a big deal."

"She seems passable." I admit, ignoring mom's raised brow. "I'm just not sure, though."

"Why?"

I shrug, shoving my hands in my pockets. "I don't think I thought this through. She isn't what I pictured."

"What did you picture?"

"I don't know… someone more like you?"

"Old, you mean?"

I laugh, biting my lip. "No… just… she can't *live* with us."

"Why not?"

"Because she's young. People will talk."

"You didn't realize she was young when you hired her?"

I tip my head. I knew she was young. I just didn't expect her to look like… that. Her profile picture reminded me of my cousin Marla. A little frumpy. But in real life, she's more of a bombshell than I expected. If people see her coming and going from my house, if they get word she lives with me, they'll start talking.

They'll say I've finally moved on.

And I would never do that to Ana.

She was the love of my life.

7.

Erin

Josh doesn't live in the big house.

I follow in my little sedan as he drives across the county road to an adjacent property.

He lives in a small ranch-style house with a tidy yard. A tire swing sways in the breeze, a frozen puddle gleaming beneath it.

Trace bounds across the yard, warming me through with his enthusiasm. I'm still not sure about all of this, but Trace is not the problem. It's his dad.

I let Trace take my hand. He's excited to show me his house, tugging me right up behind Josh. Maven leans over her daddy's shoulder, watching me with big, brown eyes.

I try to estimate how tall Josh is. He's got at least a foot on me, which would put him at 6'4" at a minimum.

And despite the lingering smell of feedlot, I catch Josh's scent and it's distinctly manly. Like leather, and cedar, and soap. I never took myself to be a cowboy kind of girl, but those Wranglers make a convincing case.

Leading us inside, he nearly catches me staring.

I turn my gaze to the snug little living room. Josh rubs the back of his neck. He opens his mouth like he wants to say something, but just turns and moves off to the kitchen.

Trace grabs my hand and tows me into the living room. He jumps up on the couch, putting his finger on the glass of a family photo frame. "That's my family. Dad, Mavey, and mom." He turns to look at me, his gaze solemn. "My mom got sick. She's in heaven now."

"I'm so sorry to hear that."

He shrugs, jumping down from the couch. I glance at the portrait again. They're at the lake. Josh and Trace wear matching white shirts. The girls are in white dresses. They're all smiling, Josh included. His wife wasn't pretty in a traditional sense, which is a bit surprising. He seems like the kind of guy who could have whoever he wants. She was tall and slender, with a distinct nose and gorgeous dark eyes.

It doesn't escape my notice that I'm more or less her polar opposite. I don't think I was *ever* that skinny. And despite my best efforts, the straighteners and the hair dye, this curly red hair is here to stay.

Trace doubles back, hanging off the corner of the hallway. "Coming?"

I follow behind Trace while he gives me a tour, showing me his room. Maven's. He demands I step into Josh's room, even though it feels like I'm treading on hallowed ground.

Josh's wife is everywhere. Not just in photos, but in her style. In the warm, comforting home she crafted.

Trace leads me back to the kitchen, where Josh is cooking with Maven on his hip.

"I can help with that."

He glances back at me, expression completely impassive. "It's okay. I got it. The kids are pretty particular about their Mac n Cheese."

"Okay. I'm going to go grab my suitcase, then."

"Oh. Are you staying the night?"

There's a brief pause between the two of us. I doubt myself for a second, but I must have read his job posting a hundred times. Lodging was part of the deal.

Something's off, though. It's like he's changed his mind. I've been on the fence, myself, but if he doesn't want me here, that makes the decision pretty obvious. I open my mouth to tell him exactly that, but Trace interrupts. "You're staying the night?" He says, eyes wide. "Like a slumber party?"

I look at Josh, catching him mid-wince. He tears his gaze away, patting Trace's head. "Go help her with her bags, bud."

Trace leaps out into the snow, boots skidding across the frozen drive. He carries my purse and I drag my suitcase up the steps.

"She's sleeping in my room." Trace calls, carrying my purse down the hall.

Josh steps into the living room, a cheesy spoon in hand. "Put her things in the guest room."

Maven struggles out of his arms. "My room!"

Josh meets my gaze. "There's a guest room by Trace's."

I nod, dragging my suitcase into a small room with an antique bed set. I smooth my hand over the worn quilt, wondering whose hands pieced it together.

Trace careens into the room, pulling Maven behind him. They both clamber onto the bed and start bouncing. He points over my shoulder. "That's your bathroom."

I peek into the bathroom, realizing it's connected to Josh's room.

Awesome. I get to share a bathroom with this guy.

My gaze catches on the counter and I spot a half-empty bottle of perfume. A makeup bag. My first thought is that he must have a girlfriend, but as I step closer, I realize the bottle has a fine sheen of dust on it.

My heart twists in my chest. This was his wife's. He hasn't touched anything, from the looks of it. Like she could just walk in at any minute and pick up where she left off.

It reminds me of my dad. One year isn't long enough to get over the heartbreak, but life moves on. It was incredibly hard to lose my dad the way we did. So suddenly. I can't imagine what it must be like for Josh. Maven slips in behind me, grabbing my legs. I bend down and pick her up. She puts her fingers around my lips and pinches, hard. "Pretty."

I boop her little nose and smile. "You're pretty."

8.

Josh

I couldn't sleep.

The entire night I tossed and turned, thinking about what to do with Erin.

She can't stay, that much is obvious. But that means I have to fire her and that is not something I ever pictured myself doing.

I don't know how other people do it. She already packed up her old life to move here, and now I'm going to tell her she has to go.

The thought has me feeling queasy.

We're sitting at the table, the kids feverishly coloring, while I rehearse what I'm going to say to her.

You're a wonderful person, but I just don't think it's going to work out.

When she steps into the kitchen, it causes such a commotion; I don't get a chance to pull her aside. Trace jumps down from his seat, waving his coloring in the air. "I made you a sign so you know which room is yours."

She squats down so that she's at eye level, studying his drawing with a big smile.

Today, she's wearing some sort of grown-up overalls and a long sleeve shirt. At least she ditched the dress and heels, but her style is a bit kooky. The braids are cute, I guess.

Ruffling Trace's hair, she stands and looks around. "Have you eaten breakfast yet? Can I get something started?"

I push my chair back, climbing to my feet. "We don't eat breakfast."

She tilts her head. "Really? Not even the kids?"

I can't tell if that's genuine surprise or if she's being judgmental. "The kids don't like it."

Maven climbs off her chair, waving her drawing over her head. Trace's enthusiasm is contagious, as always, and Maven wants to give Erin a drawing, too.

Erin scoops her up, studying Maven's scribbles with a serious eye. "Is this for me?"

Maven nods, wrapping her fingers around Erin's braid. "My hair."

She pats her own head, tugging violently on Erin's braid.

Erin just grins. "You want a braid, too?"

Maven nods.

Erin glances at me. "Do you have any hair ties?"

"I know where they are!" Trace shouts, disappearing down the hallway. He sprints back, a brush and one of Ana's hair ties in his hand.

A pang of loss shoots through my chest. I don't like having Ana's stuff disturbed, but it surprises me that Trace knew where to find her things. Ana's been gone for two years, and I've started wondering how much Trace actually remembers. Sometimes, I forget Ana is gone. I'll think of things I want to tell her, only to remember she isn't here anymore. It hurts my heart to think Maven won't remember her at all. But maybe Trace is holding on to more memories than I realized.

Erin sets Maven down on a kitchen chair and starts brushing her hair, starting at the tips and working her way up. I watch, realizing I've been brushing their hair all wrong. I always start at the top, wrestling with the rat's nests that form on the way down. No wonder it gets so tangled.

Maven doesn't have enough hair for a braid, but Erin puts it in a little ponytail on top. "It's a cute little pumpkin stem."

It's amazing how the little rubber band instantly transformed Maven from a feral toddler into a little grown up. As her chubby little hands feel the way her hair is gathered at the top of her head, I can't help but realize how big she's getting.

How did that happen?

Life has been stuck in a holding pattern for me ever since Ana got sick. Maven was just a few months old. Trace was the same age Maven is now. Time is moving on, tearing me in two. Sometimes, I miss Ana so much it overwhelms me. Feeling my throat getting thick again, I cough and scoop Trace up.

He tries to make a case for staying home from preschool. It's Erin's first day. He claims she's going to need him to show her around.

But his teacher is a stickler and would not approve. After a bit of a debate, he lets me drag him to the truck.

He sits in his car seat, watching the frozen fields blur by. "Is Erin going to be home when I get back from school?"

I'm not sure. If I fire her first, she'll be long gone. "Maybe."

"Is she going to live with us now?"

"We'll see, bud."

He's quiet for a bit. "I hope she does."

"You do?"

I glance at him in the rearview. He nods. "We need a mom in our house."

I wince. "She wouldn't be your mom, bud. You already have a mom."

"Not around, though." Trace says. "I like her. She's pretty."

"Is she?"

He nods. "Like a Disney princess. Do you think she sings?"

I laugh. "I'm not sure, bud."

"I hope she does. Princesses are supposed to sing."

9.

Erin

I lay Maven down in her crib and slowly back away. Leaving the door open a crack, I pad back through the house, looking for my phone.

Ana's ghost is everywhere I look. There are a few still frames, places Josh has left completely undisturbed. Ana's toiletries.

Her baking supplies.

She must have been a crafter. There's a desk in the corner of my room with a stamp set spread out, as though she just walked away for a moment.

The love those two must have shared is palpable. Heartache hangs in the air.

It's clear that there isn't room for another woman in this house. Even if she is just the hired help. Josh isn't very good at hiding the emotions that flit across that handsome face of his.

He regrets hiring me. It's obvious.

I'm having regrets, myself.

What made me think I could be a country girl? I was picturing bullfrogs and summer sunsets. I obviously forgot which state we live in. This is a frozen wasteland devoid of coffee shops and Targets. And it's a solid hour from my mom's place.

I find my phone by the coffeemaker and call mom right away.

She picks up on the third ring. "How's it going?"

"Terrible."

She laughs. "Oh, Erin. Come on."

"It is. I swear to God, mom. There's a cow farm across the street."

"A cow farm? You mean a feed lot?"

"Whatever. It smells like bullshit."

"Erin."

"My apologies. It smells like cow shit."

She laughs again. "I hope there aren't any little ears nearby."

I lean up against the counter. "One of them is at school, the other is taking a nap."

"What are they like?"

"The kids are amazing. Trace, the little boy, is so sweet and energetic. And Maven is so lovable."

"And their parents?"

"It's just the dad. Their mom passed away."

Mom sighs. "Oh, that's so terrible."

I glance at the Christmas card taped to the fridge. White sand and turquoise water fill the frame. They snuggle together, happy and totally unaware that their lives were about to get upended.

"It's a little like living with her ghost, mom. I don't think Josh has moved on."

"I don't think you ever move on, Erin. I still miss Gary every single day."

"I miss him, too."

She pauses. "So, other than that, how's it going?"

"He won't let me do anything. He's treating me like a guest." I pause, looking around the tidy little kitchen. "Honestly? I think he's still deciding if he wants to keep me or not."

"Are you sure? Everyone loves you, Erin. You're so happy-go-lucky."

I shrug. "Something's up. I'm not sure I want to stay, anyway."

"What's he like?"

"Josh?"

"Is he handsome?"

Oh, yes. Very. "He's okay."

"I think you just need to give it some time."

I frown. "You don't want me to come back?"

"I'd love it if you came back, but you need this, Erin. You've been down in the dumps ever since you and Matt split up."

"You make me sound like a lovesick puppy."

"I think you're a creature of habit. This move is going to stretch you, but it's going to be good, Erin. I can feel it. You just have to be patient."

Maven starts fussing in the other room. "I got to go. Maven's waking up."

"Okay. Good luck, honey. Love you."

"Love you, too."

Setting my phone aside, I go in search of Maven.

Her room is light and airy with a woodland theme. I can almost picture Ana picking out every detail. Maven stands in her crib, face grumpy and tear-stained. I pick her up and she pulls back, looking up at my face. Now that it's just the two of us, she isn't so sure about me.

That's to be expected. I'm a stranger to her.

"How about we go make some play dough?"

She nods, slinging an arm around my neck.

I don't know how long I'm going to be working for them, but as long as I'm here, Maven is pretty good company.

10.

Josh

I step inside, kicking the snows from my boots before slipping them off. For a second, I think I must have left the radio on, but then I realize I don't have a radio anymore.

That's Erin's voice, clear and pretty, spiraling out from the kitchen.

Guess that answers Trace's question.

She sings beautifully.

I pause in the living room, noticing the new additions to the buffet. Fingerpaint dries on a piece of paper, Maven's tiny hands imprinted all over it. I lift a plastic container and pull the lid off. I shove my finger into the soft, red play dough. How did they find time to paint and make homemade play dough?

I step into the kitchen without either girl noticing. Maven has a chair pulled up and the two of them are chopping vegetables. Maven has a play knife and is making a mess of a tomato, but she's burbling away, happy as can be.

I tilt my head, taking Erin in from head to toe.

I study the way soft tendrils of hair have escaped her braid. Despite the shapeless overalls, it's plain to see that this woman has the classic hourglass figure. I've never been into buxom ladies, not like my friends are. Ana and I were together from puberty on, so my taste crystalized around her exact form.

But I have to admit, Erin's soft curves have their own appeal. I find myself wondering what she would feel like pressed up against my hips.

My brain supplies me with a very visceral depiction and my cock stirs against my jeans. It shocks me a little. I haven't really thought about sex for two years. Sure, I jerk off in the shower now and then, but no woman has caught my attention. No one can stack up to Ana. But Erin's stoking old feelings to life, things I haven't felt for a long, long time.

As though sensing I'm thinking about her, Erin turns to look at me. She yelps in surprise, pressing a hand to her chest. "You scared me."

A bright laugh spills from those soft lips. I'm picturing them wrapped around my shaft, and then I'm frowning at her.

It's not her fault, it's mine, but I can't help but feel like she's tempting me in some way.

I immediately shift my focus to Maven. Erin hands her a baby carrot.

"She can't eat those." I automatically say.

Maven accepts the carrot, chomping away on it.

Erin's gaze flicks back to me. "Is she allergic?"

I shake my head. "No. I didn't think she liked them."

Erin shrugs. "I made salad, if you're interested."

I was just going to grab a frozen burrito, but Erin's salad looks infinitely more appealing.

It's strange seeing the kitchen being put to actual use. I pretty much stick to the microwave, occasionally using the stove to make noodles for the kids.

Ana's mixing bowl sits by the sink, along with the frosting dye she used to make the kids' birthday cakes. Baking was one of Ana's things. I left all of her tools, even the flour and sugar, untouched because I didn't have the heart to move them. But Erin pawed through it all, disturbing precious memories.

It makes me feel a little panicky.

She follows my gaze, misreading my expression. "We made a bit of a mess. I'll clean up later when Maven's napping."

I scrub a hand through my hair. "Those were Ana's things. I haven't really touched them."

"Oh." She looks back at the mess, cheeks coloring.

I feel a little guilty, which then makes me feel defensive. "I would have cleaned it out, eventually."

"Of course."

I can't tell what she's thinking. Those eyes are blue. Very, very blue. They threaten to pull me in and take me under.

I don't want to abandon Ana. It was a mistake bringing another woman into her house. She's disturbing Ana's memory, distracting me. She needs to go.

The sooner the better.

I'm forming the words on my tongue when there's a giant crash by the sink.

And Maven starts wailing.

11.

Erin

Maven slips off the chair, grabbing the cutting board on her way down. Vegetables topple down on top of her, the board catching her on the side of the head. I kneel down by her, checking that she isn't seriously injured, but then Josh is swooping in.

He bundles her up, holding her protectively to his chest. He snuggles her under his jaw, pacing anxiously, shushing her rhythmically. When she stops crying, he peers down at the goose egg forming on her forehead, before turning to me with anger in those brown eyes. "This is why I don't let her climb on furniture."

I shrug helplessly. "She wanted to help."

I step closer to check on the bump on her head, but he spins her away. He may as well have slapped me. The look in his eyes says it all.

"What if the knife had fallen on her?" he asks.

I glance at the knife resting safely behind the sink. "I would never leave a knife where she can reach it."

He huffs a breath, angling his chin so that he can kiss her head.

Even when he's angry, or maybe *because* he's angry, he's still hot.

I'm distracted by the way his nostrils flare, so I don't initially process the words that come out of his mouth.

"I don't think this is working out."

I look up at him. "What?"

"I'm sorry. I thought we were ready to hire a nanny, but I don't think we are."

I look around at the mess. Chopped broccoli and carrots litter the floor.

"I could tell."

He tilts his head, his big hands easily cradling Maven's tiny body.

"You haven't really been letting me help."

His jaw tenses. "I don't know what you mean."

"Supper last night? Putting the kids to bed? I could sense you're not ready to move on." Oh, crap. Why would I say that? Maybe it's the fact that I already have one foot out the door, but I'm not filtering myself the way I normally would.

"Move on?" He repeats the words, looking adorably befuddled. But then he's frowning, which is still adorable, but spells trouble for me. "You make it sound like we're stuck."

I hold up my hands. "I didn't mean it like that. I understand. That's all I'm trying to say."

"You understand?" He snaps. "Have you lost a spouse, too?"

"No, I…"

"Then you can hardly appreciate what it's like." He shakes his head. "You know what? I'm not getting into it. I think it's pretty clear you need to leave."

I stare at him, my cheeks catching fire. Things have taken a spectacularly sharp dive, and that's even by my standards.

"Okay, yeah. I agree. This hasn't been a good fit."

He clutches Maven in his arms.

"Do you want me to finish out the day?"

He shakes his head. "It's fine. I've got it."

Wow. Okay. My eyes start to burn, tears threaten to make a humiliating appearance. I bend down, hiding my bloodshot eyes, by gathering up the spilled veggies. There's nothing I want to do more than run from this house, but then I think of Trace.

He said he had a secret to show me when he got home from school. I don't want to throw myself at Josh's mercy, but I'd feel terrible about disappearing on Trace like I didn't care about him.

Because the truth is, I'm already way more attached to these kids than I expected to be.

"Can I hang around until Trace gets home from school? He had something he wanted to show me… I'd feel bad if I weren't here…"

I chance a look and read surprise on Josh's features. "Yeah. I guess. If you want to."

Maven turns, demanding to be set down. Josh relents and she scampers over, using her chubby fingers to push vegetables together. "I help."

Josh hesitates. "If you're okay watching her, I guess I'll head back out?"

"That's fine." Get out of here, you grumpy bastard. I peer up at him, feelings of guilt catching up to my stinging ego. "I'm sorry I let her fall."

He rubs the back of his neck. "Accidents happen."

"I know. But not on my watch. We'll be more careful."

12.

Josh

I stare into Betsy's big, doe eyes and try to understand what just happened.

She's the one who let Maven fall, around knives, no less. And somehow, I'm the one who feels like the bad guy.

The tears might have something to do with it.

I've never been very good with tears.

My sisters know this well and have weaponized the fact.

Erin was the one who messed up, but I take no pleasure in making her feel bad.

In fact, I feel awful about it.

Betsy bats her long eyelashes at me, and I scratch behind her jaw. She twitches her tail, ignoring the rest of the cattle milling about.

Of course, dad immediately sensed something was wrong when I came stomping back out of the house without lunch.

It's not a surprise when I spot mom's truck barreling down the drive. There's no secrets between those two.

She hops down from the cab, fixing me with her patented 'mom' look. Part frustration. Part disappointment. It gets me every time.

I lean against the fence, watching her pick her way over to me. She stops, planting her hands on her hips. "What's this I hear about you firing that poor girl?"

"I didn't fire her."

Mom tilts her head. "You didn't?"

"No. We just both agreed it wasn't a good fit."

"A good fit?" Mom throws her hands up. "Josh, if you two were any better of a fit, you'd be on top of each other."

That calls to mind a very visual image, one that I'm not prepared to think about with my mom standing right here. "I'm not ready to bring another person into the house."

Mom's gaze softens. "I know, Josh. I miss Ana, too. But she wouldn't want you living like this."

A small kernel of anger sparks to life in my gut. "Living like what?"

"Stuck." Mom says, her voice gentle. "Either way, those two kids of yours need a woman in their life. Since you're not in a hurry to start dating again…"

"That's not happening."

She tips her head. "I know, but all the more reason to give Erin a fair shot."

"She let Maven fall."

"Did she push her?"

I huff a breath. "No."

"Your dad let Maven fall off a hay bale last week."

My eyebrows fly up. "He did what?"

"We didn't mention it because you're so overprotective."

"I am not."

"You are. You'd wrap those kids in bubble wrap if you could get away with it." Mom steps closer. "Maven's a precocious girl. She likes to explore. Climbing and falling go hand in hand. But that doesn't mean you should stop her from trying."

I get the feeling she's not just talking about Maven anymore. Mom and dad have been incredibly patient with me, but they're worried. It's been two years and I think they just want to see me get on with my life.

The fact is, I'll never get on with it. Ana took part of my heart with her. I'm happy with the life we had together. I don't need more.

But the kids do. They deserve so much more, and I can't raise them inside a mausoleum.

Even I can see that.

Mom has a sharp eye. She spots the crack in my defense and drives the point home. "I want you to march back in there and apologize. Get on your knees if you have to."

"A little strong, don't you think?"

"No, I do not think. That girl is perfect for this family, and you are not going to let her slip away. Not without putting up a good fight first."

She literally pushes me towards the house.

I step inside but hesitate by the door.

What the hell am I supposed to say to the poor girl?

Her voice travels back to me. She's singing some soft song.

She sounds… sad.

No surprise there. Some surly farmer was just a complete dick to her.

I stop in the kitchen doorway, watching her work at the sink. She's scrubbing Ana's mixing bowl, handling it like it's made from spun glass.

I'm almost hyper aware of her now.

Her scent fills the kitchen, like peaches and cream.

She seems to sense me watching her, turning to look at me with wary eyes.

I run a hand through my hair. "I think we should talk."

13.

Erin

I don't want to talk to him.

We already talked.

What's left to say?

But I'm a people pleaser and if Josh wants to talk, we'll talk.

I dry my hands off and follow him into the dining room. There's a wooden panel on the wall that says 'family' and is surrounded by family photos. Vacations they took. Ana in a beautiful lace wedding gown. The rest of the family is in that picture, too, but she steals the spotlight looking heartbreakingly beautiful.

I sit at the table, watching him lower that big body into a chair across from me. Still cute, even when he's being a dick. "Where's Maven?"

"Napping."

He nods, resting his hands on the table in front of him. "I should apologize."

My eyebrows shoot up.

He glances at my face and winces. "I overreacted. I'm sorry."

I shrug. "Maven fell. It was an understandable reaction."

He rubs his neck, a nervous habit. "I'm told I'm a little overprotective."

"You care about them. That's not a bad thing."

He studies my face. I want to shrink under his scrutiny but hold my chin high.

"I'm having a hard time adjusting." He admits. "I guess I leaned on my parents pretty hard these last two years. And now that they're retiring, it just throws me back to square one." He forces himself to meet my gaze. "We have a pretty small circle. It's hard letting someone else in. Especially having someone else in the house."

I shrug. "Your nanny doesn't have to be a live-in. They could find an apartment in town."

He shakes his head. "We're going to start calving soon and that means sometimes I'm out all night. I need someone here when I'm not."

"Okay. So, what's the answer?"

"The answer is that I need to get over my hang-ups. If you're willing to overlook that little tantrum back there, I was wondering if we could try again?"

An apology.

Huh.

I hardly know how to respond. Matt was never one to admit he'd done something wrong. He'd usually just crack a joke to get me laughing.

I find an apology from this handsome man to be rather disarming. I sigh. "Sounds good to me, Josh. Let's give it another try."

Josh's mom, Lisa, drops Trace off later that afternoon. She looks happy, and maybe even a little relieved, to see me.

Trace's secret was squirreled away in an old shoe box. He shows it to me like it's the best thing ever.

An owl pellet.

He puts it on the kitchen table and dissects it while I prepare dinner. I hear Josh step inside. He's so quiet when he does that. I have to familiarize myself with the barely audible sounds, otherwise this man is going to scare me right out of my skin one of these days.

He appears in the kitchen with a sleepy Maven in his arms.

I glance up at him, pausing at the stove. "Was she awake?"

He shrugs, smiling sheepishly when she snuggles under his jaw. "I just went in to look. I might have woken her up."

He's a bear with everyone else, but that little girl just melts his heart.

Throwing a quick supper together, I set the table and retreat to the kitchen to let them eat in peace, but Trace drags me back into the dining room so we can all 'eat as a family'. Shooting Josh a wary look, I reluctantly sink into my chair.

I introduce the family to spaghetti aglio e olio and you would think I discovered a new continent.

It's a simple recipe. Oil and garlic. But the kids eat it up like mana from heaven.

Josh watches Trace slurp the last noodle from his plate with awe. "I can never get this kid to eat."

Apparently, the way to this man's heart is through his stomach, because I've earned enough trust from him to brush the kids' teeth.

He still puts them to bed, but I would call it a small step in the right direction.

The next morning, I decide to double down on the whole comfort food approach. I set my alarm for an ungodly early time. Creeping into the kitchen, I'm relieved to find that I guessed correctly. I'm the only one who's awake.

I'm not usually a morning person, but it's kind of nice to get so much done so early in the day.

There's a coffee cake in the oven and I've just started the coffeepot when Josh ambles into the kitchen. He's yawning, one hand sleepily rubbing his stomach, but we both freeze when we see each other.

He obviously wasn't expecting to find anyone in the kitchen.

And I was not prepared to see Josh Olson in nothing but a pair of gray sweatpants.

Damn.

I already thought he was pretty handsome. I did not need to know how deep that rabbit hole went. The image burns itself into the back of my eyelids. I turn quickly, but it's already done. I can't unsee what I saw.

Sexy, tousled bedhead.

And abs. Abs on top of abs.

Good lord. I know that can't be just from feeding the cattle. This man must work out.

A lot.

But the part that is etched into my retinas, the part that will probably haunt me for the rest of time, is the situation south of that very tempting stomach.

He's sporting a morning wood.

Not a full staff, or anything, more of a little chubby. A hint of what lies beneath those sweats.

And judging by the general length, little wouldn't be the right word.

I realize I turned away from him without saying a word. Forcing what I hope to be a neutral expression on my face, I turn back, moving towards the coffee pot.

He's still rooted to the spot, a mesmerizing bloom of color on his cheekbones. It's almost good enough to distract from that very generous package down below.

Almost.

My eyes flicking downward, as though my brain needed to confirm we didn't hallucinate.

Yep, still there.

Still impressive.

14.

Josh

Well, this is awkward.

I stumbled into the kitchen with the intention of drinking a cup of coffee before the rest of the house woke up.

I did not expect to find Erin, bright-eyed and bushy-tailed.

And is that… cake?

She's already dressed and ready for the day in jeans and a pink t-shirt. Her curly hair has been bullied into a topknot. She wears a handkerchief headband. It's looks cute. The kids are going to love it.

But she's looking at me with horror on her face.

No, I don't run around in public in just my sweats, but this is my house. Am I going to have to start each morning fully dressed and raring to go?

Judging by the look on her face? Yes. That's exactly what I have to do.

A little judgmental for a girl with Sesame Street plastered across her chest, but what do I know?

I'm about to turn around when she thrusts a mug of coffee into my hands. "Kids sleep okay?"

I accept the mug, staring down at its dark contents. "Yeah. Maven only woke up once."

"I can always grab her when she does that." Erin offers.

"I don't mind." I sip the coffee, stifling a happy groan. "Is this the coffee from my cupboard?"

She grins. "Yes."

I stare down at it. "How?"

"Is that a good how or a bad how?"

I take another sip, nodding. "Good. Did you add something?"

"A pinch of salt. Helps even out the bitterness." A timer goes off and she bends down, pulling a coffee cake out of the oven. Steam swirls out of the oven, filling the kitchen with the scent of cinnamon and butter. I'm instantly transported back to my mom's kitchen on Christmas day. Except my mom's kitchen didn't have a buxom redhead bending over to pull things out of the oven.

Trace wanders in, rubbing his eyes. "I smell doughnuts."

"Close." Erin says, grinning at him. "It's coffee cake."

"Cake for breakfast?" He lights up, looking over at me. "Is that even allowed?"

His expression warms my heart. I grin at him. "You bet."

Erin gets the kids to finish their breakfast and drink their milk. My kids usually pick at their food like birds. I gave up trying to make them finish their food long ago. She makes it look easy.

When they're done eating, they all disappear down the hallway, reappearing in record time, dressed and pressed. Trace wears his favorite sweater and khakis. Maven is clearly proud of the sweater dress Erin put her in. She's got little pigtails that dad is going to lose his ever-loving-mind over. Even Trace has his hair gelled.

I don't think he looked that good on picture day.

They all move into the kitchen, where Erin starts throwing together a cold lunch.

"Not doing hot lunch today, bud?" I ask, watching her pull out a loaf of bread.

"Nope. It's fish sticks."

"You like fish sticks, right?"

He makes a face. "No. They're disgusting."

I make him fish sticks regularly. And this kid has always eaten them. Makes me wonder how much of their light appetite has to do with my cooking.

I take Trace to school, but the whole fish sticks thing is really bothering me. I glance back at him in the rearview. "You really don't like fish?"

"Fish is fine." He shrugs. "Fish *sticks* are the worst."

"Why didn't you tell me, bud?"

He shrugs.

"You can tell me if I make you something you don't like."

He turns to look out the window. "It's okay, dad. I know you're trying."

"You do?"

He glances at me. "Yeah. You're doing your best. I don't mind if we have to eat fish sticks sometimes."

I drop him off and he gives me a bigger hug than usual. But I'm still thinking about it hours later. I'm supposed to be separating cattle, but my mind is elsewhere. How many things was I coming up short on?

How did Erin get this nugget of information out of him? He was too afraid to tell me and that's just not sitting well.

A shriek interrupts my thoughts. My head whips around, looking for danger, but my gaze lands on little Maven. She's bundled up in her snowsuit and winter coat. She looks like a swaddled starfish, walking around with stiff limbs and a huge smile on her face.

Erin chases behind her, heedless of the fact that she's wearing sneakers and jeans. She scoops Maven up with a mighty roar, eliciting peals of laughter.

I glance back at the cattle, wondering how they're taking all this ruckus, but they're implacable as ever.

Mom never had that kind of energy. She loves Maven, that's undeniable, but she just doesn't have the stamina to keep up with Maven.

For the first time, my mom's words are really starting to sink in.

The kids really did need a change of pace. I glance at Erin, careful not to get caught staring.

She's loud and energetic and… pretty. My brain supplies me with an instant replay of the naughty dream I had about Erin the night before.

I remind myself I am not trying to get in this woman's pants, no matter how cute she is.

This is especially true since the kids love her so much. I need to make sure I don't do anything stupid that might jeopardize that.

15.

Erin

Maven's completely enamored with the snow, that is, until she spots daddy.

Then she's a single-minded machine.

Relenting, I put her on my shoulders and carry her over to Josh.

He spots us almost immediately, making me wonder if he was watching us the whole time.

Probably checking to make sure I don't let her fall again. His gaze travels up to Maven's face, and I realize maybe he doesn't like her being quite so high. I ease her off my head, letting her reach out to Josh.

He takes her while I dust the snow and muck off my jacket. I have two maven-shaped boot prints on my chest. I scrub at the marks, realizing both Maven and Josh are watching.

A third creature is watching, too.

"That cow is staring."

He glances back, grinning at the ginormous cow poking its head through the fence. "They all stare." He grins. "But this one is a friend of mine. Betsy, meet Erin. Erin, meet Betsy."

I walk forward, trying to act like the giant animal isn't freaking me out. When Maven puts her little gloved hand on Betsy's head, I decide to woman up and do the same.

She leans her furry cheek into my hand and I pull my glove off so I can scratch under her jaw. "Look at these eyelashes." I murmur. A horrible thought occurs to me. "Will you eat her?"

He laughs. "No. Not Betsy. She'd probably be pretty tough by now."

"Why's that?"

"She's thirteen. Elderly, by cow standards."

I tilt my head. "Why haven't you…"

"Butchered her yet?" He chuckles again. "You haven't met my sisters yet. They fell in love with her and long story short, she was granted clemency."

"That's sweet."

He tilts his head. "You really don't eat meat?"

I shrug. "Sometimes I do."

"So, it's not an animal lover thing?"

My lips quirk up. "That's a fringe benefit." I glance at him, trying to decide how much I should share with him. "Heart disease runs in my family. After my dad's heart attack, I decided to clean up my diet."

"How's your dad now?"

I look away, tucking my hand back into my glove. "He passed away."

"Oh, shit. I'm sorry." He takes his hat off and scrubs a hand through his hair. "When did he pass?"

"Last year."

"Recently, then."

I pause, meeting his gaze. He has got to be the first person I've come across who calls one year 'recent'. Matt was sick of hearing about it about three months after the funeral.

Maybe that should have been my first sign that he wasn't the right guy for me.

I clear my throat, trying to rid myself of the funk threatening to descend on my shoulders. "What are you up to today?"

"Got to give these ladies a round of shots."

I glance out at the full feed lot. "All of them?"

He looks out over the herd and nods. "Every last one."

"Won't that take a long time?"

"I'll be at it all afternoon. I got to pick Trace up at three, but other than that, this is all I'm going to be doing for the next several hours."

"You want me to pick Trace up from school?"

He meets my gaze. "You'd do that?"

"Of course. I'd love to."

Josh gives me the information for Trace's school and calls ahead, so they know I'm coming. I'm not sure how Josh thought he was going to vaccinate several hundred cattle and stop for a school pick up. But it is becoming pretty apparent that the man needs help.

He just doesn't know how to ask for it.

Trace is thrilled to see Maven and me at school pick up. He introduces me to his teacher, the bus driver, and anyone who will stop. Every adult we come into contact with studies me with open curiosity. I'm used to living in anonymity, but I guess small town life is different. They all know Josh Olson and when Trace lets it drop that my bedroom is next to his, the interest doubles down. I wince, knowing that the grapevine is going to be active tonight.

The whole way home, Trace chatters on. He made a Thanksgiving craft at school and he can't wait for his dad to see it.

As soon as we get in the house, he's barreling around the house, looking for a good place to display his cornucopia. I suggest the buffet in the dining room and his eyes get super round. "We can put it in there?"

I nod. "Of course, Trace. Something this nice needs to be front and center."

Finding a box in the garage, I clear the buffet. Carefully stowing the basket and dried flowers inside, we make room for Trace's crafts.

He arranges and rearranges the cornucopia, the collection of paper maché gourds, before settling on an arrangement that meets his high standards.

When Josh opens the front door, Trace practically vibrates with excitement. We hear Josh walk through the house, floorboards quietly creaking underfoot. He finds us in the dining room, gaze bopping from my face, to Trace's, before landing on the buffet.

But instead of smiling kindly and complimenting the craft, his face hardens. "You moved Ana's flowers."

My stomach drops. It's instantly apparent that I've touched something sacred.

Shit.

I made the mistake, but it's Trace's feelings that are being clobbered.

I glance down at him, noticing the way his lower lip is wobbling. My gaze flits back up to Josh's. "I'm sorry, I didn't realize…"

"Can you just…" Josh interrupts me, squeezing his eyes shut briefly, before looking at me. There's no warmth in those eyes. Only steely anger. "Can you just leave things the way they are? You don't need to go putting your touch on everything."

That feels particularly pointed, but at the moment, I'm more worried about Trace's feelings than my own. "You're absolutely right. I made a mistake. I can put it all back."

"No." He says sharply. His eyes widen. "You didn't throw it all away, did you?"

"Of course not." I say, lifting the box from the floor. "It's all here. I was really careful, don't worry."

"I'm not worried." He huffs, taking the box from my hands. "I just don't like having things disturbed."

"Message received. Won't happen again."

He turns away, box in hand. I can see how tense his shoulders are.

Josh pauses at the doorway, not looking back. "I'm going out. I won't be back for supper."

It's not until the front door closes again that Trace breaks down. I pull him into a hug and he sobs into my shirt.

16.

Josh

Twangy country music floats overhead, and I stare at my beer, watching bubbles float to the surface.

Bo slaps my shoulder, shocking me out of my funk. "Penny for your thoughts."

We've known each other since kindergarten. I can still remember the playground football game that went south and the brawl that followed. The entire kindergarten class was involved, but only four of us got sent to the principal's office, noses bleeding, grins on our faces.

We've been fast friends ever since.

The bartender, Tia, slings a beer over to Bo without asking. We're predictable, the two of us.

He's wearing his typical Carhart jacket and jeans. Grease streaks his knees.

"Working on that John Deere again?"

He nods. "Damn thing has it out for me."

I give him a sly look. "You know what the problem is, don't you?"

He rolls his eyes. "Don't get started on that Case versus John Deere bullshit again. I've heard it all. If I want to drive green tractors, that's what I'll do, God damn it." He takes a swig of beer to emphasize the point. "I heard a rumor about you today."

I glance over. "Oh yeah? A good one, I hope."

Bo smiles so big that his crooked tooth shows. "It's a good one, believe me."

"Just spit it out. I don't have the energy for guessing games."

"Alright, don't get tetchy. Why didn't you tell me you were getting yourself a nanny?"

I turn to face him, putting a hand on his shoulder. "I'm getting a nanny."

He grins, shrugging out from under my hand. "From the sounds of it, she's just perfect for you."

"What's that supposed to mean?"

"Just that she's a cute little thing. I heard she has a nice… face." He motions in front of his chest, holding two imaginary melons in front of him.

I'm used to the guys talking about ladies. I never took part in it, because for as long as we were interested in girls, I had Ana to occupy my thoughts.

But hearing him talk about Erin's anatomy like she's just another chick sends a small flare of irritation through me.

I turn away, sipping my beer. "She's alright, I guess."

"Just alright?" Bo asks, studying my profile.

A smile tugs at the corner of my lips.

He laughs, pounding me on the back. "You got any pictures?"

"If I did, I wouldn't show them to a no good horn dog like yourself."

"Just humor me, then. I haven't gone on a date in months. I'm dying over here. What's she like?"

"She's cute."

"Just cute?"

I shrug.

He sighs. "I need more details, man. What kind of cute? Like baby bunny cute or Playboy bunny cute?"

"The latter."

I'm almost surprised by the concession. It sort of rolls off the tongue without me really taking the time to think about it. I can't say I ever saw myself thinking a chick who wears bright pink Sesame street t-shirts was hot. My brain may not understand her sense of fashion, but my body is a big fan.

Her face flashes in front of mine, reminding me of the last conversation we had.

Well, she was having a conversation. I was just throwing another tantrum.

But those weren't just flowers she cleared away; they were memories of some of the last good days we had with Ana. She clipped those blooms from my mom's garden. She kept going on and on about how amazing it was to still have blooms so late in October. A miracle, she called it.

She called the sudden snowstorm that followed a miracle, too. I remember calling it a pain in the ass. If I'd known what would follow, I would have called that snow a curse.

"Earth to Joshy."

I shake myself, glancing over at him. "Hmm?"

"I was asking you a question, man. Where'd you go just now?"

I scrub my hands over my face. "Nowhere. I'm just tired." I turn to face him. "What's your question?"

He grins, waggling his eyebrows. "Is she really living with you?"

"Where'd you hear that?"

"From Lydia Carlisle."

"The school secretary?" I ask. "How in the hell does she know about that?"

"So, it's true?"

I shrug. "Well, I mean, I need someone to watch the kids and I'm always coming and going. Especially with calving season coming up."

"Holy shit, man." He crows. "It's about damn time. Maybe you'll finally get some action. Lord knows you need it." He kneads my shoulders. "You been getting pretty tense these days, my friend."

I shrug out of his grasp, anger simmering in my stomach. "It's not like that."

"Sure, sure."

"I'm dead ass serious, Bo. It's not like that."

Except for the part where I had a sexy dream about her the night before. But that's neither here nor there. I can't stop the brain from concocting whatever it wants when I fall asleep. The other night, I had a dream that Betsy and I had a BBQ together. I'm not going to start feeding her burgers, and by that token, I'm not going to act on the dream about Erin.

Bo can be a little crude, but he usually catches up, eventually. He holds up his hands. "Okay. You're not banging the babysitter. Got it."

"I'd never do that to Ana."

He winces, turning back to his beer. "We all miss her, you know."

I look over at him, surprised. We rarely talk about Ana. I don't want to burden them with the depths of my sorrow; and I think they're trying to keep things light for me.

"But, Josh? Don't you think Ana would want to see you live a good life?"

"Yeah. Of course."

"She'd understand if you moved on."

"If moving on means leaving her behind, I won't do it."

He nods, picking at the label of his beer. "Nobody wants to forget about Ana. She was special, man. But we miss seeing you smile."

"We? You guys been talking about me?"

He huffs a laugh. "If you don't think we've been talking about you for the last two years, you're off your rocker. You're our friend, Josh. We're worried about you, like it or not."

"Not." I say, fighting back a small grin. "I like it not."

But that's not entirely true.

I've spent the last two years thinking I was in this all alone. I didn't know it, but they were there too, looking out for me.

It's a good feeling.

"Now, about this nanny." Bo says.

I shove him, laughing. "Man, shut up."

17.

Erin

Josh never mentioned the flowers again and I'm afraid to bring it up.

Actually, I'm afraid to touch anything. I already made a mistake with the baking supplies.

And with the flowers, that's two strikes. I don't want to know what happens on a third strike, so I'm extra careful about rearranging things.

I can understand where he was coming from. My dad's work bench still sits untouched—there's even a half-finished cigar sitting amongst his tools that I won't let mom throw away. Eventually, we'll need to sell his bike and clean out the garage. I know this. I'm just not ready to deal with it.

And I'm not in the business of making anyone else move on, either.

It's like I've designated a safe path through his house and I stick to it, avoiding anything I'm not sure about.

I doubt he knows how much he hurt Trace's feelings, but I don't have it in me to hold his feet to the fire over it. He's obviously trying as hard as he can, and those kids are the center of his universe. He needs grace and compassion more than he needs a lecture.

And maybe he already knows he overreacted, because ever since then, he's been extra polite.

We're making things work. I'm doing more housework than I envisioned myself doing, but the pay is so much better than anything I've had before, I don't mind.

It's a lot more fun to cook for a household of four, than trying to figure out portioning for one.

Humming, I stand at the stove buttering bread for grilled cheese.

I glance over at the clock.

It's six.

Any minute now.

The front door opens, and like clockwork, Josh comes inside to eat dinner with the kids.

The kids are sitting at the table coloring, but like an enthusiastic pair of golden retrievers, they perk up and dash off towards the door.

I smile to myself, listening to that taciturn man greet his kids with a loud, joyful ruckus. They're in a rare mood tonight. I chop veggies with a smile on my face, listening to the increasingly noisy commotion. As it usually is with kids, the excitement rides the razor-sharp line between pure, unbridled joy and terror.

When Trace starts shouting my name, I step into the living room with the intention of telling Josh to knock it off. A little excitement is fun, too much usually ends in tears.

But Josh is the one who probably needs help. He's buried under a pile of couch cushions. Trace is straddling his chest, doing his best to keep his dad submerged. Maven has both fists buried in Josh's hair and is pulling with all her might.

"Erin! Help!" Trace laughs. "I trapped the monster."

Josh springs to life, tickling Trace with a mighty roar.

Trace twists towards around. "Save me!"

I snag a pillow from an armchair and wade in. Winding back, I swing at Josh, hitting him with more force than I intended. He pretends to fall back, and I take the opportunity to grab Trace. I've got him under the arms, but Josh perks up, grabbing Trace's ankle.

Trace is laughing his head off, losing his mind. Josh is laughing, too. I don't think I've ever seen that particular expression on his face. His smile is so bright it almost hurts my eyes.

Josh capitalizes on my stupor, jumping to his feet. He circles us, a predatory gleam in his eyes.

I hug Trace to my chest, who is flailing at his dad, peals of laughter spiraling out of him.

Josh starts swinging his arms, hooting like a big monkey. It's both incredibly amusing and slightly terrifying. Trace and I are both laughing, backing up.

Josh lunges, tickling Trace, trying to tug him out of my arms. Trace is kicking and swinging, no doubt landing a few painful blows, but Josh isn't deterred. When tickling Trace doesn't work, he switches tactics, poking at my sides.

This was a critical mistake.

Josh didn't realize how ticklish I am.

An unladylike yowl comes out of my mouth, shocking the entire family into brief silence. And then Josh's eyebrows lower wickedly. He prowls forward, clearly intent on getting another reaction out of me. My ankles hit the pillow pile and I can't back up any farther.

Josh reaches towards me just as Trace wrenches his body to the side, colliding with Josh and throwing all three of us off balance.

We all go down in a tangle of limbs. Somehow, I've ended up in Josh's arms. Trace leaps up, pummeling his dad with a pillow. But we're both temporarily frozen.

I've got my hands planted on his chest and my entire body runs the length of his. And he feels so good. Hard muscle and warmth that radiates out through his shirt. Our gazes connect and find myself staring at those eyes, marveling at how thick his dark eyelashes are. Then my gaze slips down to his smooth lips. I'm really not sure what might have happened next if we weren't interrupted. But Maven decides it's finally safe to join the fray by jumping directly onto her father's head.

18.

Josh

Thank God Maven knocked some sense into me. I was two heartbeats away from kissing Erin.

I needed a good slap in the face, and Maven is delivering that with gusto.

Erin's struggling to climb off of me, but she's only making matters worse. Her soft body felt nice pressed up alongside mine, but this wiggling is taking matters to a stage that is far less family friendly.

I know she's trying to extract herself, but she's squirming along my hips and that isn't helping anybody. I put a hand under her arm, trying to steady her, but then Trace comes barreling back in, knocking her flat against me with a mighty roar. "Avenge me!" He yells to no one in particular. Which is pretty damn funny, but also there's a lot of touching going on between the grown-ups that is more than either of us is bargaining for.

And of course, that's the moment when my mom decides to walk in.

I need to get a better lock.

Or an alarm system.

"What in the heck is going on here?" She asks.

All four of us freeze, caught in our chaotic tableau. Trace recovers first, hopping off us with a gleeful shout. "Grandma!"

She wraps her arms around him when he barrels into her.

Trace peers up at her. "We caught a bear."

Mom looks at me. "I see that."

Erin seems to snap out of it, suddenly struggling against my chest to get upright. I hook a hand around her upper arm, helping her to her feet, climbing up behind her.

She pats her hair, a look of horror crossing her features. "The grilled cheese!"

There is a hint of smoke in the air. I watch her go, reluctantly bringing my gaze back to my mom.

I don't know why I'm embarrassed to look at her, other than I feel like I just got caught in some sin I can't quite put my finger on.

My feelings are pretty tangled up. I can't help but to feel a little guilty towards Ana, but that's odd, because Erin and I weren't doing anything romantic, we were just playing with the kids.

Right?

Judging by mom's face, it might have at least looked like more was going on.

I finger comb my hair back into place while I try to concoct some sort of explanation.

Mom beats me to it. "I haven't seen Monkey Josh since you were ten years old."

Monkey Josh. I forgot about that one.

She smiles, looking nostalgic. "You used to rile the girls up so much and we'd get so mad at you."

Trace and Maven slip back into the kitchen, obviously bored with the grown-up talk.

Mom bends down, picking up a couch cushion. "You were the goofiest kid. We were sure you'd grow up to be a comedian or an actor."

I help her clean up the living room. "Yeah, right."

She pauses, a cushion in her arms. "I'm serious, Joshy. We really thought you were destined for the stage. But then puberty hit and you sort of grew out of it."

"Oh, God, mom. Don't start talking about puberty."

She pauses. "I never thought I'd get to see this side of you again. It's nice."

I shake my head, picking up the rest of the pillows. She acts like I never horse around with my kids. But admittedly, this evening did get a little out of control. Erin's had that effect on us, though. If she's not singing Disney songs at the top of her lungs, she's got the kids dancing and spinning.

It's like she's breathing life into this old house. She's breathing life into all of us. Myself included.

She makes it safe to be as loud and goofy as we want.

Throwing the last of the pillows back into place, I glance at my mom. Did I really change that much when I was a kid?

I do remember how hard it was to walk the tightrope between masculinity and childhood. Thank God for my friends. We would occasionally get silly together, but I remember there being an intense pressure to grow up.

I can hear Trace singing with Erin in the kitchen. A heavy weight settles on my shoulders at the thought of Trace going through the same thing.

Mom pats my arm. "I'm going to go help Erin with supper. I haven't gotten to spend much time with her yet. Something tells me I should get to know her."

19.

Erin

I pull up to the big house, making note of the half dozen trucks and cars parked in the lane. Lisa comes down the porch, opening the car door for me. "Thank God."

"Good to see you, too." I grin at her, unnerved by the wired look in her eyes.

"How was your Thanksgiving?"

"Good. We got together with my aunts in Kearney."

"And they didn't mind you flitting back to Clark the next day?"

I shrug. "Mom and her sisters are all nurses. They had to work today, anyway."

Lisa nods, but she looks distracted.

I crane my head, trying to decipher the look on her face. "Are you feeling okay, Lisa?"

She meets my gaze. "I have a confession to make."

"Okay." I say slowly.

"I might have twisted Josh's arm a little… to get you here today."

"Okay, that answers some questions. He was a little weird about asking me."

"It's just Keith's family is a lot, and I just wanted back up. And you're such a calming presence, I thought maybe you'd rub off on them."

I turn on heel, pretending to go back to my car. She flutters after me and I let her pull me up the steps. The truth is, Josh is paying me time and a half to be here. It's a nice little bonus right before Christmas and I didn't have anything else going on.

Right before we step inside, she looks over at me. "Just be warned, they can be a little loud."

At her words, the living room erupts in a chorus of boos and complaints.

Husker football.

It's the most important thing in this state, right behind God and family.

Maybe even in front of family.

When we step inside, the game switches to commercial. It's unfortunate timing, because now the Olson clan is looking for a diversion.

I try not to blush under the weight of a dozen pairs of eyes.

I tug at the sleeve of my sweater, realizing too late that I wore the other team's colors. Green.

I had one job. Wear red. Couldn't even manage that.

Josh is sitting on a recliner with Trace on his lap.

A tall woman, presumably Josh's aunt, turns to look at him. "Joshy, who's this?"

Trace leaps off his dad's lap. "Erin! You're here!"

He barrels into me, wrapping me in a hug. Pulling back, he fixes the room with a proud smile. "This is Erin, and she's my nanny."

"My nanny!" Maven squawks, clambering off Keith's lap. She joins her brother, and they engage in a brief struggle over my legs. I break up the scuffle by sweeping Maven into my arms. It certainly beats responding to the collective stare of twelve people.

"You got a nanny?" Another man asks. He looks like a shorter, pudgier version of Keith. Must be an uncle.

Josh glances at me, and I'm surprised to see the faintest tinge of pink on his cheekbones. He introduces all twelve of his family members, finishing up just as the commercial break comes to a close. I only really paid attention when he introduced his sisters. It doesn't seem like I need to know who his cousins are, but the sisters might be more relevant.

He has three of them.

Parker is tall and willowy. She takes after their dad.

Reese is short and curvy like Lisa, with her warm smile.

Charlie is a perfect blend of the two: petite, but skinny.

Having staked her claim, Maven wiggles out of my arms and returns to her throne on grandpa's lap. Charlie squats down by Trace, cajoling him into playing with her.

Within moments, both kids have abandoned me and I am left with nothing to do.

I glance around the crowded living room. I've never been a big football fan, as much of a sin as that is for a Nebraskan to say.

And I don't relish sitting amongst the Olsons while they watch. Each play seems to be punctuated by their loud and bombastic outcries.

I can see why Lisa wanted back up.

With nothing else to do, I make my way into the kitchen and start tidying up.

Despite watching her grandkids for a few weeks now, I've never been inside Lisa's kitchen.

It's beautiful.

Maybe it's a bit out of date, but it's still charming. It's got that old Victorian style that was so popular in the eighties. The sheer size of the room is impressive. I can easily picture the family gatherings in here, kids getting ready for school.

I wipe the countertops down, making my way over to the fridge. My gaze catches on the photos taped there.

Charlie looking like a little, petite fairy in her prom dress.

Parker standing tall and proud with a volleyball tucked under her arm.

Reese looking fine as hell in her dance team uniform.

And then, there's Josh in his football uniform, a gleaming plastic crown on his head.

"Fucking figures." I mutter to myself. I called it on the day we met. Between his good looks and perfect body, the man is a prototype for high school popularity.

"Did you say something, dear?" Josh's Aunt Kim is standing in the doorway, watching me with an expectant gaze.

"Just talking to myself." I laugh, feeling my cheeks heat. "Don't mind me."

"You're tidying up? That's so sweet of you."

I shrug, rinsing the dish towel. "Just trying to stay busy."

"In that case, they've turned the living room into a real pigsty. Would you mind clearing some of that up?"

I stare at her for a few beats. "You want me to clean the living room while they're in it?"

"If it's not too much trouble."

20.

Josh

Uncle Kyle has always been a bit of an idiot.

He's my dad's older brother and he never really got over the fact that grandpa passed the farm down to my dad, bypassing him. But even back then, Uncle Kyle spent more time getting to the bottom of his whiskey glass than farming. It was sort of a no brainer, but my uncle never saw it that way.

"You got yourself a nanny?" He asks, plopping down in the chair beside me.

I nod, trying to keep my eye on the game. It's been an effort ever since Erin walked in the house. My gaze keeps straying, trying to figure out where she went.

That sweater keeps making an appearance in my thoughts. It clings to her curves. The neckline had a delicate lace trim, an innocent touch, but it's got me thinking about what's under that sweater and those thoughts are anything but innocent.

"Does that make you Daddy Warbucks?"

I spare him a quick glance. He's got a mean glint in his eye. I turn my attention back to the game. "Just needed some help with the kids."

"Why don't you just get married again?" He asks. "You ain't going to find a wife as long as you've got a woman living with you."

I turn to him, surprised he knew about the cohabitation. His gaze goes over my shoulder, and I turn to see Erin gathering dirty snack plates under Aunt Kim's careful eye.

"What are you doing?" I ask.

The conversations in the room lull momentarily before people go back to talking. They pretend they aren't hanging on every word.

Erin shrugs, picking up an empty glass. "Just tidying up."

"You don't have to do that." I say, my voice coming out harsher than I intended.

Aunt Kim hands her another glass, pasting on a guileless smile. "She's on the clock, isn't she?"

"Yeah, but not for *you*." I push to my feet, ignoring the stares burning holes in the back of my head. I take the plates and glasses out of Erin's hands, marching through to the kitchen.

She follows a few moments behind me with more plates.

I'm filling the sink with water. "No matter what my dear Aunt Kim tries to tell you, we didn't ask you to come here so that you could be her personal maid."

"I know." She says, drifting closer to set the plates down. "But Maven is with your dad and Charlie has Trace. I don't have anything to do."

"Then sit down and watch the game."

"I don't like football."

I stop, turning to look at her. "Really?"

She laughs. "You should see your face."

"You're joking."

"Oh, no. I'm not. I don't understand the game. They spend so much time setting them up, just to knock them over fifteen seconds later."

"By *them*, you're referring to the players?"

She nods, biting back a smile.

"You do realize I played in high school, right?"

She tips her chin towards the fridge. "There's the evidence."

I follow her gaze and wince. "I wish she'd take that damn thing down."

"Why? I think it's cute."

I huff, but inside I'm smiling. "That's what I was aiming for. Cute."

There's a loud outburst in the living room, followed by a chorus of cheers. I peer into the next room, trying to divine what just happened.

"Go watch the game." Erin says, nudging me to the side. "I can finish this up."

"I'm right where I want to be."

She gives me a skeptical look.

Hell, I'm skeptical, too.

But searching inside myself, I realize it's true. I love football, but I've seen hundreds and hundreds of games.

I've never seen the way Erin looks in the fading November light.

The sun is setting, slanting warm, gold light into the kitchen. It lights up her eyes, makes her coppery hair glow. I'm kind of fascinated.

I find myself wondering what she'd look like under the moonlight.

If I'm being truthful with myself, I'd admit that I want to know what every square inch of her looks like under the moon and the stars.

But I'll settle for how she looks when she's scrubbing dishes.

Even that is better than any old football game.

21.

Erin

It is very difficult to play it cool when you've got six and a half feet of smoking hotness breathing down your neck.

I thought his aunt was a bit pushy, but I don't mind being put on cleanup duty. Beats the heck out of being bored.

But Josh had to go and make it a *thing* and now we're stuck in here together, playing some sort of game of chicken that I don't fully understand the rules to.

And I swear he keeps sneaking glances at me, which is nuts, because a man like *that* isn't looking at a woman like me.

Whether he is or isn't, I still feel outgunned when I stand next to him.

He's like the big bad wolf and I'm a shivering bunny.

But that just reminds me of the time I saw him in just his sweats. And I saw something else that was also big.

"Are you blushing?" Josh asks, breaking into my thoughts.

I glance up at him, wishing I could wipe the smirk from his face.

Actually, I'd like to kiss it off, but that would be inappropriate.

"No." I hand him a dish. "Rinse."

He chuckles. "You are. What's going on in that head of yours?"

"You don't want to know." I mutter.

"Oh, but I think I do." He replies, his voice smokey and low. It sends a thrill down my spine.

I'm so startled I momentarily forget how to wash a dish. He nudges me and I commence scrubbing dishes that don't need to be scrubbed. He's distracting me. I didn't know it was possible to make rinsing dishes look sexy, but he is accomplishing this with flying colors.

"I think that one is clean." He laughs, plunging his hand into the soapy side of the sink. Our fingers connect, and he slides his thumb over the back of my hand before pulling the plate out of the water.

My cheeks are completely on fire. Glowing.

"Now you really are blushing."

"I am not."

How is it this asshole looks completely cool and collected while I feel like a glowing top, spinning out of control?

I want to be pissed at him, but he's too damn cute to stay mad for long. I don't understand what this man wants from me.

On an intellectual level, I am all too aware that it's a mistake to flirt with this guy. He's my boss. And if we screw things up, make them too awkward, then that means I can't keep looking after Trace and Maven.

It's only been a few weeks, but I'm already getting pretty attached to those little cuties.

Josh reaches into the sink again, obviously thinking I'm moving too slowly, and extracts another dish, sliding his pinky finger along mine. I jerk my gaze up to his, but he's looking away, all innocence and ease.

These touches might be accidental. Or he might be fucking with me.

Either way, it's sending me into a lust spiral, and I feel my resolve slipping.

We've washed all the dishes, but I keep my hands submerged. He reaches in, feeling around. When he realizes the sink is empty, his hand slides alongside mine. When I don't pull away, he laces his fingers through mine.

For a brief, glorious moment, I just let the feeling wash over me. His touch sends sparks jumping and jittering across my body. There's no question now, no misinterpreting things.

Josh is holding my hand.

Under soapy water, yes. Which is a little weird. But also, kind of cute.

If I could just turn off my thoughts, I might be able to enjoy it. But questions batter around my head. What does it mean? What does he want?

A surge of panic fills my chest, and I jerk my hand out of his.

I take a few steps back, trying to harden my heart to the look of pure concern on his handsome face.

"I need to use the bathroom."

And with that, I speed down a hallway, diving into the first room I find.

22.

Josh

Well, shit.

Now I've gone and done it.

I'm not really sure what impulse compelled me to grab her hand like that, other than the fact that I just wanted to know what it would be like.

And that was a little like tipping the lid off Pandora's box, because I didn't expect holding Erin's hand to feel *that* nice.

It was a reckless thing to do, and now I get to deal with the consequences. I follow behind her, trying to form an explanation for my behavior, but I'm coming up short.

My head's a mess these days. And her presence is the only thing I can count on.

I walk down the dark hallway, stopping in front of the room Erin dived into. My knuckles rap quietly on the oak panel.

"Someone's in here." Her voice is muffled and small.

My lips tug into a half smile. "Using the bathroom?"

There's a slight pause. "Yup."

"In Charlie's bedroom?" A grin is stretching from ear to ear. "I don't think she'd take kindly to that, Erin."

I can hear her muttering a string of unladylike words on the other side of the door.

I press my forehead to the panel. "Can I come in?"

There's a pause and then she opens the door. I slip inside, closing it behind me.

Was she always this short?

For some reason, she's striking me as being particularly pocket-sized.

Her plump lips twist into a smile. "This isn't the bathroom, is it?"

"No. Doesn't seem like it."

"Huh."

I laugh, biting back a smile. "Were you trying to hide?"

"Maybe."

I tuck my hands into my pockets to keep them from reaching out. "Why?"

She sighs, blowing a losing lock of hair from her forehead. "I might have panicked."

My lips want to tug into a grin, but I muscle them into a straight line. "Why?"

"Damn it, Josh. Are you going to make me say it?"

"Say what?"

She tosses her hands. "You make me nervous."

I tilt my head. "Why?"

She growls at me. "Because you're hot, you big dummy."

And now I'm smiling from ear to ear, feeling amused and just a bit giddy.

She backs up a little. "I always feel outgunned with you."

I move closer. "Why?"

"I swear to God, if you say that one more time." She steps back, legs running into Charlie's bed. "Are you just fucking with me?"

Her voice comes out as little more than a whisper.

"Definitely not."

She has to tip her head back to look at me. "So then, what are you doing?"

"I don't honestly know." My gaze follows the curve of her lips. Warmth kindles in my chest.

"I don't understand what you want from me."

I catch one of her curls and wind it around my finger. "I would think that's pretty obvious."

"It's really not." She says, her eyes are snared by mine, but it's like she has to keep talking. "You're so out of my league."

What?

I pull back, stopping long enough to really look at her. There's more there than just nerves on that pretty face. Some sort of pain lurks behind those eyes, too.

I never thought she was below me and I don't like hearing her talk about herself like that. A possessive sort of energy takes over my body and I find myself closing the distance.

Weaving my fingers through her soft hair, I angle her face towards mine and press my lips against hers.

I've wanted to know what those lips felt like since the first moment I saw her.

And I wanted to show her that I think she's beautiful and worthy.

I did not expect the rush of sensations that followed that kiss.

Our lips just brush against each other, a whisper of a touch, but it's like my entire body comes alive in a shivery, staticky feeling. I press into her mouth, deepening the touch. A tiny sound, something between a squeak and a moan, comes from her throat. My hand slips across her lower back and, with only a slight tug, she melts into me.

It feels so good to have her soft body leaning into mine; I wrap both arms around her and hold her tight.

This touch, this connection, is cracking me open. I'm a deep root, waiting for winter to end, and she is sunlight.

I feel everything that was buried so deep start to unfurl.

My thoughts are messy, chaotic. But the thread that sews it all together is a feeling of relief.

There's a thump in the hallway outside and we both spring apart.

Her fingers slowly rise up to brush against those lips, and I barely stop myself from diving back in for another kiss.

With a strange little frown on her face, she pushes past me and slips out the door.

23.

Erin

The thing about awkward work experiences as a live-in nanny is that when you go home, your troubles follow you.

We take Maven and Trace back to Josh's house a few hours after dinner. I offer to take them back by myself so Josh can hang out with his family, but he just shrugs off my suggestion.

I've got Maven in my arms and he has Trace sleeping on his shoulder. He settles Trace into the truck, buckling his car seat, before turning to take Maven from me. "Got to love having kids. They're an easy excuse to leave."

I watch him gently settle Maven in her seat. Her little chin is drooping towards her chest. "You didn't want to stick around?"

He shakes his head. "God, no." Glancing up at the house, he closes the truck door. "Parker and Charlie are up in arms because mom and dad are moving."

"They're moving?"

He tilts his head, giving me a strange look. "Yeah. We didn't tell you that? It's what precipitated the whole nanny thing. Mom looked after the kids before, but then they decided it was time for retirement."

"Were you upset about them moving too?"

He leans against the truck, shoving his hands into his pockets. "I've had to learn perspective over the last few years. I don't like it, but in the grand scheme of things, this is not something to lose your shit over." He glances up at the house. I wonder what he's looking at, which memories are playing through his mind.

He shrugs, looking away. "Anyway. My sisters won't be very good company tonight. And Uncle Kyle and Aunt Kim are bad company on a good night." He thumps the hood of the truck. "Hop in. We can get your car in the morning."

"Or I can just drive it back tonight." I say, not quite filtering the snarky tone from my voice.

He shrugs. "Suit yourself."

Without another word, he circles the truck and climbs in.

I stand there for a few heartbeats, looking and feeling like an idiot. What did I expect? Was he supposed to beg me to ride with him?

My boots crunch through the frozen slush as I make my way back to my car. It's freezing cold inside, and the car is almost reluctant to start up. By some small mercy, the engine grumbles to a start and I bounce and careen down the icy drive.

His taillights glow ahead of me. He's so close and yet completely cut off. I should have ridden with him. We're going to need to talk about that kiss.

My lips tingle at the memory and I slide my fingers across them.

We have to talk about it, right?

It's not like we can just carry on like nothing happened.

Except, that's what we were just doing. The healthiest thing to do would be to sit down and hash it out. We need to discuss boundaries.

Feelings.

Ugh. Feelings.

But I'm not really sure how I feel about it and I don't think talking it over with Dreamboat up there is going to clear anything up for me.

It's obvious that he's not over his wife and maybe never will be.

He's permanently out of reach.

Whatever feelings I have for him, whatever that damn kiss meant, none of it can be long term.

Maybe he wants to use me to scratch an itch.

The idea is a little daunting.

Matt and I were together my entire adult life—I've never been in this position.

I'm not sure if I'm capable of being a no strings attached kind of person. But I also don't think I'm ready for another long-term relationship.

Maybe a quick and easy rebound would do me good. My lips curve into a smile, imagining the look on Matt's face if he saw me in the grocery store with Josh on my arm.

If it was just Josh and me, I think maybe I'd throw caution to the wind and say, fuck it. Let's have fun.

But there are two little people involved and I cannot stand the idea of them getting hurt in the process.

It's pretty obvious that both kids, but especially Trace, are missing having a mommy in their lives.

All Trace would need is the slightest hint, the barest suggestion that Josh and I are together, and he'd run with it.

By the time we pull up to the house, a mere quarter of a mile down the road, the decision seems pretty clear.

Josh and I need to put the kids first.

That means no hashing it out.

No second kisses.

We need to erase this night from our minds and act like it never happened.

24.

Josh

I shouldn't have grabbed Erin's hand.

I for damn sure shouldn't have kissed her.

A small part of me is mortified.

The bigger part of me, and the southern parts of me, can't stop thinking about the way she felt in my arms.

In a word, delectable.

I half-expected her to bring it up. She's so outspoken. But last night, she helped me put the kids to bed without a word about it. It's like it never happened.

Except that it did. I can still feel those soft curves on my palms.

I wake up in the early hours of the morning, staring at the ceiling.

Maven made her way to my bed and is snuggled up in my arms. I run my fingers through her soft hair, turning thoughts over in my mind.

I'm not sure I can go backwards from here.

I might need to fire her.

Or apologize.

Or throw her over my shoulder and carry her to the bedroom like a cave man.

Maybe all three, in reverse order.

I slip out of bed, careful not to disturb Maven, and pull on a pair of jeans. Tugging a sweater over my head, I pad out into the kitchen.

I'm not surprised to see Erin in there. Aside from that first morning, she's always the first one up. She's always one step ahead of me, looking wide awake despite the early hour. She has all that hair up in a high ponytail. Her turtleneck sweater ought to be modest, but it only serves to emphasize her chest.

"Morning." She pours me a mug of coffee without needing to ask.

I take it, trying not to stare at those perfect lips.

I'm definitely not remembering the way they felt against mine.

My gaze is anchored to her mouth. She bites her lower lip, sending a zing of hunger through me.

Okay, fuck it. I can't do this. We need to face this head on. I raise my eyes to hers, trying to form the words on my tongue.

"Is it Christmas yet?" Trace comes pelting into the kitchen. He wears footie jammies and his hair is mussed—defying gravity.

Erin smiles, hands gliding over his shoulders when he dives in for a hug. "Not yet, Trace. But maybe we can decorate."

He cranes his head, looking up at her. "Can we cut down a tree just like your family does?"

She meets my gaze. "I told him how we used to go to the tree farm."

Trace backs up. "Can we go with you?"

"To the tree farm? My family probably won't go this year. That was always my dad's job."

She's smiling, but there's a hint of sadness in those eyes.

Trace turns to look at me. "Then Erin can go with us. Right, dad?"

"We don't need to go to a tree farm. There's a whole pasture full of cedar trees right out back."

Trace's eyes light up. "So we can get a real tree this year? Not a fake one?"

We always had an artificial tree because Ana thought real ones were a fire hazard. But if cutting down one of those cedars would make Erin feel better, I'll gladly do it. It's the least I can do.

Trace practically vibrates with energy, but Erin forces all three of us to sit down and eat a full breakfast before we can go outside.

Maven doesn't know what's going on, but she picks up on Trace's excitement and by the time we get them bundled up, they're both spinning in circles.

Erin stands beside me, Maven's mittened hand in hers, while I unhitch the fence gate. Trace climbs over it and is tumbling over the snow-covered slope before I can even swing the gate open.

"No cows in here?" Erin asks when I leave the fence open.

"Not yet. But soon. Once the heifers start calving, I'll bring them over here so they're closer to the house." I nod at the barn between the house and the pasture. "That's the calving barn."

"Aha."

Maven demands to be picked up, so Erin settles Maven on her hips, ignoring the muddy snow tracks Maven leaves on her jacket. Both kids are decked out for the snow in snow pants and coats. But Erin's trudging through eight inches of snow in skinny jeans and canvas sneakers.

We're going to have to get her some coveralls and work boots if she's going to be sticking around. Don't want her getting frostbite.

"I found one!" Trace's voice echoes back up the pasture.

He's little more than a speck at the bottom of the ravine. I grin, shaking my head. "He's a fast little devil."

25.

Erin

Josh leads the way, boots carving a path through the snow. I try to step in his boot prints. I already have a boatload of snow in my shoes, but the air is so crisp and fresh and I can't help but to feel happy.

I thought I wouldn't have the energy to look for a Christmas tree this year. That was always dad's favorite thing. But Trace's enthusiasm is contagious. And this part of the country is snow-covered and beautiful. "I'm really glad we're doing this."

Josh looks back. "Not too cold?"

"Oh, I'm cold." I laugh. "But it's fun doing it with the kids. I don't think mom and I would have been a barrel of monkeys this year."

"Your mom won't feel bad to be left out?"

I shake my head. "She didn't like doing it when dad was alive. I'm sure she wouldn't like it now."

He doesn't prod, but it's nice to talk about things like this with someone who would understand. My mom has gone through a different grieving process than I have, most of which involves chinning up and not talking about it.

Trace has stopped in front of a particularly large cedar. Josh plants his hands on his hips and tips his head back. "Might be a little too big, bud."

"No, it's not." Trace says, scooting around the far side of the tree.

"It's taller than our house." Josh points out.

Trace looks like he's bracing for a showdown. I squat down beside him, gasping theatrically. "Trace. Look at that one over there."

He follows where I'm pointing. I lower my voice to a whisper. "It's just perfect, don't you think?"

He squints his eyes at me, skepticism giving way to agreement. He raises a mittened hand to point at the smaller tree. "That's the one, dad. Hack it down."

I pull out my phone, ignoring the biting cold, to take a few pictures of Josh with the kids. He hunkers down by them and Trace barrels into him, knocking him flat on this back. Maven capitalizes on his position and then the two of them are dog-piling on their dad. I snap a few more shots, laughing when Trace shoves a handful of snow down Josh's shirt.

"You think that's funny?" Josh asks, climbing to his feet with a mischievous glint in his eye.

I take a step backwards. "I do, actually."

He reaches down, scooping up a handful of snow. "Really funny?"

I put my hands up, warding him off. "Put that down."

He takes a few steps towards me, and I spin on my heel. His arm hooks me around my waist, lifting me off the ground. Squawking indignantly, a peel of laughter rings out of me.

I don't really like being picked up. I'm always afraid I'm going to be too heavy. But Josh spins me around like I weigh as much as Trace.

It's flattering, if not anywhere near accurate.

Trace, little hero that he is, charges in to the rescue. He pelts his dad with snowballs while Maven tangles herself up in his legs. He sets me down before pretending to be tackled to the ground by the kids.

Maven switches sides, turning on me. She holds her hands up and gives me an adorably ferocious bear growl. Wrapping her arms around my legs, she tugs and tugs until I pretend to fall over.

Snow is sneaking in my collar, at the waistband on my jeans, but Maven's too cute to put off. Trace yanks my phone out of my pocket, attempting to unlock it with his mittened thumbs. "We need a group picture."

I unlock it for him and Josh leans over, tugging the phone from our hands. Trace hooks his arm around my neck and pulls me flat. "Scoot in close, dad."

Josh holds the phone above us with his long arm. I look up at our little group, pink-cheeked and happy—we look like a living Christmas card.

Trace settles in closer, accidentally shoving more snow down my collar. A shiver wracks my body and Josh feels the tremor. He sits up. "Okay, that's enough frozen selfies for one day."

I scoop Maven up and hold her on my hip while Josh and Trace kneel by the tree trunk. Josh lets Trace pass the saw through the trunk a few times before taking over. The tree goes over with a quiet whisper of pine needles.

I carry Maven back up the slope. Josh tows the tree and Trace scampers ahead, an endless bundle of energy.

Josh looks askance at me. "It's not too cold out, is it?"

"It's cold." I laugh.

His face is dead serious. "I don't want you getting sick."

I'm not sure how to take that. "I'm tough. You don't have to worry about me."

He frowns at that, jaw tensing. "As soon as we get back to the house, we're ordering you decent boots and some coveralls."

26.

Josh

Sometimes fresh snow gives me anxiety.

This snow is good, though. It's hard. Dingy.

It's not at all like the perfect, soft snow that fell on the worst day.

We didn't even get one more Christmas with Ana that year. I didn't have the heart to put up Christmas decorations. Trace was only two, so he didn't know any better.

Last year, I just told him grandma had the tree at her house and he accepted it as a fact.

It's good that we're putting up our own tree this year. Trace and Maven deserve a real Christmas. It's such a relief to have someone help.

My mom offered to help put up the tree, but she misses Ana too, so I knew it would just be depressing. But Erin isn't stained by all that. She's separate from the muck and the mire.

Imported joy.

I drag the tree into the house before climbing up into the attic. I find Ana's Christmas decorations and an antique tree stand that my grandparents used.

Erin's got hot cocoa going on the stove by the time I get back, and the house smells so warm. It's alive with music and noise. A feeling of hope whispers through my chest.

But then I sit down on the couch and open the box of decorations. Right on top is the glass star I gave Ana on our first anniversary. Beneath that is the shell ornament she picked out to celebrate Trace's first Christmas.

Erin quietly sits at my side. "We don't have to use those."

"It's fine." I say, aiming for a light-hearted tone, but it comes out strangled.

She swipes her thumb across my cheekbone, catching tears. "No, it's not."

When did I start crying? Jesus Christ. "Must be something in my eye."

Erin pushes up to her feet. "Besides, I had big plans to make homemade decorations." She holds out her hand. "Come on. The kids will love it."

I suspect she is learning to weaponize the kids to get me to see her side of things. In this case, she might have a point. I carry the box back to the garage, taking a few seconds to pull myself together. By the time I come back inside, Erin has the kids working on paper garland.

Maven's just making a mess, but Trace's garland is already pretty long. He staples ring after ring together, his little tongue poking out in concentration.

I lean into the counter beside Erin. She hands me a mug of cocoa and I breathe it in. "Thanks for all this."

"The holidays can be hard." She shrugs. Judging by the look in her eye, she's missing her dad. "You got anything stronger we can spice this up with?"

I grin. "Whiskey?"

She makes a face.

"Rum?"

She shrugs. "Getting closer."

"Peppermint schnapps?"

"Now you're speaking my language."

I've never really helped with Christmas decorations. Ana had her own way of doing things.

Even when I was a kid, I preferred being outside with dad. Calving always struck me as infinitely more interesting than ornaments and tinsel.

But watching Erin conjure decorations out of thin air is an impressive sight. I shouldn't be so surprised. She studied childhood development in college, has worked in childcare for years.

But the woman literally turned applesauce and cinnamon into gingerbread shaped ornaments.

The day passes easily in a lazy swirl of garland and spice.

When the kids start getting a little snarly she switches on the TV, putting The Grinch on. Making sure both kids have popcorn and their water bottles, she carries a huge bowl of popcorn over to the couch where I'm sitting.

I scoop out a big handful and she lightly slaps the back of my hand. "That's for the tree."

"The tree isn't hungry."

She chuckles quietly, threading a needle before handing it to me.

"I have literally no idea what you expect me to do with this."

"Patience, my friend." She makes me pinch the needle between finger and thumb, stringing a piece of popcorn along its length. Her shoulder leans into mine, arm brushing along my lap as she sweeps the kernel down the string.

She plucks another piece of popcorn from the bowl. "Now you."

I bend down, snagging the piece from her fingertips with my teeth. My teeth gently graze her thumb, and she squeaks. She scowls at me, but her cheeks are flushing a pretty shade of pink.

27.

Erin

Josh eats more popcorn than he threads, but bit by bit, his garland grows.

With each inch, he seems to relax, one foot tucked up under his thigh. And the more he eases back onto the couch, the more he's pressing up against me.

I should probably move. My thoughts are like a dog chasing its tail when it comes to Josh. Until I know what I want, I'd be smart to stay away from him.

But I don't want to be smart, I want to be happy.

And Christmas is turning out to be harder than I bargained for. I miss my dad and Josh's presence is the only thing that eases the ache in my heart.

So even though I should slip into the kitchen, get some distance, I lean into him instead. Having made a five-foot string of popcorn, Josh retires from elf duty, throwing an arm over my shoulder. He pretends he's not sneaking popcorn by the handful and I pretend to be annoyed, but the truth is, I like the weight of his arm on my shoulders. I like the way he smells mixed up with the scent of a fresh cut cedar tree and popcorn.

Touching him like this, absorbing his warmth, makes me feel almost giddy. When his fingertips start threading through my hair, coiling and uncoiling a curl around his finger, I tumble right past giddy and straight into buzzed.

If it weren't for the kids, I might be inclined to climb right onto his lap and see if he kisses as good as I remember.

Trace has fallen asleep with one hand curled in his popcorn bowl. Little Maven is curled up like a puppy, kicking and squirming in her sleep.

She coughs and settles down.

But then, there's another cough.

And another.

Josh is grower more tense by the minute. When the cough turns particularly barky, he's on his feet, scooping her up. He turns to me with a hardened expression. "She's burning up."

"Let's see." I stand and he brings her to me. I put the back of my hand on her forehead, then rest my cheek against hers. Bending closer to him, I can almost hear his heart racing. "She's warm. I'll go get the thermometer."

He follows me, cradling Maven to his chest while she suffers through another fit of coughs. "Do we need to take her to the emergency room?"

I glance back. "I don't think it's that serious."

We check her temperature and I check the reading. "It's low grade. Nothing dangerous."

She coughs again, and he looks at me with skeptical eyes. "Can we give her something?"

"What do you usually give her when she has a cold?"

He shrugs helplessly. "She doesn't get sick very often. She hardly ever goes anywhere. We don't do preschool or Sunday school. And it's just my mom who looked after her before."

"Okay. That's not a problem." I pause, smoothing a hand over the back of her head. "Do you have any baby Vaporub?"

He shakes his head. "Should I go get some from the store?"

"Is there anywhere around here that would still be open?"

He thinks that over and shakes his head. "No."

"Can I hold her?"

He pauses, reluctantly handing her over to me. "Can you put Trace in bed?"

He nods, padding back down the hallway.

I carry Maven into the little bathroom that separates my room from Josh's. Closing both doors, I turn on the shower, cranking it as hot as it will go. When the room is starting to fill with steam, Josh knocks lightly on the door. "Are you taking a shower?"

I smile. "No. Come on in."

He slips inside, spotting me sitting on the floor with Maven in my arms. She's sleeping soundly, the steam having loosened up her congestion. He sits next to me. His knees draw up and he rests his elbows on them. "I'm not very good in these situations. I don't know what to do."

That might be an understatement. He looks completely wrecked. I knew he was protective, but this is closer to fear.

"You've had super healthy kids. That's a blessing."

He nods, but he only has eyes for Maven. "Can I take her back?"

"Of course."

I pass Maven to Josh like she's made of spun sugar. He holds her with a tenderness that almost breaks my heart.

28.

Josh

I would have stayed in that steamy bathroom all night, slept on the damn floor, but Erin said Maven only needs a few minutes at a time.

We carefully lay her in her crib and Erin tiptoes away, but I stand there, watching for her chest to rise and fall. When I'm absolutely convinced she's okay, I start to worry that I might wake her up by standing too close. Reluctantly, I step back into the living room and spot Erin sitting on the couch.

Erin. Our guardian angel.

She looks upset.

I collapse on the couch next to her, knees akimbo.

She turns to face me, almost in tears. "This is all my fault."

I sit up a little. "Your fault? How do you figure?"

"The whole Christmas tree thing. That was my idea."

I glance at the tree in question, glowing merrily by the window. My kids are present on every branch in their handprints and their artwork. It's not a perfect tree, but it was made with love, and that makes it picture perfect in my book.

I nudge her. "That was Trace's idea. And you were gracious enough to indulge him."

"But it was too cold."

I plant my hand on her knee and give it a little shake. "It's not your fault. I heard Charlie telling mom she was just getting over a cold and she had Maven all day yesterday."

"You're sure?"

I shrug. "I can't be sure, but even if it was the cold weather, that's just life, you know?" I stop short, taken aback.

"What?"

"I just never thought I'd hear myself say something like that." I pause, hesitating over how much I should tell her. "Has anyone told you about Ana?"

Her gaze meets mine, and she shakes her head.

Everyone around here knows what happened. I haven't had to explain it to anyone, but by the same token, no one talks about it. The topic is taboo. But so is Ana's name.

After two years of being trapped in my head, forming that story into words feels like rolling a boulder uphill.

"Remember a few years back when we got that big blizzard on Halloween?"

She nods. "Yeah. They had to cancel Halloween in Lincoln because the ice took power lines down."

"It was a freak storm."

"Yeah."

"Ana loved the snow." I clear my throat, wishing I had some whiskey to ease the pain. "We had some early calves that year and I was out in the barn all night and she came out with wet hair to keep me company." I clear my throat again. "She was like that. Always trying to tough shit out. I don't know for sure if that was when she got sick, but in my heart… anyway, she caught this cold that wouldn't go away and she never told any of us how bad it was getting. By the time she finally let me take her to the hospital, she had septic pneumonia."

Glancing back at Erin, I'm surprised to see tears tracking down her cheeks. I reach out and catch them on the back of my hand. I can feel my eyes burning, but I already cried in front of this woman once today. That's my quota. I wipe away the fresh torrent of tears on her cheeks. "Why are you crying?"

"I'm so sorry, Josh."

My heart lurches in my chest. "Me too."

"Is that why you were so worried about Maven?"

I heave a deep breath. "Yeah." I glance over my shoulder in the direction of Maven's room. "Think we can hear her okay from here?"

"It's probably the best place in the house. I can go get the baby monitor, though."

She gets the monitor and I get some extra quilts. Turning the TV all the way down, I put on the most festive movie I can think of and plop down on the couch.

Erin returns with the baby monitor. "Die Hard?"

"Is that okay?"

"Best Christmas movie ever." Erin says, sitting down.

I glance over, a surprised grin on my face. "I've been trying to convince my sisters of that fact for the last two decades."

"I'm team Die Hard." Erin says, tugging a quilt over her lap.

She's full of little surprises like that. If I could, I'd pick them all up and store them in my pocket.

Instead, I reach out and drag her closer.

She rolls her eyes, but she's biting back a grin.

And maybe it's shitty to talk about my wife with another woman. But I think I'm finally starting to understand what my mom and Bo and all the guys have been saying. And I think they're right—Ana wouldn't have wanted me to be alone.

Right now, I'm not thinking about sex, I'm thinking about how it's a little less lonely when I've got her in my arms.

She fits just right. Her head is right at chest level. Cupping my hand around the back of her head, I guide her onto my chest. Nerves flutter in my stomach, but she relaxes against me without complaint. Something inside my chest loosens at that.

29.

Erin

Maven has one more coughing spell. It's back in the bathroom for another steam bath, before she finally falls asleep again. Somewhere around two in the morning her fever breaks, but Josh and I stay in the living room just in case.

He doesn't strictly need me there, but I get the feeling he wants the back up. We watch old reruns on TV side by side. He puts his arm around me again and I lean into him, breathing him in. At one point, he turns and presses his lips to the top of my head.

I'm really not sure what to make of all of it. I've been out of the dating game for so long, I don't know what in the hell I'm doing.

And we can't date anyway, not without putting everything else at risk. But some little part of me says there's nothing wrong with a little physical affection. I'm trying to tell myself I can handle it without getting attached. It's delusional, but his pull is so strong, I want to believe it.

I've had a rough year. Between my dad passing away and getting dumped, I'm tired of being strong all the time. It's nice to feel protected. Safe.

Josh's fingertips absentmindedly trace patterns on my shoulder, lulling me to sleep.

The next time I wake up, the TV is stuck on a screensaver and Josh is padding back into the living room. "I just wanted to check on her."

"She doing okay?" I murmur.

He nods, settling onto the couch. Stretching onto his side, he tugs me down alongside him. No preamble. No warning. And I just melt into him. My mind is shorting out, but he wraps an arm around my waist and tugs me into his chest. I knew he was in good shape, but seeing those abs and feeling them snugged up against my body are two entirely different things.

I stare straight ahead, cataloguing every point of physical connection. His chest against my shoulders. My ass presses into his hips. His lips graze my hair. I can feel his breath, soft and warm.

"You're wide awake, aren't you?" His voice rumbles against my back.

"No."

I can feel him chuckling. "Go to sleep, Erin."

Easy for him to say.

Every nerve is firing and my lizard brain is telling me to turn around and kiss the man—finally get a look at what he's packing in those jeans.

But he's got his arm around me so tight, I'm not sure I could turn even if I was brave enough to try. I focus on the feeling of his chest rising and falling against my back, eventually drifting off to sleep.

Josh follows me into my dreams. My subconscious is far less reserved than my waking self. In the dream, I find him in the kitchen. Overcome by a tidal wave of lust, pull him down into a deep, delicious kiss. My hands travel up and down that fine chest before slipping beneath his waistband.

His hand arrests mine and I feel myself straddling the line between the dream world and the waking world.

My mind slowly pieces facts together. The hot make-out session was a dream. But my hands are definitely trying to burrow into Josh's jeans.

I slowly become aware of him, his ragged breath.

I try to jerk my hand away, but he keeps it pinned. Warmth suffuses my entire middle like a soft glow.

"Were you dreaming?" He asks, his voice husky and low.

I'm too embarrassed to look at him, but the early dawn light is casting his shoulder in a blue glow. I nod my head, thankful that the dim light is hiding my burning cheeks.

His fingers move to encircle my wrist. "About what?"

"Please don't make me say."

He chuckles. "About me?"

When I don't answer, he shifts over me so that his elbow is braced just over my shoulder. He leans down, lips grazing my ear. "I was dreaming about you."

My gaze meets his. Pushing past my embarrassment, I slowly become aware that it's not just his hips poking into my side.

My body subconsciously sways against him, noting the length pressing into my thigh. He groans quietly, brushing his nose along my cheekbone. "Can I kiss you?"

I stare up at him for a few seconds, temporarily distracted by the heat in those dark eyes. He almost looks like he's suffering, and it's hard to wrap my mind around the fact that I could be the source of that desire.

"Erin?"

I nod my head. My fingers reach up, tentatively threading through his short hair. He leans into my hand, kissing the inside of my wrist.

It's a move that's so unexpectedly tender, he crashes through the last of my reservations.

30.

Josh

She lies beneath me, looking like a gift, and I hardly know where to start.

I'm rusty. I haven't been with a woman in over two years.

And I've never been with another woman.

My hand grazes along her side, following the soft curve of her waist.

It helps that she's so different. Ana was slender and willowy.

Erin is like a juicy peach.

I know I shouldn't compare them.

I shouldn't be thinking about Ana at a moment like this. It's not fair to Erin.

And I want to be here with her, not trapped in the past.

Her fingernails scratch soft lines against my scalp and she tugs me closer. I let my lips brush hers. Her tongue flicks across my lower lip and my cock twitches in response. I'm distantly aware that this is a mistake. That I need to get up and go take a cold shower.

With a cute little whimper of impatience, she pulls me closer, deepening the connection. Her tongue sneaks between my lips and I'm so gone.

All of my worries erode like sand in a windstorm.

My focus narrows down to the exact points where our bodies touch.

Her lips are plush and her body is so soft.

She is pleasure.

She is happiness.

I smile into the kiss, bringing my hand to the back of her neck. My fingers work their way up through all those pretty copper curls.

She shifts under me, drawing her thigh up between my legs, running the length of my shaft. My hips react automatically, pinning her hips to the couch. She squirms against me, taking my lower lip between her teeth.

Her hand slips down my chest, over my stomach. When her fingers trail past my hips, curving around my bulge, my hips twitch. A muffled grunt escapes my lips and I bury my face into the crook of her neck. She gives me a little squeeze and my entire torso tenses. "Ah. Fuck me."

She curls her fingers around my waistband. "Yes, please."

I look down at her and she's got a hint of a smile on her lips.

Naughty thing.

I don't have to be told twice.

But not here. Both of the kids have a history of making early morning appearances.

Climbing to my feet, I drag her upright. Before she can find her feet, I sweep her up into my arms. She yelps indignantly, clearly not a fan of being picked up.

But I'm a fan of picking her up, so she's going to have to get used to it.

I carry her to the guest bedroom, closing the door behind us, locking it.

I set her down on her feet and she stares up at me, looking a little impatient. Her hair is mussed from having my fingers in it. Her clothes are disheveled. And it's a good look on her.

Prowling forward, I slip both hands along her jaw, bringing her in for a kiss. She braces her hands on my chest, parting her lips for me. I pull her sweater up and we break apart long enough for me to tug it over her head. I want to stop and admire the way she looks in the early morning light. But I also want to kiss her so deep she doesn't have room for anything but me. I settle for kissing her while my hands explore her bare skin.

"So soft." I murmur, trailing kisses down the curve of her neck. My hand lays flat against the small of her back and I pull her in. She grinds her hips against mine, hands slipping under my sweater. Bunching it up, her fingernails chart a course up my chest. I tug the sweater over my head and she scrapes her hands against my torso before gliding south.

Her fingers find the button of my jeans and as she works on pulling off my pants, I feel like I'm coming undone. She shoves my jeans down and my cock springs out, slapping against her tummy.

Her lips part prettily and she looks up at me, wide-eyed.

It's rather… gratifying. I grab hold of her hips and pull her into me, feeling her soft skin against my shaft. Slanting my lips over hers, I thrust my tongue between her lips.

31.

Erin

I'm starting to wonder if this guy saved a country in a previous life.

It hardly seems fair for one man to be so heartbreakingly handsome and be equipped like *that*.

I suspected he was well-endowed. I've been curious since he walked into the kitchen with a morning wood weeks ago.

But even my colorful imagination did not prepare me for the sheer size of that thing.

I'm not sure what a person does with something like that. It doesn't seem like it would fit… anywhere.

But he's mashing it up against my stomach and my body is very much interested in giving it a try. My body is ready. I'm soaking wet, but my brain isn't quite ready to go all the way.

I haven't been with another guy since Matt, and I was with him for years. My experience is extremely limited. To say I'm nervous is a vast understatement.

But I want more than just kisses. And judging by the way he's straining against me, he wants more, too.

I decide to split the difference by dropping to my knees.

He sucks in a surprised breath, revealing that maybe he wasn't sure what the next step was supposed to be, either.

Misery loves company and so does insecurity. Knowing he might be nervous too gives me a little surge of confidence. I take him in my hands, marveling at the fact that my finger and thumb don't meet. Squeezing him around the base, I drag my fist up his length, enjoying the contrast between velvety skin and hard flesh. He shivers from my touch.

Shivers.

Because of little old me.

The power goes straight to my head. My lips quirk into a grin, and I glance up at his face. He's watching my every move, eyes hazy with desire. The look on his face sends sparks shooting right to my center. Keeping my gaze locked on his, I lower my mouth, taking his tip between my lips. A soft grunt spills out of him. He gathers up my hair in his hand, hips almost vibrating with tension.

He's a mouthful. I swirl my tongue along his underside, earning an involuntary thrust from his hips.

I've never liked giving head, but Josh is opening new horizons for me. Touching him like this has me so hot I'm afraid I might spontaneously combust.

I want to experience all of him. I want to blow his mind.

My fist works up and down his shaft, making up for what I can't accommodate in my mouth. My cheeks hollow out as I suck on him, tugging him out of my mouth with a quiet little *pop*.

I kiss his length, caressing him with my tongue. When I take him back in my mouth, I brace both hands on his hips, encouraging him to thrust into my mouth.

"Fuck, baby. You feel so good." He murmurs, voice low and raspy. My fingertips dig into his glutes and he tightens his grip on my hair, pumping his shaft into my mouth.

I move my hand to his balls, his entire torso tenses. When I play with them, he groans. "I'm not going to last much longer if you keep that up."

I pull back, running my hand up and down his length. "Don't hold back. I want to see what you've got."

His fist releases my hair and then both of his hands are wrapping around the back of my head. "Take it."

I happily take him back in my mouth, hands working on his shaft, his balls.

"Fuck." He grunts. "I'm close."

I pull back a bit, cupping his tip with my tongue. I slide my fist up and down, listening to his haggard breath. Marveling at the effect I'm having on him.

His entire body tenses up and then he's coming with a soft, surprised grunt. I close my lips around his shaft, taking everything he gives me. His hands weave through my hair, caressing my head while he gently pumps into my mouth.

When he's finished, he helps me to my feet, kicking his jeans the rest of the way off. He lifts me onto the bed and crawls in behind me.

Manhandling me a little, he arranges my body alongside his. His fingers find the button on my jeans, my zipper. And then he's tugging my jeans off, slipping them down my legs.

I'm a little nervous he's going to want more. And even though my body is fully on board, my heart is still a little scared.

He seems content to just explore my stomach, my hips.

It makes me a little self-conscious. This man clearly works out. His body is hard. Mine is… soft.

His fingertips dimple my love handles and he buries his face in my hair. "God, you feel so good."

He sounds so genuine, I can almost believe him.

Something eases in me a little.

I relax back against him, wishing I could bottle this feeling.

32.

Josh

I didn't realize how tense I'd been until all the stress left my body.

I feel like I've got a new lease on life.

Contentment suffuses my body in a warm glow. She feels like a million bucks pressed up against me. Everything about this body is luxurious. I want to squeeze her harder, fill my hands with her soft curves, but I'm afraid I might hurt her. I have to content myself with light touches.

I nuzzle my face into her neck, filling my nose with the sweet scent of her shampoo. She shivers when my nose grazes the sensitive spot behind her ear. Ticklish, then. I nip at the spot, and she squirms against me with a muffled giggle.

So fucking cute.

My hands glide up her side, slipping over her chest. She fills my palms, scratching an itch that's been there since the day I first laid eyes on her. It's not enough. I tug her bra down, bringing my hands back down on bare skin. Her nipples harden against my palms. When I squeeze her, she arches against me. I slip my arms around her, bracing her, supporting her, while my hands explore her body. She lets her head fit into the crook of my neck, soft curls spilling across my shoulders.

Keeping one hand possessively on her breast, my other sails down her stomach, past that cute little belly button. She tenses slightly when I nose my fingertips under the lace band of her panties. I pause, but then she wiggles her round ass against my hips.

That's all the encouragement I need.

My hand glides under her panties, fitting between her legs. I can feel her warmth beneath my fingertips and I pause there, liking the way she feels against my hand, the way her body feels tucked inside my arms.

My finger parts her folds, dipping inside, and I groan, kissing her shoulder. "So wet."

She squirms against me, threatening to breathe new life into my shaft. But I already had my moment in the sun. It's her turn.

Pushing her panties to the side, I slip my finger deeper. Her hand glides down my forearm, encouraging me to take more. My second finger squeezes inside, stretching her. She's incredibly tight. If we ever do have sex, I'm going to have to be extra careful with her.

I curl my fingers, and she arches her back, pressing her hips against mine.

I can feel her clit hitting the fleshy part of my thumb. Pressing down, I increase the pace as I thrust my fingers in and out of her wet pussy.

She squirms in my arms and I hold her against my body. Peppering her neck and shoulder with kisses, I pinch her nipples with one hand, the other is buried between her legs.

I can feel her chest rising and falling, can almost feel her heart pounding against her chest. And then, with a muted little cry, she comes against me. Her muscles clamp down on my fingers, making me wonder what it would feel like to have my shaft buried inside instead of my fingers.

When the last twitches of her orgasm are spent, I pull my fingers out and bring them to her lips. She takes them in her mouth, tongue wrapping around my knuckles, taking the entire length of my fingers into her mouth so that I could almost tickle the back of her throat. I press a kiss to her temple and wrap her up in my arms.

I can't remember the last time I felt this content. This relaxed.

We just woke up, but I slip into a light cat nap.

"Dad!"

My eyes snap open.

"Dad. Where are you?"

Fuck it all.

We spring apart, scrambling for our clothes. I can hear Trace banging the door open on my bedroom. All he would need to do is pass through the adjoining bathroom and he'll catch us with our pants around our ankles.

Literally.

It's a little funny, but mostly, very embarrassing. I feel like I'm back in high school again, scrambling to not get caught by my parents.

She manages to get dressed first. She's got her jeans and sweater back in place, but her hair is still tousled. And those cheeks are flushed. I have the strongest compulsion to scoop her up and kiss those swollen lips, but something about those wide eyes tells me I need to give her space.

With a look over her shoulder, she slips out the door. I can hear her voice filtering through the wall. "Trace. What are you doing, buddy?"

"Where's dad?"

"He's around, I'm sure. What do you want for breakfast?"

Capitalizing on the diversion Erin is creating, I slip through the bathroom and emerge from my own bedroom.

He turns around, wide-eyed. "Where'd you come from?"

I give him a sleepy, befuddled look, feeling a little guilty. "I was in my room."

As soon as the words are off my lips, I regret them. I don't like lying to him. It was necessary, because I don't think he'd understand what's going on between Erin and me.

Hell, I don't even know what's going on between the two of us.

But I do get a creeping feeling of shame. Like we've made a terrible mistake.

33.

Erin

Josh slips through the kitchen without a word. He steps into his boots and shrugs his heavy, canvas coat on before stepping outside.

He checks the cattle every morning. But lately, he eats breakfast first.

That's my second hint that he's having some regrets.

The first was the way he looked at me while we raced to get dressed.

You don't have to be a genius to know what regret looks like.

I get it.

It hurts.

But I get it.

This is what I was afraid of—messing up a good thing.

Being in his arms was a good thing, too. But if I can't have both, then I at least need a paycheck.

For the first time in weeks, I start to wonder if I should think about finding another job.

Both kids are eating pancakes at the table when Josh comes back in. I listen to him methodically pull off his boots. He always washes his hands when he comes back in. When the water turns off, I count the seconds until the floorboards creak under his feet. He always moves so damn quietly.

"Coffee?" I don't bother to turn around.

"Yes, please."

Filling a mug, I hand it to him, finding him leaning against the counter. He has one hand braced the edge of the countertop, the other accepts his coffee. Our fingers brush and I do my best not to think about what those fingers are capable of.

The kids are watching PBS on their iPad. They're not listening to us, but he pitches his voice low, anyway. "We should talk."

"Uh oh." I smile weakly.

"I'm serious."

I frown. "Yes. I gathered that."

He tips his head towards the living room, and I follow him. The room is almost blindingly bright with morning sunlight. Our tree sits in a pool of crisp, white sunlight.

He rubs the back of his neck. "About last night."

"You mean this morning?"

He gives me a tight smile. I find myself wondering what happened to the tender guy who held me in his arms.

His gaze is pinned on mine. "I want you to know how much I respect you."

"Oh lord, Josh. Spare me."

"Let me finish."

"Not necessary." I glance back at the kitchen. "I know what rejection sounds like. I was treated to one quite recently, if you'll recall."

"What?"

"My ex-boyfriend."

He pauses. "I didn't know you just broke up with someone."

I'm surprised I didn't tell him about that. But then again, why would I have? "I mean, it was last summer. So, not that recent. But we were together forever. That's besides the point." I wave my hand airily, trying to act like I'm not internally squirming. "I know what you were going to say, and we can just skip it."

He crosses his arms. "What was I going to say?"

"You were going to say you think I'm a swell gal, but we need to cool it. For the kids' sake. And you would be right." I shrug. "As far as I'm concerned, nothing happened. It's no big deal."

I should have stopped after I mentioned the kids. Everything after that only made him frown. When I said it wasn't a big deal, he even looked a little taken aback. Part of me wishes I could reel those words back, but the truth is we really do need to cool it. If acting like I don't care is what it takes, then that's what I need to do.

I can tell he's not satisfied with my response, which is frustrating, because that means I'm probably in for another conversation.

But his mom saves the day by knocking on the front door. Without waiting for a response, she pushes the door open. "Knock, knock. It's grandma."

Josh crosses the room, stopping by me to mutter in my ear. "We're not done here."

His voice, low and sultry, sends a shiver down my spine.

He wraps his mom in a quick hug. "What are you up to?"

"It's Small Town Christmas in Clark. We're taking the kids, remember?"

"Oh shit. That's today, isn't it?" He glances at his mom, doing a double take at her raised eyebrow. "I mean, oh shoot."

"Better." Her tone is dry. "You'll come too, won't you, Erin? You'll love it. All the little boutiques and coffee shops have open houses and crafts for the kids. And they bring Santa in on a fire truck."

"Oh, I'd love to." I say, wondering how convincing my brittle tone is. "Maven's sick though. I better stay back with her."

"Oh, no! Little Mavey? Where is she? Is she okay?"

I nod towards the kitchen. "She's eating breakfast."

"Oh, thank goodness." Lisa says, crossing the room to peek in the kitchen. "Can't go outside, though, if she's got a cold. How about this? You and Josh take Trace, and I'll stay back with Maven."

"Oh, mom…" Josh struggles for words. "You have to go. You love Small Town Christmas. I'll stay back and you ladies can go. I'm not a big shopper, anyway."

"Nonsense." Lisa says, her tone definitive. "Maven needs her grammy. I'm staying. You two are going."

34.

Josh

Erin was spot on. She predicted my rehearsed script to the line. She was just missing one part—the part where I say how big of a deal it was to me.

Ana was the first and only woman I ever slept with.

Erin stretches the list to two.

If you can count a blow job and getting fingered as sleeping together.

Maybe she doesn't. She certainly isn't acting like we did anything consequential.

I'm not going to lie. That hurts a little.

And when I get hurt, I get surly.

This is not the best time for me to drag Trace to a crowded holiday festival. I don't like those things when I'm in a good mood, let alone when I'm taking my one-night-stand along for the ride.

But when my mom makes a decision, her will is iron clad. Fifteen minutes later, Erin and I both find ourselves bumping down the icy drive, Trace merrily chatting away in the backseat.

Erin spots Reese before I do. "Is that your sister?"

She's short and compact, not unlike my mom. In fact, mom is always calling Reese her mini me. They have the same dark hair and sleepy eyes.

I'm not surprised to see Reese coming back from a walk. She was always like that, rain or shine, out walking by herself. She said she needed the air; I think she just needed away from our full house.

I pull over, tires crunching in the ice and gravel, and roll down the window. "What are you up to?"

She leans on the edge of the truck door and waves at Erin. "I had to get out of the house. Charlie and Parker are driving me nuts."

"Want to go to Small Town Christmas?"

She wrinkles her nose. "Not particularly."

"It's that or go back to the loving arms of our dear sisters."

She laughs. "Fair point."

My shoulders sag a little in relief as she slides into the backseat, bumping fists with Trace.

She is the buffer Erin and I needed.

Scooting to the middle of the backseat, she leans forward. "What'd you think of the Olson family Thanksgiving?"

Erin glances back at her. "Yeah. They're great."

Her tone is too light. Neither of us believe her.

Reese laughs. "We're not particularly fond of that side of the family, so you don't have to worry about our feelings." She thumps me on the arm. "I heard your boyfriends are driving the firetruck this year."

"You bet. Bo and Skyler."

She laughs. "What fool gave the keys to the fire truck to the Thomas cousins?"

"They probably gave them to themselves. Did you forget that Bo's captain of the department?"

"I didn't forget. I just can't believe it." She angles her body towards Erin. "Josh and his buddies were the town golden boys, but naughty as all get out."

I frown at her. "And my son is sitting in the back, listening to every word, no doubt."

"No, I'm not." Trace pipes up.

Erin bites back a smile.

Reese glances at Trace with a grin. "Then I'll talk about the Thomas boys instead."

Reese spends the next twenty minutes regaling Erin with G-rated versions of my high school exploits. Thanks to Ana, I was probably the best behaved of the four of us. But with all the dumb-shit things we did, it's amazing we survived into adulthood.

The traffic starts to get congested about a mile outside city limits. "Here we go." I say with a dry tone.

This festival brings visitors from as far as Lincoln. It's elbow to elbow at times.

We climb out of the truck and I toss Trace up on my shoulders.

He leans precariously from his perch, pointing for Erin's benefit. "See the tree?"

It's hard to miss. It's two stories tall and strung with Christmas lights and beach-ball sized ornaments.

I've seen it about twenty-five times and if you've seen it once, you've seen it enough.

But Erin's eyes go round. This girl is a sucker for Christmas joy. No surprise there. She's basically the human embodiment of holiday spirit.

I hate this festival, but I love the look on her face.

35.

Erin

From the way Josh was moping around, I set the bar very low for this event. I am pleasantly surprised. This is no small affair. It's a sprawling festival with vendors and food trucks. The air literally smells like cinnamon and spice. It's enough to take the edge off this morning's embarrassment. Reese is helping, too. She's a chatterbox, but so am I. It's easy to keep the conversation going with this particular Olson.

I glance up at Trace, who's busy pointing out every festive detail to his grumpy dad. It's my responsibility to watch Trace. And quite frankly, I'd feel a little less awkward about being here if Josh let me do my job.

But he's holding onto Trace like the kid's a human shield.

We thread our way past an absurdly long line and just as I'm thinking, *let's avoid whatever this is*, Trace notices the end of the rainbow leads to a balloon guy. He's dressed up like a Christmas elf, twisting balloons into swords and crowns and little dogs.

"Balloons!" Trace crows. "Can we get a balloon, dad?"

"That's a long line, Trace."

"Please?" Trace whines.

Josh glances at me and I shrug. So we plant ourselves at the back of the line, resigned to our fate.

We're only in the line for about five minutes when the wail of a fire engine sails out across the crowd.

Reese grins ear to ear. "It's Santa, Trace! Look!"

We all turn to see a fire engine rounding the corner. A guy in a Santa suit sits on top, waving his mittened hand to the crowd.

"Can I go talk to Santa?" Trace asks.

Josh squints at the line. "You don't want a balloon?"

Trace bites his lip, torn.

"I'll take him over there." Reese says. "You two hold our spot."

Before we can respond, Reese helps Trace scramble down from his dad's shoulder. The two disappear into the crowd, hand in hand.

Josh and I glance at each other uneasily before digging our phones out of our pockets. I'm doom-scrolling on Instagram, not even registering the pictures rolling by when someone calls out. "Joshy Olson."

Joshy?

I look up in time to see a very handsome, very tall blonde sweep in to wrap Josh in a bone-cracking bear hug. He braces his hands on either side of Josh's cheeks, squeezing a little so Josh is making a fish face. "Where you been, man? We never see you these days."

Josh shakes him off, rubbing his cheek. His expression is annoyed, but there's laughter in his eyes. "Fuck off, man."

The blonde presses his hand against his chest. "Language, Josh. This is a family event."

Josh shakes his head. "Erin, this is my idiot friend, Dusty."

Dusty turns the full wattage of his blinding charm on me. He's *cute*.

It shouldn't surprise me. Beautiful people tend to travel in packs. But Dusty looks like a walking, breathing Calvin Klein ad. He's got a scruffy jaw and fascinating blue eyes. Just looking at him makes me blush. Judas. I need to pull it together.

Dusty offers me his hand. "Dusty Larson. And you must be the mysterious nanny I've been hearing about."

My cheeks flame to a new depth of color.

Josh speaks first. "Who's been talking?"

"Bo, for one."

"Fucking Bo."

Dusty laughs. "How do you put up with this grouch?"

"Carefully." I reply, earning a full-throated laugh from Dusty. It wasn't that funny, but I'll take what I can get.

Josh watches the interaction with a skeptical expression. He tugs on my jacket, towing me behind him as the line moves forward. Dusty notices the interaction, gaze travel between the two of us.

Josh plants his feet, shoving his hands into his coat pockets. "What are you doing here? There's no booze or ladies."

Dusty grins. "Correction, there are plenty of ladies." He glances at me, winking.

Josh rolls his eyes. "They're all here with their kids, Dusty."

"What's your point?" He shakes Josh's shoulder. "I'm kidding. Kind of. Not really."

Josh gives him a dry look. "Sienna made you drag her here?"

"You got it, sir."

Josh glances at me. "His little sister."

"Sister's a generous word. I prefer demon. Teenagers are terrifying these days." Dusty grimaces. "She told me to act like I didn't know her, so obviously, I have to track her down and give her shit. But first things first, I need to go greet our resident firefighters."

"You bummed they wouldn't let you ride on top?"

Dusty thinks that over, a wicked grin stretching across his face. "You lined that joke up for me, but since there is a lady present, I'll leave it be. We still watching the game at your place tomorrow?"

Josh gives me a sidelong glance. "Planning on it."

"Cool. Until then." Dusty slaps Josh's shoulder, winking at me *again*, before threading through the crowd. His blonde head bobs well above everyone else, drawing gazes as he goes. He parts the crowd like Moses parted the sea.

"How many of you are there?" I murmur, my thoughts spilling off my tongue before I can filter them.

"What?"

I want to know how many heartbreakingly gorgeous friends Josh has, so I can mentally prepare for tomorrow. I wonder if it's too early to fake a headache. "How many friends are coming over?"

"Tomorrow?" He shrugs. "It'll just be the four of us."

Four of them.

Great.

36.

Josh

Usually, when the guys come over for the game, we drink our supper.

In beer form.

Maybe somebody gets ambitious enough to bring a bag of chips.

Erin doesn't know this.

She's been working away in the kitchen all afternoon, even after I told her she didn't need to trouble herself.

I lean on the doorframe, watching her roll dough out on the counter. "Now what are you making?"

"Synonym rolls." Trace declares.

Erin and I glance at each other, mutually amused.

I tilt my head. "To go with the antonym soup?"

Trace looks at me like I've lost my mind. "It's chili."

Erin laughs. Trace glances at her with a big grin. "He doesn't know much about cooking."

"Not like you." She says, booping his nose. Her finger leaves a smudge of flour on his nose.

"Are you helping?" I ask him.

He nods. "It was my idea."

Erin smiles, showing him how to sprinkle cinnamon and sugar on the dough. "He said cinnamon rolls were his favorite."

"Dad's too." Trace declares, giving me away.

She glances at me, looking almost shy.

This woman is going to be my undoing. She's got on a white sweater than exposes both shoulders. Big hoop earrings just draw the eye to her delicate neck and then back down the slope of her bare shoulders. I want nothing more than to lift those soft curls from her neck and see if she tastes as good as I remember.

Cinnamon rolls from scratch and wearing that sweater? I'll be lucky if none of my friends tries to carry her off.

The front door creaks open and Bo's voice booms out. "Honey, I'm home."

In her room, Maven starts wailing.

"Oh, shit. I've got her." Bo calls from the living room.

Dusty and Skyler walk in next. It probably says something that none of my friends bother knocking. But we've known each other our whole lives. Not much is off limits between us. They're like brothers to me. They even treat my kids like their niece and nephew.

Dusty strides into the kitchen, depositing two six packs in the fridge before turning to lean up against the counter next to Trace. "What are you making?"

"Rolls." Trace says, giving me a flat look. Clearly, he knew we were having a joke at his expense before.

"From scratch?" Dusty asks, almost reverently. He looks at me. "She cooks for you?"

Erin shrugs, not lifting her focus from her work. "All part of the job description."

I tilt my head, looking at her. Was it?

"Come work for me." Dusty says, grinning at her.

"You don't have kids." I point out.

"I've got a dog." He cranes his head, trying to catch her eye. "Whatever he's paying you, I'll double it."

"Okay, get out." I say, shooing him away from her.

Bo comes to stand in the doorway, holding Maven high against his chest. She's got her hand wrapped around his ear, a grumpy look on her face.

Skyler comes closer, scratching her back. "Did you wake the baby up?"

Bo smiles, guilt scrawled all over his face. "She missed her Uncle Bo."

Skyler and Bo both have the trademark Thomas dark skin and black hair. They even have matching short-cropped beards. The biggest difference is that Bo has a few inches on Skyler and Skyler occasionally wears glasses.

The door opens and shuts and a very feminine "Yoo-hoo" rings out from the front room.

I glare at Skyler. "You didn't."

Skyler holds his hands up. "Reese twisted my arm."

As though summoned by some evil spell, all three of my sisters squeeze into the kitchen. Aside from my friends, there are no people in this world who enjoy busting my balls quite as much as this awful little trio.

37.

Erin

In very short order, the kitchen becomes very crowded.

I don't mind people.

I'm a dyed in the wool extrovert.

But this crowd is overwhelming me. They have an intimate knowledge of Josh and his kids. And despite the connection I'm making with my little crew, these people just serve to remind me that I'm an interloper.

The hired help.

The youngest, Charlie, swans closer. She has a vicious sort of beauty. All angles and creamy skin. Her hair is the same color as Josh's, but her eyes are a mesmerizing hazel. "Are you baking?"

Trace puffs up his chest. "I'm helping."

"I see that." Charlie rustles his hair. She tosses a smile over her shoulder. "You're wasting your time with these heathens. They won't appreciate your hard work."

Maybe it's unintentional, but I catch a patronizing note in her voice. I don't know much about her, other than the fact that she's doing pre-med at Drake. And she doesn't know much about me, other than the fact that I went to community college. I can tell she isn't particularly impressed with my career choice.

Even though she's three years younger than me, she manages to make me feel small.

"Game's on." Dusty calls from the other room.

Charlie scoops Trace up and carries him into the living room. "You're coming with me, Mister."

They filter out of the kitchen, thank God, leaving just Reese behind.

She leans on the counter across from me. "She's got some growing up to do."

"Hmm?" I murmur, rolling the dough into a log.

"Chuck." She grins at my confused expression. "Charlie. She can be a turd sometimes. For what it's worth, she's that snotty with all of us."

"Who's snotty?" Skyler asks, returning to the kitchen. He swings the fridge open and pulls two beers out.

"Nobody." Reese says, winking at me.

Skyler leans on the counter next to Reese, watching me slice the dough. It's hard not to feel self-conscious with two sets of eyes on me. One set belongs to Josh's sister. The other belongs to a very sexy, bespectacled beef cake.

I lay the rolls on a pan, a row of perfect spirals. He grins. "Paul Hollywood would approve."

Reese turns to look up at him. "I wouldn't have pegged you as a Bake Off fan."

He pretends to look offended. "That's sexist, Reese."

"How's that beer coming?" Josh calls from the living room.

Skyler straightens, grinning at me. "His lordship calls."

Reese trails behind him.

It's like there's a rotating door on the kitchen entry. As soon as they leave, Dusty pushes his way back in. He hops up on the counter, watching me cover my baking pan. "I'm very excited about this."

"The game?"

He grins. "The cinnamon rolls."

I lean on the counter opposite him. "What, do you guys never get real food?"

"Four bachelors? No."

"None of your moms like to cook?"

"Ah." He shrugs, looking uncomfortable for the first time. "My mom wasn't much of a cook, but my little sister's been experimenting lately."

It doesn't escape my notice that he talks about his mom in past tense. I decide not to push him on it. "Your Home Ec teacher should be ashamed."

He grins. "Our Home Ec teacher had her hands full with us."

"Reese mentioned you boys were a bit wild."

"She tends to exaggerate."

I bite my lip. "Actually, I think she was downplaying things. Trace was in the truck at the time."

"Ah."

"Did you all go to high school at the same time?"

He glances towards the living room, but his gaze is distant. He looks back at me, a dimple appearing in his cheek. "All of us except Chuck."

"Does she like being called Chuck?"

He grins mischievously. "Hates it."

"Got it. Were all of you boys in the same grade?"

"Kindergarten on."

"You've been friends a long time."

He nods. "We lucked out, landing in the same grade. I'm sure our teachers would disagree."

"And Reese?"

"She was a junior when we were seniors. Parker was a freshman."

"What year did you all graduate?"

He tells me, and I do the math. "I was a sophomore when you were a senior."

He tilts his head, eyes sparkling in that disconcerting light blue shade. "A baby, then."

I shrug. "If you want to look at it that way."

Josh appears in the doorway, eyes shooting daggers at both of us. "Did you get lost, Dusty?"

Dusty hops off the counter, winking at me on his way by. "Just getting to know your new friend."

38.

Josh

We're not even two minutes into the first quarter and these guys are sniffing around Erin like bloodhounds.

Bo's the only one who hasn't wandered into the kitchen, but I suspect he was just waiting his turn. I gave Dusty a few minutes, but when he didn't come back, I started to worry.

He's a smooth operator. Of the four of us, he's always been the best with the ladies.

I don't want to tell them what's going on between Erin and me, because they'd read into it too much.

She's the first woman I've had any interest in since I lost Ana. I'm not sure what that means for me, or if I'm ready to pursue it; but I know one thing—I don't want their opinions. And if they knew, they'd never let me hear the end of it.

That leaves me in the precarious position of guard-dogging a woman who, to all intents and purposes, doesn't belong to me.

She catches me staring, and okay, maybe I'm scowling. But she shrugs, flicking an eyebrow upwards in challenge. "Can I get you something?"

Yeah. You can help me get my head on straight.

I shrug, shoving my hands into my pockets. "Nope. I'm good."

I leave her alone in the kitchen and she busies herself in there so long I start to suspect she doesn't want to come out. The living room is pretty full. She'd almost have to sit on the floor. Or someone's lap. I'm sure there would be more than a few volunteers for that position.

Maven abdicates the Bo's lap, toddling into the kitchen. He climbs to his feet, following her. I can hear his booming laughter as he chats with Erin. I expected Dusty to be a problem. Bo is a bit of a surprise. I'm thinking about dragging him back into the living room when Skyler nudges me with his knee.

"Hmm?"

Skyler laughs, adjusting his glasses. "Where's your head at, man?"

In the kitchen with Erin. I shrug. "Didn't get much sleep last night."

That's true.

"How's the whole nanny thing going?" He keeps his gaze trained on the commercials, tipping his beer back against his lips.

"I wasn't too happy about it at first, but it's really nice having someone here to help all the time."

He glances at me. "She really lives here, then?"

I nod. "She's got the guest room."

"And that's not weird?"

Shrugging, I crane my head to peer into the kitchen. "At first, yeah. But we're getting used to each other."

"Are you and her…"

Fucking? I wish. I huff a laugh. "No. Definitely not."

Not sure why I added the definitely.

He follows my gaze, peering towards the kitchen. "So you don't mind if one of us takes a crack at her?"

I roll my neck, trying to loosen the tension growing at the base of my neck. "Take a crack at her? She's not an egg, Skyler."

He laughs. "She's cute. And she can cook. That's all I need to know."

She's more than cute. And there's a hell of a lot more to her than just her ability to throw baked goods together like it's no big deal. The scent of baking bread mingles with cinnamon and caramel. Okay, maybe that is a magical skill set worthy of note, but I don't like hearing her reduced to two lines.

I roll my neck again, agitated. "Listen, man. I don't care what you do, just don't make things awkward for me. The kids love that girl and if I have to find another nanny, I'm holding you personally responsible."

He holds up his hands. "Whoa, who's talking about her quitting?"

"I'm just saying, if she got upset because of you and ran back to Lincoln…"

"Okay. Message received. I won't mess with her."

"I can't tell you what to do."

"No, I know. It's cool, Josh. I didn't think about the big picture. I don't want to do anything that would have an impact on those kids. Or you. Bros before
h—"

I cut him off with a single steely glare.

39.

Erin

Hanging out with Josh and his posse is a little like being back in high school.

And not in a good way.

Who am I kidding? There was nothing good about high school the first time around, either.

I thought I had outgrown the whole swing choir nerd thing, but being around these massive guys is like being forced to sit at the cool table with all the jocks. I'm just doing my best to keep up and not make a fool of myself.

I'm actually kind of impressed by how well I'm doing so far. I'm stringing all of my words together in complete sentences. And my cheeks are merely a permanent shade of light pink, which is better than beet red.

It's taking everything I have in me to not be bowled over by them. But it's like running a gauntlet. I swear to God, they're taking turns coming in to talk to me.

They're just curious about the stranger who's been inserted into their buddy's life. They obviously care about Josh, but their protectiveness is wearing me out. It's like one long interview.

When it's time to put the kids to bed, I'm grateful for the excuse to hide. I have to physically wrestle Trace away from Charlie. In the end, she lays claim to the right to put Maven to bed. She might come off as a bit of an ice queen, but of all the girls, she's particularly smitten with the kids. And that fact alone makes me like her. Just a little.

Trace falls asleep in record time. Which just figures. The one night I wanted to linger, and he's out like a light.

I pass Skyler in the hall and he waylays me, asking me a ton of questions about my cinnamon rolls. Apparently, he's more than just a passive viewer when it comes to the Bake Off show. He likes to try his hand at all the technical challenges, but hasn't had much luck. I'm laughing at his tale of woe and soggy bottomed pies, when I catch sight of Josh watching us from the couch.

He looks a little perturbed and I'm not sure why.

Excusing myself from Skyler, I pad back into the kitchen. When I'm elbows deep in dishwater, I sense rather than hear, someone stop behind me. Only one person can walk that quietly. "What can I do for you, Josh?"

He braces his arms on either side of me, just barely holding his body away from mine. But I can feel the heat rolling off him. Smell the scent of his soap. His nose barely grazes my hair, and he leans in, putting his lips near my ear. "Why are you messing with me?"

His low voice fills my head with a hazy feeling.

I straighten, accidentally bumping into his hips with my ass. "What are you talking about?"

"You're awfully chatty."

Anger simmers in my stomach. "I'm always chatty."

"Hmm." He murmurs, his voice vibrating through his chest. My body wants to lean into that sound, to feel his hard chest against my back.

"If you don't want me talking to your friends, why didn't you just give me the night off?"

There's an unspoken rule between us where we act like we're just buds. Roommates. Like he's not my boss and I'm not his employee. Mentioning time off sort of prods at that flaw in our relationship.

He's quiet for a beat. "I don't want you to want my friends."

Those words swirl around in my mind, refusing to assimilate.

He gathers my hair in his hand and slides it over one shoulder. His lips brush along my neck in a feather-light touch. My neck automatically bends to his touch, curving towards his mouth. But just as quickly, he steps back, slipping out of the room.

I stand there, feeling confused and horny.

And very annoyed.

With no viable outlet, I stew and stew until the game is over and everyone finally leaves.

When the door closes behind Charlie, I lean against the doorframe to the kitchen, arms crossed. "We need to talk."

He turns around, shoving his hands in his pockets. "Okay." He says slowly, studying my face. "About what?"

"About earlier."

"What about it?"

"You've got to make up your mind." I say, exasperated.

"About what?"

My face reddens slightly. I frown. "If you don't want me to date your friends, then just say so."

"I thought I did say that."

"Are you harboring feelings for me?"

The words sort of hang in the air between us. He winces. "No."

"But I can't talk to anyone else?"

"I just don't want you going down the line, dating each of my friends."

It takes me a few seconds to respond. My heart is in my throat. "I can't believe you would think I'm that kind of girl."

"I don't know what kind of girl you are. You screwed around with me and I'm your boss."

"Nice, Josh. Real nice." I spin on heel, marching down the hall before he can see the tears.

40.

Josh

Am I a total dick?

I believe the answer to that question would be a resounding *yes*.

I want to be the kind of guy who knows exactly what to say. Who knows what he wants and never hurts the people he cares about.

But I'm the type of guy who sometimes has a hard time getting out of bed. I'm the sort of guy who loves his kids more than oxygen, but sometimes gets so frustrated with them I feel like a pot boiling over.

I didn't set out with the intention of hurting Erin, but those words fell off my lips before I could think them through.

I'm petrified I might have done irrevocable damage and yet, I cannot summon the courage to apologize. Because she's going to need more than a simple, I'm sorry. She's going to need an explanation and damned if I just don't have one.

When the sun rises the next day, I half expect to find her loading up her little sedan with her bags. But she's in the kitchen, making coffee with a pinch of salt.

I could almost cry with relief. Instead, I sip my coffee. "It's moving day."

She looks up, momentarily confused. She's not wearing any makeup today. Her hair doesn't have any product and she's just got on an oversized hoodie and jeans. And I think this might be my favorite look yet. I didn't realize her eyelashes were that color. Like strands of copper. I want to cup her face in my hands so I can get a closer look, but I keep them firmly tucked away in my pockets.

"Are your parents all packed up?"

I nod. "Yeah. It's been a process. Parker's been a big help." I rub the back of my neck. "I think mom wants the kids over there today, but if you can help keep them…"

"Out of trouble? No problem."

"The guys offered to come help."

She turns away, trying to look disinterested, but I can't help but to notice the way her shoulders tense. It's still a raw subject. Probably will be until I can get my act together.

She shrugs. "Well, let me know if there's anything else I can do to help."

That feels like a dismissal. Feeling like an asshole, I shove my boots on and step outside, breathing in the chilly December air.

Things seem clearer out here. I've moved the heifers over to the pasture by my house and I watch them mill about in the snow.

This right here, this is the stuff that makes sense.

That's all I need. My kids. Fresh air. And the farm.

Hopping in my truck, I head over to the main house. The second I step into the house, a heavy feeling of oppression settles on my shoulders and I realize I would have been better off with Erin. I can hear the girls yelling at each other from the second floor.

That's not news. Ever since they were little, they were feisty little things. We'd go to other places and people would tell my parents what angels they were, and we'd just laugh. At home, they were little demons.

Reese is hollering at the top of her lungs. "Just take a chill pill, you witch!"

She slams the door and comes stomping down the steps. She slows down slightly when she sees me. "If you were smart, you'd turn right around and act like you were never here."

I grin. "That bad, huh?"

"Parker and Charlie are at it again." She comes to a stop at the base of the steps. "You had coffee yet?"

"Yes, but I never say no to coffee."

She grins, leading me into the kitchen. Mom's kitchen is twice as big as mine. She's made countless birthday cakes in here. Christmas meals. Sack lunches for school. It's kind of sad to see her leave all that behind, but she seems excited. Who am I to rain on that parade?

More doors slam, followed by stomping. Parker appears in the kitchen, looking owlish and surprised to see me. She's always been quiet, economizing each word as though it costs her to speak to people. Unless she's fighting with Chuck. Then she lets loose like a howler monkey.

I grin at her. "Hey."

She tucks her hair behind her ears. "Hey."

"You ladies need to try to act civilized when the guys get over here."

Charlie isn't far behind. "Your loser friends are coming over?"

"My loser friends are coming over to lift the heavy shit. Unless you ladies are volunteering?"

Charlie gets a faraway look in her eyes. My brows lower. I point at her. "No."

She tilts her head, a mischievous glint in her eyes. "What?"

I point at all three of them. "No."

The girls exchange looks, rolling their eyes with a smattering of giggles. Nothing can unite these little banshees like making their big brother squirm.

"You three are my little sisters and they are my friends. And since I don't want to have to remove their balls, please stay away from them."

Charlie sashays into the kitchen, pouring herself some coffee. "You tell your man whore friends to stay away from us, then."

41.

Erin

Josh's friends arrive in a procession of oversized pickup trucks. Between their trucks and Josh's, they almost don't need the cattle trailer that's backed up to the house.

It's the strangest moving day I've ever witnessed because they don't move all the furniture—only the boxes and things with pink sticky notes attached to them. The rest of it is staying behind.

Lisa wanders around with a balled-up tissue in her hand, oscillating between excitement and nostalgia. The girls, on the other hand, are firmly rooted in gloom. This is their childhood we're dismantling. When tempers come to a boil over a grandfather clock, I lead Maven and Trace outside.

They love fresh air, no matter how chilly it is. Trace bounds ahead, making a beeline for an overgrown apple tree. I take Maven's hand and walk with her as she tries to put her little feet in Trace's boot prints. Despite the fact that he's wearing bulky snow boots, he grabs hold of the lowest branch and scrambles up. Maven and I make our slow progress, finally arriving below the branches. I crane my head back, a little dismayed at how high Trace has gotten. The branches have a thin skim of ice coating them. "Trace, come on down, bud. That isn't safe."

"Look at how high I am." He calls back.

"Like an eagle." I reply. "But come on back. Grandma will want us back in the house."

He doesn't hear, or doesn't want to, because he's climbing ever higher. I look down at Maven, torn. I can't climb up after him, not without leaving Maven alone. There's a scrabbling sound and I look up in time to see Trace's boot struggle to find purchase. He rights himself, but my heart is in my throat. "Trace. That's enough, now. Come down."

After a few heartbeats, his voice comes out in a squeak. "I can't. I'm stuck."

"Shit." I mutter, scanning the farmyard.

I spot Dusty carrying a stack of boxes to the bed of his truck. He glances in my direction and I wave him over. He trots across the yard, coming to a stop just a little too close to me. I have to tip my head back to look at him. These boys never cease to amaze me with their sheer size. My memory never does them justice.

"Trace is stuck." I say, trying to keep my voice even.

He peers up through the branches, a laugh tumbling off his lips. Glancing back at me with a grin, he squeezes my shoulder. "If I had a nickel for every time one of us boys got stuck in this tree." He grabs the lower branches. "Don't worry, I've got this tree charted out."

He pulls himself up into the branches, climbing up like an oversized kid. I hear a brief exchange between Trace and Dusty, along with a smattering of laughter. Then Dusty's on his way back down, his body caging Trace as they descend. I grab Trace when he gets close and lift him to the ground.

Wrapping my arms around him, I squeeze him tight. "Don't do that again."

"No way." Trace agrees. "I thought I was a goner."

Dusty drops the last four feet, landing lightly on his feet. He grins at Trace. Cuffing him gently on the jaw. "Little hellion."

I'm so relieved to have everyone back on the ground, and in one piece, I fling my arms around his oversized frame. After a little pause, he puts his arms around me.

"I was so worried." I admit. Disentangling myself from his arms, I look up at him with a sheepish smile. "Thanks, Tarzan."

He grins back. "Any time."

Trace and Maven both take the opportunity to wrap themselves around his legs. The four of us make our way back to the house and I make a mental note. Stay away from trees.

Bo and Josh stand by the trucks, watching our slow progress. Trace scampers ahead. "I almost fell out of the tree!"

Josh's gaze flits back to me before he bends down to scoop Trace in his arms.

His expression was completely neutral, but I can't help but feel horribly guilty. Like he's disappointed in me.

"Let's head in." Josh says, glancing at me over Trace's head. "We're all done and mom and dad wanted to make a toast."

I trail behind the guys, smiling at Maven as she peeks over Dusty's shoulder. The entire family is gathered in the living room. It's empty now, and their voices knock around like pins at a bowling alley.

Keith claps his hands together as I step inside. "Now that we're all here, your mother just wanted to have a little toast."

Lisa passes around plastic cups, and Keith cracks open a bottle of champagne. The girls protest loudly when it spills over on the floor. Trace and Maven are given apple juice, but everyone else, including Charlie, is given champagne.

Keith holds up his glass. "Thirty years ago, I stopped to help a little bookworm from my senior class with a flat tire."

Lisa grins fondly, nudging him.

"I didn't know everything that would happen after that. If I had, maybe I would have been too tongue-tied to talk to her. But I'm damn glad I did. This house served us well. We raised up some decent kids. Made lots of memories. I wouldn't trade those years for the world, but I'm so excited to see what this next chapter holds for us. To the future!"

Everyone lifts their glasses. I sip the champagne, letting the bubbles fizz across my tongue.

Parker has to speak twice to be heard over the group. "What's going to happen to the house?"

An awkward silence descends on the room.

Keith tips his chin towards his son. "It's Josh's."

All three girls whip around to look at their brother. He shifts uncomfortably, setting Trace on his feet.

Charlie stares at her dad. "He just *gets* the house? What about the rest of us?"

Keith frowns, clearly not thrilled to be discussing this in front of a handful of non-family members. "Josh is taking over the farm. It just makes sense that he takes the house."

I glance at Bo, who nods his head, gesturing for us to slip out.

Before we can, Josh clears his throat. "I don't want it."

"What?" Keith stares at his son.

Josh straightens his back. "I said, I don't fucking want it. Y'all can fight over it."

And with that, he strides out of the room, leaving eight people shellshocked and speechless.

Lisa pulls the girls into the kitchen and Keith stomps after them. Dusty and Skyler sweep up the kids, distracting them.

Bo comes to stand next to me. "Go talk to him."

"Me?"

He gives me an exasperated look. "Yes, you." His expression softens, and he lowers his voice. "Look, you've already given him a hard time today."

"How?"

"You and Dusty." He searches my eyes. "We saw you two under the tree."

My cheeks color. That was an innocent hug.

He nudges my shoulder. "I know Josh. And I'm certain you're the only person he'll tolerate right now."

42.

Josh

I sit on my old bed holding a bottle of champagne, staring up at the ceiling. There's a Ninja Turtle sticker stuck up there and I'm trying to remember how I managed to put it up there.

The floorboards in the hall creak and I look over, the tips of my ears heating up when I see Erin lingering in the doorway. "Room for one more?"

I pat the bed beside me. "If you can stand the company."

She crawls onto the bed, leaning against the wall. Her shoulders brush mine and I hand her the bottle. She tips it to her lips and takes a little sip before passing it back.

"I made quite an exit, didn't I?"

She shrugs. "Your sisters have been a handful today."

"That's one way of putting it."

She's quiet for a bit. "You really don't want the house?"

The hollow feeling in my chest widens, threatening to steal my breath. "At one point, I did. I had all sorts of plans for this old place."

"What changed?"

She nods, fingers brushing mine when she grabs the bottle. "What were you going to do?"

I lean into her, and she rests her head on my shoulder. I clear my throat. "That kitchen is due for an update. I wanted to refinish the cabinets. Put in granite countertops. Maybe marble."

"That would be beautiful."

I put my arm around her shoulder. "And I wanted to restore the fireplaces."

"What fireplaces?"

"Exactly." I smile, warming to the topic. "They walled them in sometime back in the eighties, but there's a big fireplace in the kitchen and another in the primary bedroom."

"Is that what that awkward nook is in the dining room?"

I nod. "Yep. The fireplace is right behind that wall."

"I would love to see that."

We pass the bottle back and forth while I tell her about my plans. I've been dreaming about it since I was a kid, but when Ana passed away, my future went right with her. Talking about it with Erin is kindling some of those cold embers back to life.

The champagne is helping, too. The bubbles go straight to my head. I'm feeling particularly thankful towards Erin. She's the little ray of sunshine my life needed and I want her to be as happy as she's making me.

"Dusty's a good guy." I say, passing her the bottle.

"Hmm?"

"I'm sorry if I've been cock-blocking you two." I rub the back of my neck. "I can understand why you like him."

"I don't." She's peering up at me. "I mean, he's a nice guy. And he's cute."

I wince.

She rolls her eyes. "But you're all cute. Disgustingly cute."

I laugh. "Disgustingly cute?"

"Four perfectly beautiful human beings. It's awful."

There's a creak in the hallway and Bo appears, looking cautiously optimistic.

I grin at him. "She says we're awful."

Bo nods solemnly. "We are."

Skyler steps up behind him. "Your parents are headed to their new house. They kidnapped your children, by the way."

"What?"

Bo nods, stepping inside Josh's room. "Trace wanted to have a slumber party at the new house."

"You've both got the night off." Skyler grins. "The girls wanted to have a little after party."

I scowl. "Sounds delightful."

Skyler shrugs, leaning against the wall. "Dusty and Reese held a little board meeting with them. I think they're contrite."

"How many years has it been since we've partied in this house?" I ask.

Dusty laughs. "Remember the time Lisa and Keith went on that cruise?"

Bo groans. "I have never been so hung over in my life."

Erin shifts out from under my arm, scooting to the edge of the bed. I didn't realize I was still holding onto her, but I don't really regret it. Short of chasing Dusty off with a club, a message needed to be sent.

This woman is mine.

43.

Erin

The guys have a natural rapport with each other. They obviously grew up together, forming around each other, until they were like four puzzle pieces. They can finish each other's sentences, tell half stories because they already know the ending. It's fascinating to watch.

I didn't know friendship like this existed.

The girls add the perfect amount of antagonism, keeping the guys on their toes.

I don't really know what to make of Josh—no surprise there. We all stand around in the kitchen, but he seems to intentionally put some distance between the two of us. Every time I look at him, though, he's watching me. His gaze is like a tether, keeping me anchored to him.

Our little party is clobbered when some of Parker's friends arrive. Like flipping a switch, the girls electrify her and she goes from quiet mouse to party diva in no time at all.

More friends start pouring in. The only person who isn't allowed to invite anyone over is Charlie. Josh says he doesn't want any babies drinking in the house.

But as the party swells, it's hard to tell who's who anymore.

There's a small-town atmosphere that's hard to wrap my mind around. These people have known each other since they were in diapers. And before that, their parents knew each other since *they* were in diapers. There's a generational interconnectedness that borders on incestuous. They know each other's stories; they know their parents' stories. There isn't a lot of room for an outsider like me.

I lose track of the guys. I eventually find them playing a very aggressive game of beer pong. Josh's sisters have all found their girl gangs, and that leaves me an odd man out.

Alone in the crowd.

The guys and Josh's sisters—they're all clearly very popular.

It's giving me high school vibes, and I thought I was done with that shit five years ago.

Excavating my coat from a mountain of winter jackets, I shrug it on and step outside. It's frigid outside, but Josh's house is just on the other side of that country road. I just have to hike through one long icy lane, cross the road and take on another long, icy lane.

It's a bit daunting, but no more daunting than hanging out with a bunch of people stuck in their high school glory days.

"Where do you think you're going?"

I jump, pressing my hand to my chest as I turn around. Josh is sitting on the porch swing, drinking a beer in the dark.

"I was going to head back."

He tilts his head. "Had enough fun for one night?"

"You could say that."

"It's like a high school reunion in there." He says, fiddling with the label on his beer. "Lots of people stuck in the past."

It occurs to me that the people in there went to school with Josh's wife. Being around them must be like standing in the middle of a living photo album.

I glance back down the lane and, with a shrug, turn back to sit next to him. He leans over and snags a fresh beer from the ground. "I was double fisting it."

I accept the beer, settling in as he gently rocks the swing back and forth. He puts his arm around my shoulder, tugging me closer. I can feel the warmth radiating off his body, and despite the cold, it's kind of nice. The stars are so clear out here. Like glitter and dust tossed across the night sky.

"What were you like in high school?" He asks.

"Me?" I laugh. "Nothing like this."

"Like what?"

"Popular." I laugh. "Don't look like that. The popular kids at my school were rich snobs. Nothing like you guys. I just tried to stay in my lane."

"Which lane was that?"

"Music nerd, I guess? I was in the swing choir. And I had blue hair."

"No way."

I laugh. "Way."

He peers at me. "I need to see pictures."

"No, you don't."

He tickles my side. "I absolutely do."

I dig out my phone and bring up Instagram, scrolling past my life. It's so different from the way the guys live out here. I've been entrenched in the art community. My friends have piercings and vintage flare. These guys have Wranglers and cowboy boots. Josh leans in, studying the images as I rush past them.

"Who's this?" He asks.

I reluctantly stop on an image from a music festival in Kansas City. "That's my ex. Matt."

"Huh." Josh says. He glances at me. "You are way out of his league."

"If you say so." I scroll to the next picture and hand him the phone. "Behold."

He smiles at the screen. "How old were you?"

"In that picture? Twenty."

My hair is ice blue. I'm wearing a bubblegum pink beret I found at a vintage shop.

He passes my phone back. "It's kind of hot."

My cheeks color and I'm thankful for the relative cover of darkness.

His fingers twine in my curls. "I like this color better, though."

44.

Josh

There's a reason we haven't thrown a party in years.

Having all these people in my house is like going through a time warp. It's like being sixteen again. The only difference is, I don't have my best friend with me anymore.

She was always the buffer, the one who did all the talking. I feel lost without her and would literally rather hide in a dark corner than face these people.

Then Erin comes sweeping out, and she's like a ray of sunshine cutting through the doom and gloom. I'm drawn to her like a moth to flames.

I've been curious about the life she left behind and seeing those pictures on Instagram is like getting the Cliffs notes version.

I like seeing pictures of her from her younger days. I do not, however, like seeing pictures of that dough ball she dated for five years.

Maybe he was funny.

Or had a great personality.

She sure as shit wasn't dating him for his looks.

I wasn't kidding when I said she was out of his league. But I'm learning she tends to undersell herself. I twine her soft hair around my finger, wondering why she doesn't see what I see.

She glows. A light in the darkness.

I wish I could absorb some of that.

My fingers slip through her hair, weaving behind her head. I know I was the one who said we needed to slow down. But unfortunately for both of us, I don't listen very well.

She tilts her face towards mine, lips parted slightly and I lean down, kissing her deeply. I'm a man dying of thirst, and she's an oasis in the desert.

Her hands find my chest, slipping inside my jacket. She fists my shirt, clinging to me.

The door bangs open and a few people spill out, oblivious to us. But I'm still annoyed. Climbing to my feet, I tow her behind me. "Let's go home."

I open the truck door and help her inside. Circling around the truck, I climb behind the wheel. She's sitting too far away, so I grab her thigh and slide her to the middle of the bench. My hand stays locked around her leg as we drive down the lane, and she leans into me, wrapping her hands around my arm.

My heart is pounding in my chest as I lead her back up onto the porch. It's reckless. I'm dimly aware of that. But there's an even greater sense of urgency. The kids are out of the house and I don't know when our next opportunity will be.

I shut the door behind us, helping her out of her coat while she kicks her boots off. Then she's pulling my jacket off while I step out of my boots.

My arms twine around that waist, pulling her hard against my body. I kiss her, letting my hands slip under her sweater. Her skin is so soft and warm. She arches her back, leaning into my body.

I'm impatient.

This is overdue.

Judging by the way she's kissing me, she feels the same way.

I start to lift the hem of her sweater, exposing her skin, and she tugs it up over her head. I get a quick glimpse of her tummy, those beautiful tits straining against a lace bra, before she snuggles into my chest, almost hiding from my gaze.

Her hands slip around my waist and she tugs at my shirt. I pull it off and haul her into me. She's so soft, melting into me so perfectly. I want more. I want to touch every square inch of her. Hunger stokes in my belly, my shaft lengthens and presses against my zipper. Turning her around, I pull her ass into my hips and bend to kiss the slope of her shoulder. With both hands pressed against her tummy, I walk her to her bedroom. I know better than to take her to my room. Too many memories in there. Too many memories in this house, in general. It's like living with ghosts. Maybe it would be a good thing to move to the big house.

I stop her in front of the bed, filling my hands with those glorious tits. They occupy my thoughts, drowning out all the background noise.

She leans back into my chest, swaying on her feet as I kiss her neck. My hands slip down to her jeans and I unbutton them, pushing them past her hips. She kicks them off, turning to pull my jeans off. Standing in our underwear, I drag her closer, pressing my hips up against her. She rocks against me, teasing me with her kisses, nipping at my lower lip. When her hand slips down to curve around my bulge, all bets are off.

45.

Erin

In my head, I know this is a terrible idea.

But my body thinks it's the best idea I've ever had.

I'm not really sure how I lucked into this situation, standing in front of a half-naked god, but I don't want to jinx it by overthinking things.

There will be plenty of time for regret tomorrow. But right now, he's so big and *hard* and he's that way because of me.

He backs me up against the bed frame, half chasing, half dragging me onto the middle of the bed.

Prowling over me, he settles part of his weight over my body. He's heavy, and it feels so good. I wrap my arms around his back and pull him down on top of me. He braces his arms on either side of my body, bundling me up in his arms while his lips chart a path down my neck, across my collarbone.

I slide my hand around the curve of his muscular shoulder, guiding him onto his side. Sidling closer, I tangle my legs up with his, letting my hands explore his chest. He's got a dark trail of hair leading from his belly button down. I drag my nails along his hips, slipping into his boxers. His hips twitch when I touch him and he sucks in a little breath.

I lean in and he kisses me, tongue slipping in between my lips. My hand slides up and down his shaft and his tongue subconsciously echoes the movement, gliding across my tongue. Delving deep.

His hand is braced on the small of my waist, fingers dimpling my skin. "I want you so fucking bad." He murmurs, his voice gruff.

A shiver wracks my body. "I want you, too."

He moves his mouth to my neck, feathering my skin with kisses as his fingers slip under my panties. He cups me there, pressing, and a frustrated rush of need builds in my tummy. I put my hand over his and he slides a finger inside. I roll my hips, pressing down on his hand.

He slides another finger in, stretching me. "You're so wet."

I don't know whether to be embarrassed or smug. He moves his lips, trailing kisses down the curve of my breast. He locates my hard nipple, gently nipping me through my bra.

I arch against him with a moan and he goes stock still.

I glance up at him. "What's wrong?"

He groans, resting his forehead against my shoulder. "I don't have any condoms."

I can almost feel him pulling away from me and there is absolutely no way he should leave this bed without fucking me first.

Preferably more than once.

I grasp onto his shoulders, attempting to lock him into place. "Have you slept with anyone recently?"

"No. Not since…"

He doesn't want to say her name. Probably wise. I'm a little surprised he hasn't been with anyone since, and yet, it completely tracks with his devotion.

There's a vague fluttering in my tummy at the thought of being his first in so long.

He pulls back, looking shyly into my eyes. "What about you?"

"Not since Matt." I admit. "And you bet your ass I had a physical after breaking up with that piece of shit."

He laughs, amused by my temper flare.

His gaze locks onto my lips. "So… you think we can skip it?"

I nod, and he bends down to press his lips against mine. He kisses my jaw, my neck. "You're sure?"

"Yes. Are you?"

"Fuck, yes." He growls.

Giddiness and hunger spiral through me as he tugs at my panties. I lift my hips and he rips them off, kicking his boxers off in the process.

His long length presses against my thigh. I run my hand along his hip, enjoying the feel of his bare skin.

He nudges my thighs apart with his knee, easing down between my legs. His shaft is hard and heavy against my pelvis. I reach down and circle my fingers around his girth, guiding him to my entrance.

"Tell me if it's too much." He murmurs shakily.

I nod, but I just want to take as much of him as I can get.

He already stretched me a little with his fingers, so I'm ready for him.

It's a tight fit, but he pushes in slowly, taking his time. He pulls back, easing his hips forward, delving deeper each time. He's murmuring sweet words against my ear, holding me so carefully. And I'm sort of lost to the moment. He's occupying my body in a way I've never experienced. When he pulls back and delves back inside, his shaft mercilessly drags along my inner wall, stoking a building pressure. I won't last long at this rate. I press my hands into his back, arresting his movement while I try to fend off the impending climax.

He peers down at me. "Am I hurting you?"

"Gonna make me come." I whisper.

His eyebrows bounce up and then he's chuckling. "That's the plan, babe."

His hips thrust forward, picking up the pace, and I gasp. He pulls my bra down and pinches my nipple. "I'm going to make you come again and again."

And between the way he's tugging at my nipple, and the way his hips are thrusting against mine, he sends me sailing right over the edge.

I roll my hips against him, moaning his name while pleasure sparkles through my entire body. Slipping an arm behind my back, he braces my body while he rolls onto his back.

His cock stays buried inside, impaling me, and I lay on his chest, trying to catch my breath.

His fingertips trace lines up and down my spine until I'm languid and sleepy.

And then his hips start rolling beneath mine, stoking the fire before it can go out.

46.

Josh

She's so damn responsive.

And vocal.

Little gasps and moans rain down on me, and I soak it up like parched earth. My fingers slip between us, pressing against her clit. It doesn't take much to wring another orgasm from her body. She comes hard, muscles tightening around my shaft.

I'm not sure how I'm holding out when this angel is coming undone around me. But maybe I just need to see what she'll do next.

She melts on my chest, slipping onto the bed beside me. I run my fingers up and down her arm and she sighs happily. "You're going to make me pass out."

I chuckle, kissing the top of her head. She turns, snuggling against my chest. Her hand trails along my chest, my stomach, charting a delicious path across my skin. It feels so good just to be touched.

Her fingers circle around my shaft.

That feels even better. She shimmies down between my legs. When she presses a kiss against my tip, my hips twitch. Curving her fingers around me, she draws her tongue up and down my length until I'm breathing heavily like I just ran a marathon.

Crawling back up alongside me, she settles onto her back, dragging my body over hers.

I push her thighs apart and she wraps her hands around my hips. She's still so slippery wet, when I drive my hips into hers, my shaft delves deeper than I intended. But fuck if it doesn't feel good.

I pull back and thrust in again, this time burying my entire length inside her. She wraps her legs around my back, dragging me against her body.

I've missed this more than I realized. This kind of connection has every nerve firing, pleasure radiating through my body. My body tenses up, abs, hips. I feel the familiar pressure building and pull out, thrusting against her soft tummy until an orgasm slams into me, ripping through my body. The first wave of pleasure splashes across her skin, catching in the little dip between her collarbones. She looks so pretty, so fucking sexy, with my seed painting across her skin.

I get the feeling she's a little self-conscious about her body. We're going to have to work on that. Because I want to look. She's too gorgeous not to.

Eventually, I get up and bring back a washcloth. She tries to take it from me, but I nudge her hand away, insisting on taking care of her myself.

I toss it aside and flop onto the bed, pulling her alongside me. She kisses my shoulder before nuzzling into my side. I slip the blanket up over us, tugging her into my body like I'm afraid she might try to get away.

Eventually, she just might. I have no idea what comes next.

But right now, I just want to revel in this feeling of complete release. My fingers tease through her curls, listening to the soft, barely audible sounds of her breath. Her chest rises and falls against mine, and I match her breath, eventually drifting off to sleep.

I'm so used to my kids waking me up in the middle of the night that I wake up on my own. It takes me a second to remember that they're with my parents.

And that Erin is in my bed.

Well, technically, I'm in her bed.

I never thought I would want to sleep next to another woman. But the worst part about sleeping with Erin is knowing that tomorrow we'll be back in separate beds.

I roll onto my back, staring at the ceiling. She sleepily follows, muttering some nonsense in her sleep. Craning my head to look at her, I chuckle a little, letting my head flop back. She stirs against me, her voice muffled against my shoulder. "Are you laughing right now?"

"You're talking in your sleep.

She wiggles closer. "I don't talk in my sleep."

"And you snore."

That part isn't true, but it's worth it to see her reaction. She pushes up against my chest, squinting down at me. "I do not."

I trail a finger down her arm. "Woke me up."

"Oh, poor baby." She says, sliding her palm across my stomach. "How will I make it up to you?"

I grin, biting my lip. "I have some ideas."

She laughs. "You do?"

I nod, pulling her onto my chest. I kind of forgot how naked we both were.

Things get serious real fast.

The smile fades from my face and I pull her down to my lips.

Having her naked curves pressed against my body is a feast for the senses. I grab her butt with both hands, squeezing before giving her a little slap. She jumps slightly, a surprised moan tumbling from her lips. I smile into our kiss. "Do you like that?"

She nods, drawing the tip of her nose across my cheekbone. Putting her lips by my ear, she bites my earlobe. "Do it again."

I obey, smacking her a little harder this time, and she rolls her hips against mine, sending my half-staff erection into full-riot mode. She reaches around, positioning my tip at her entrance and eases back onto me.

I lift my hips, driving deeper, and she groans lustily.

A laugh rumbles in my chest. "Fuck, baby, you're so damn sexy."

47.

Erin

Josh really knows how to make a woman feel appreciated. He's not stingy with compliments, murmuring sweet nothings as he fucks me silly. He likes my ass. My 'tits'. My 'dirty little mouth'.

I like everything about his body. I wouldn't even know where to start. Besides, I can barely string two words together, let alone think of sexy little things to say to him.

I'm only capable of saying yes.

Please.

Harder.

This time, when he comes, his cock is pressed between my tummy and his abs. I can feel his shaft throbbing between us and the groan that rumbles in his chest resonates from my head to my toes. We clean up in the bathroom and there's a brief hesitation afterwards. His room is to the right and mine is to the left. I want him to come back with me and judging by the lingering look in his eyes, that's what he wants, too. So I grab his hand and lead him back to the bed. I wiggle back into my panties, slipping into a t-shirt, while he pulls his boxers back on.

He lies on his back and tucks me into his side. I curl up next to him, planting my hand on his warm chest.

"What happens now?" He asks, fingers playing with my hair.

"That's a complicated question."

He blows out a deep breath. "I know."

I'm quiet for a long time, thinking it over. He waits patiently. My fingers slip along his collarbone. "Living together kind of puts us in a fishbowl. The kids pick up on everything. I think… for their sake, we need to carry on. Business as usual."

He presses his lips to the top of my head. A deep breath fills his chest and cascades over my skin as he releases it. "Think we can pull that off?"

"I think we have to."

His hand rests on his stomach, and I run my fingers over the back of it. He flips it over, weaving our fingers together. His arm slips along my side, supporting me, holding me close. "If that's what you want."

I nod, but who the hell knows what I want?

I'm not sure if we're doing the right thing. Maybe we made a critical mistake by sleeping together.

But there was an attraction between us that was bound to boil over at some point.

We're both so tangled up in our thoughts and our pasts that neither of us has a clear direction.

The only thing I know for sure is that I don't want those kids getting hurt in the process. With that pole star as our guiding light, we have to feel our way forward.

For the time being, we have the house to ourselves and we can live in the dream space between our pasts and whatever the future holds. For a little while longer, anyway.

We can't seem to decide between snuggling and fucking, so we split the difference. Josh wasn't kidding when he said he was going to make me come again and again.

There's a desperation to our touch, like we're not sure if we'll ever get a second chance together.

By the time the sun cracks over the horizon, I'm thoroughly exhausted, but satisfied.

Josh rolls over, kissing my shoulder, before slipping out of bed. I hear the shower running and my stomach twists a little. The fantasy, the illusion, is fading like smoke and reality comes painfully into focus.

We get ready together, trying to slip back into our old rapport. It's a little hard at first, but by the time we're drinking our coffee, I can almost pretend like it doesn't sting.

This was my idea.

I have to remind myself of that.

But the truth is, if I hadn't said it, I'm confident that he would have.

It was going to hurt either way, but at least this way, I saw it coming.

We drive together to pick the kids up. Lisa and Keith want to host a brunch in their new house.

Somehow, this woman has managed to conjure up a full spread from scratch, despite the fact that they are very much still living out of boxes.

The girls are there. Dusty even makes an appearance.

I smile and chat with Reese.

Pretending like there isn't a pleasant ache to my body, an assertive reminder of who was inside me hours before.

His gaze meets mine and I let mine slide on by.

It never happened.
Everything is fine.
I'm fine.

48.

Josh

I love that Erin loves my kids.

But I kind of wish she wasn't so selfless.

She might be able to compartmentalize that night, but I feel like I'm living with constant temptation.

Everything she does commands my attention.

It's pure torture, but it's a welcome distraction. A good kind of pain. Thinking about how cute her ass looks in jeans is a hell of a lot more enjoyable than thinking about the holidays.

Because, the truth is, this is a really hard time of year for me.

It's only our second year without Ana and the memories are crystalized in all the traditions, the rituals. Even the food.

Last year, I coped by spending a lot of late nights at the bar with the guys. The kids had a lot of sleepovers at grandma's.

This year, I make it all the way to Christmas Eve without thinking about getting smashed. I haven't gone to the bar since Erin moved in and that's no coincidence. I can't stand to be alone with my ghosts. I love my kids, but I obviously can't burden them with my sorrows.

Erin fills the house with so much noise—laughter and singing—it crowds out all the sad memories. But Christmas Eve rolls around and not even Erin can blot out that pain.

Trace is getting older, and this year, his preschool class is in the Christmas Eve service. I can't skip again, as much as I want to. My head is in a fog all day. I'm trying to be a good dad, trying to stay in the moment with my kids.

But it's hard.

Thank God for the people around me.

I don't know, maybe Erin sensed it.

Maybe she's running from her own ghosts. But she offered to stay through Christmas Eve. I said she could go home if she wanted to, but the truth is, I need her here. She keeps everything on the rails.

We go to mom's for lunch, opening presents and sitting down for a meal that rivals Thanksgiving. But I have no appetite. It's a struggle to keep up with the jokes and the stories. The more I withdraw, the more my family crowds in, trying to pull me out of this quicksand I'm stuck in.

At some point, Erin's fingers brush across my shoulder. I glance up at her, focusing on her steady expression. "When do you want to go back? Maven's going to need a nap and we still need to get the kids ready for the Christmas program."

I launch at the chance to escape. "Yep. We better take off."

Maven falls asleep in the truck and I carry her inside, feet slowing when I step inside. Memories, like a faded film reel, play in front of my eyes. I'm lost in thought when I hear Erin struggling in behind me. Trace must have fallen asleep, too. I lay Maven down, doubling back to take Trace off her hands.

When I come back to the living room, she's curled up on the couch. She holds out a beer and I accept it, slumping onto the couch beside her. "What are we watching?"

"Krampus? It's got David Koechner in it."

"Who the hell is David Koechner?"

"What, are you some sort of heathen?"

I laugh, shrugging. "I have no idea who that is."

"Champ Kind in Anchor Man?" She pauses. "Tom Packer from The Office?"

"Okay, I've seen those. I'm just not a name guy." I settle back. "So it's a comedy, then?"

"I think so."

It most definitely is not a comedy.

It starts out that way. Then gets dark.

And terrifying.

We both recede into the couch like we can get away from the horror that's unfolding on the screen. At one point, Erin jumps, spilling her beer.

"Ah! Fuck me." She mutters. I take one look at her face and start laughing.

It's more or less downhill from there. We crack up at the most inappropriate parts.

Laughing until tears run down our faces.

I'll take these tears all day long over the ones I would have spent if I'd been alone.

Laughing is infinitely preferable to crying.

49.

Erin

I decided to stay through the afternoon because I thought the Olsons needed my help.

But I'm not completely selfless.

I didn't want to go home because I couldn't stand to see the house without dad in it. Couldn't stand to see mom carrying on like her world didn't come crashing down around her feet.

She went to spend the day with my Aunt Marla and her brood of children. I consider the fact that I won't see my cousins this year to be a silver lining.

I picked Krampus because I hadn't seen it and I figured Josh hadn't either. The horror part sort of came out of left field, but that was a silver lining, too, because it serves as an outlet for the swirl of emotions in my chest.

Josh seems to like it, in any event. He's wheeze-laughing at all the wrong parts, a fact that I find to be a little twisted, and therefore, incredibly endearing.

He catches me staring at him and his smile slips a little. Tucking a stray curl behind my ear, he leans in, drawing his nose along mine. I tip my head up and our lips brush each other.

And, oh shit, this is why I've been avoiding this honey trap. I swear sparks fly when we kiss. His tongue traces the seam of my lips and when I part them for him, he delves inside, dominating my thoughts, my body. Wrapping his hands around my ass, he drags me onto his lap. We kiss like it can solve all our problems. Like it can make all the bad things go away.

And for a few minutes, it works pretty damn well.

But then Trace's door squeaks open.

Scrambling in a tangle of limbs and disheveled clothes, we spring apart.

He fumbles for the remote. Hitting the power button on poor Krampus. "Nope."

Trace wanders into the living room, gaze darting back and forth with suspicion. "Were you watching a movie?"

"Hey, Trace." Josh says, tugging a pillow over his lap.

Trace tilts his head. "Aren't we supposed to be getting ready for the program? Are you going to wear jeans to church, dad?"

"No. I'll change."

Trace pauses, expectantly. Josh and I both know why there's a pillow over his lap.

Josh glances at me, eyes beseeching me for help.

I bite my lip to keep from laughing. "Yes, Josh. Aren't you going to go get dressed?"

He smiles, speaking through gritted teeth. "In a minute."

I grin at his condition, climbing to my feet. "Come on, Trace. Let's go see what grandma got you to wear to the program."

"It better not be itchy." Trace announces, leading me to his room. "She likes to buy itchy sweaters."

I find his sweater in a department store bag and sure enough, the darn thing is wool. We put a long-sleeve dinosaur shirt under it, protecting his skin from the dreaded itchiness.

"Are you going to dress up, too?"

"Oh. I'm not going to church with you."

His eyebrows scrunch up. "You're going to miss my program?"

"Your dad is going. And grandma. You won't even miss me."

"I will, too!" He wails, barreling out of the room.

I follow after him, running into Josh in the hall. We both wince when the door to the bathroom slams shut.

"What got into him?" Josh asks.

"He's upset because I'm not going to church with you."

"Oh." He nods. "He'll get over it. This is your holiday, too. You should be with your family."

He's right, but the only problem with that is that I can't be with my whole family. Not anymore.

He rubs the back of his neck. "But if you wanted to stay… it's a really pretty service. Candlelit and all that. I think you'd like it."

"I mean, I could go to church with you guys and then head home after that."

He meets my gaze. "I don't think I want you on the road that late at night."

I laugh. "What, you think I'm a menace behind the wheel?"

"No, it's just not real safe."

"Good Lord, Josh. I'll be fine."

He still looks reluctant. The concern in those dark eyes is hitting me pretty hard. I don't know whether to laugh or cry.

Taking a page from Krampus's book, I elect to laugh.

50.

Josh

Thank God for preschool tantrums.

I felt like having a tantrum about going to church, too, but being twenty-six, I thought it might look unseemly.

Erin disappears into her room with Maven and a few minutes later, both girls emerge looking like they got visited by their fairy godmother.

I don't know where to look first. The dress my mom picked out for Maven is ridiculously over the top. The forest green skirt is so poofy it nearly swallows her up. She looks like a God damn princess and it's making my heart feel so full.

I'm avoiding looking directly at Erin, because I know that'll do other things to my heart. Maven prances forward and I scoop her up. She turns back, pointing at Erin. "Pretty."

I force myself to look, hoping my ears aren't turning beet red. "Yes. Very pretty."

Erin looks good in anything, but tonight, she's pulled out the big guns. Her dress is green, too, and velvety. It skims her shoulders, sloping down her chest. She put on more makeup than normal. I usually prefer a natural look, but this look is out of this world. She's said she thinks I'm out of her league, but I'm realizing she had it backwards. I'm just a redneck from the sticks.

She's a star.

Eyes that I thought were blue might actually be green. But it's those lips that have their own gravitational pull. She put on cherry red lipstick and its making her lips look good enough to eat. My brain supplies me with an image of what they might look like wrapped around my shaft and then I really am blushing.

With a cough, I turn and beat a hasty retreat.

Keeping my mind out of the gutter is going to take all of my focus, but that's a good thing. I'd rather be struggling with that demon than the ghosts that are threatening to pull me apart.

We drive to church, listening to Trace's entire program as he rehearses, loudly, from the backseat. When we get there, the parking lot is already full. I pull Maven out and hold her close. Erin takes Trace's hand and we walk towards the church.

It seems to loom over us. The closer we get, the slower my feet become until I'm stopped in the middle of the lot, staring at the spot where the hearse was.

Erin looks back, tilting her head.

I clear my throat. "I haven't been back since the…"

The funeral.

I don't have to finish the statement. Her face softens in an expression of compassion that makes my eyes burn. Reaching out, she takes my hand and the four of us walk into the church.

Dad and Charlie are waiting in the lobby for us. Dad practically melts when he sees how gussied up Maven is. I set her on the ground and she scampers over to him. Trace and Erin follow behind. Charlie pulls me aside. "You brought the nanny?"

"She wasn't going to come, but then Trace flipped out."

Charlie flips her hair over her shoulder. "Well, it's a packed house. I'm not sure where she's going to sit."

"With me."

"We're already squished in the pew like sardines, Josh."

"Then I'll sit somewhere else."

I ask my dad if they mind taking the kids during the service. Of course, he doesn't. As long as he's got Maven, he doesn't care if I sit on the moon.

Erin watches my family filter back into the sanctuary. "Why aren't you going to sit with your family?"

"Too crowded." I say with a shrug.

"You should be with your family, Josh. I can find a seat in the back."

"You're sitting with me." I say, my voice a little gruffer than I intended. "Honestly? I didn't want to come at all. This is going to be… hard. I'm not sure if I'm going to make it through the whole thing. I'd rather be able to slip out the back."

She reaches out, squeezing my hand. "Okay, yeah. Let's sit in the back."

I'm sure tongues will be wagging. Erin is a bombshell beauty. She draws the eye just by merely existing, but she's touching my hand. The tragic widower. The story will spread like wildfire.

And yet, I don't want her to let go.

Her touch is the only thing keeping me from falling to pieces.

51.

Erin

Some years, we went to church on Christmas Eve.

Some years, we didn't.

We weren't exactly a devoted, church-going family. This culture is a little foreign to me. We sit in one of the back pews, in the corner. I'm on the end and when another couple sits in our row, they cause a domino effect of people scooting down the pew. Josh ends up squashed up next to me. He shifts, putting his arm around my shoulders.

It's cozy and very distracting.

They've dimmed the lights, and people are taking turns playing solos. A guitar. A flute. Two sisters performing a hauntingly beautiful duet of silent night. I'm kind of amazed by all the home-grown talent in this little church.

Trace and his preschool class perform an adorable rendition of The Little Drummer Boy. Trace can't stand still, but he does the motions like a pro. I can't stop grinning.

I can feel a chuckle rumble through Josh's chest and we glance at each other, sharing an amused grin. Josh tightens his arm around me and I feel myself just melting into him. It's nice, the familiar music. The soft glow of a candlelit service. I can see the appeal.

If every church service was like this, maybe I'd think about coming more often.

When they start passing out candles, I lean in to whisper to Josh. "What's happening?"

"We're going to sing now."

"Christmas carols?" I whisper.

He nods, tipping his candle against his neighbor's. When his is lit, he turns and lights mine.

"By candlelight?"

I'm probably grinning like an idiot. I can feel the smile stretching across my face. But I'm just so damn excited. I didn't think I'd get a chance to sing carols this year, and here I am melding my voice with hundreds of people. Josh holds his candle in one hand, slipping the other around my waist. We don't need to look at the hymnals. I know these words by heart. I let the words sail from my lips, joy suffusing my body from head to toe. I was in the choir in high school, but that was pretty much the end of my singing career. Singing with a group is like a balm for the soul.

Josh's thumb slides up and down my spine and I glance up at him, realizing he's not singing at all. He's just watching me with a quiet smile on his lips.

Almost like… he's just listening to me.

My cheeks get warm and I lean my head into his chest to avoid his searching stare. There's something kind of magical about the church on a night like this. It just sweeps you up. I find myself caught in the spell, until just as quickly, it's over.

The thing about candle lit services is that they're late at night.

Too late for a gussied up two-year-old and an energetic preschooler. Maven must have fallen asleep at some point during the service. Keith carries her to the truck himself. Josh carries Trace, who insists he's not tired in the least.

About a mile down the road, both kids are sound asleep.

I glance over at Josh. His features are just visible in the dim light from the dash. He's got a faraway look in his eye. I'm betting he's trying to wade through the memories dredged up by the Christmas season.

I doubt he wants to talk about it. I sure as shit don't want to talk about dad. But I want him to know he isn't alone. So I just reach out and brush my fingers over the back of his hand. He glances at me; the frown easing from his features, and weaves his fingers through mine.

We drive down Josh's lane. His house is lit up with colorful lights. I carry Maven and he takes Trace. We quietly pass through the house, settling them in their beds.

I stop in the living room, glancing at the tree. "We forgot to put out cookies. You should take one of the gingerbread men and pretend Santa took a bite out of it."

"Okay," He turns to the kitchen and I follow behind him.

I start to button up my coat. "I wrapped all the presents. They're in the garage underneath that old blue tarp."

He puts two cookies on a plate, pausing to look at me. "Wait, are you going back tonight?"

"Yeah." I glance at his worried expression and laugh. "Josh, we already talked about this."

"Yes, we did. And I thought we agreed that you'd stay." He starts stacking more cookies on Santa's plate. "Just spend the night and go in the morning. It's too late to be on the roads."

"You're being silly."

He pauses, looking at me with exasperation. "You're being silly."

I grab my purse, giving him a lopsided grin. "Maybe. But unfortunately for you, you're not the boss of me."

He comes closer, gently grabbing the lapels of my coat. "I'm not?"

He tugs me into his body and all my snappy comebacks dry up. I peer up at him and he leans down to kiss me. It's a breath-stealing kiss, full of promise. When he pulls back, we're both breathing harder, and my lipstick is smudged on his lower lip. I reach up and drag my thumb along his lip, feeling the rough scruff of his beard.

"Do you really need to go?"

I try to picture my mom spending Christmas Eve alone. Waking up by herself. "Yes."

He sighs, pulling me in tight, pressing his lips to the top of my head. "Text me when you get there."

"Okay."

52.

Josh

Nothing says Christmas like having a four-year-old body slam your head while you sleep.

I groggily come to, watching Trace bounce on the bed, shouting. "It's Christmas morning! Up and Adam!"

Maven plants a wet kiss on my ear, whispering loudly. "Chrissum."

I roll to my side, glancing at the alarm clock.

It's seven. Last year, Trace was up at five, so this feels like a Christmas miracle.

Trace runs a quick circle around my body before leaping onto the floor. "I'll go get Erin."

"No, bud." I climb to my feet. "She's not here."

But he's already gone.

He comes barreling back in seconds later. "Where's Erin?"

"She went home, Trace."

A look of pure confusion contorts his little features. "So, she *is* here?"

"Not our home, her home."

"Erin has another house?"

"And a mom and everything."

That was the wrong thing to say, because his face screws up and then he's wailing. "We have to keep her here. Why'd you make her leave?"

I squat down beside him, putting my hands on his shoulders. "I didn't make her leave, bud." His expression is heartbreakingly sad. "I gave her the day off."

"Day off from what?"

"From work."

He's got tears rolling down his cheeks. "Where does she work?"

"Aw, bud." I pull him in for a hug. Now does not seem like the best time to tell him that watching him is a job we have to pay Erin to do. "She'll be back in a few days."

"A few days?" He squeaks and then he's wailing again. "You gotta go get her, Dad. What if something happens to her?"

Maven climbs down from the bed and wraps her arms around my neck. I put my hand over her little arms. "Nothing is going to happen to her. Why would you think that?"

"Because something happened to the last mommy."

Oh.

That's what this is about.

I sit cross-legged on the floor and pull him into my lap.

I clear my throat a few times, trying hard to keep the wobble out of my voice. "Erin's not sick, bud. She texted me as soon as she got home. She's snug as a bug in a rug at her mom's house."

He sniffs. "Can I talk to her?"

I think that over. I don't want to bother Erin on Christmas, but considering the circumstances, I don't think she'd mind.

We FaceTime her and even as the phone is ringing, it occurs to me that this is rather early to be calling anyone.

She takes the call anyway, to my immense relief, but it's another woman's face who fills the screen.

My first thought is that we've somehow called the wrong number, but then I recognize blue-green eyes. Round cheekbones.

This is Erin's mom. She's smiling into the camera like the cat who got the cream. "You must be Josh."

"Yes, ma'am. Are you Erin's mom?"

"You bet. I'm Donnita."

"I'm Trace."

Maven tumbles into my lap. "Maven!"

"Oh, my stars. They *are* beautiful. She wasn't exaggerating."

Trace's face fills the screen. "Where's Erin? Is she safe?"

Donnita laughs. "I sure hope so. She stepped into the shower just a few seconds ago."

Trace flops in my arms, melting to the ground. "I want Erin."

"You should come visit her."

Trace perks up. "Right now?"

"Oh." Donnita pauses, grinning. "Well, why not? I would love that."

I'm sitting there, waiting for her to insert a 'but'.

She doesn't.

I squirm internally. My mother trained me never to invite myself over to someone else's house. Inviting yourself over on *Christmas Day* seems like a particularly grievous sin. "Oh, we couldn't impose. Trace was just missing Erin, so I thought we'd try to catch her on a video call."

"Let's go surprise her, dad." Trace says from his new position on the floor.

"Trace, we can't interrupt someone else's Christmas."

He starts crying again. This time it's less of a wail and more of a heartbroken burble.

"Oh, listen to the poor thing." Donnita's face is full of concern. It's a strange echo of the expression I've seen on Erin's face. "Listen, I can understand if you want to spend the day in your own home, but we really would love to have you here. This is our first year without Gary and it's awfully quiet. I think it's hitting Erin pretty hard. She was such a daddy's girl."

"Please." Trace wails.

I sigh. "If you're sure we're not going to be a burden."

Donnita lights up. "Oh my dear, quite the opposite. Actually, I like Trace's idea. What if we keep it a surprise?"

"Are you sure she'd like that?"

Donnita grins mischievously. "Who doesn't like a little Christmas magic?"

53.

Erin

Mom's giving me whiplash.

In the time it took me to take a shower, she went from saying let's get Chinese later, to let's make an entire Christmas feast. From scratch.

It's not that we aren't capable of cooking.

My mom is an excellent cook when she feels like it.

Which isn't very often.

Cooking was more my dad's thing. He was an amateur pit master, but could tackle just about anything if it went well with barbecue. He and I spent hours in the kitchen perfecting his spice rubs. We even made a special Thanksgiving turkey blend. I can recite it by heart.

Brown sugar.

Paprika.

Celery salt.

I grab a pad of paper and start making a list of the things we'd need. Marvin, dad's beagle, flops down on the mat by the sink.

Mom stands on the other side of the counter, watching me scratch *rosemary* and *onion powder* on the paper. "Is that for Gary's turkey rub?"

I nod, squinting at the list to see if I've remembered everything. "We won't have time for a whole turkey, but I could get a roaster chicken."

"You'll deep fry it just like he did?"

I meet her gaze, surprised to see so much emotion there. "Yeah. I can."

"This is good." She pushes away from the counter. "I know Gary would be smiling down on you, seeing you carry on the tradition."

My pen pauses over the paper and I watch her for a few moments, wondering what's gotten into her.

I can count the number of times she's used his name this year on one hand.

She hasn't wanted to talk about him. And last I knew, her game plan was to ignore the holidays as much as humanly possible.

"Make sure to get a really big chicken when you go to the store." She pulls the flour cannister down from the cupboard. "I'm going to want leftovers. The biggest chicken you can find."

It's better than moping around, so I take my list and head out.

I park in the grocery store parking lot, surprised by how many cars are parked around me. It's a reminder that not everyone celebrates Christmas. Some people don't ascribe to the cultural practice.

But others are just trying to outrun it.

I can relate.

It feels like I already did the whole Christmas thing with Josh and his kids. Now that I'm back here, I'm just ready to mute the Christmas music and tear down the decorations.

Stopping by the bell ringer at the entrance, I drop some cash in the Salvation Army bucket. Our gazes meet. He's about my dad's age. We're both probably thinking the same thing.

What's your story?

Why aren't you home on a day like this?

But what I say is, "Merry Christmas."

And what he says is, "God bless."

Maybe he should have said that last part a little louder. I don't think anyone upstairs was listening.

Because standing at the orange display is my ex and his girlfriend.

"Oh, for fuck's sake." I mutter, remembering too late why I didn't want to go to this grocery store.

Matt glances in my direction, doing a double take when he sees me. He's spotted me and there's no graceful way out of this. I can't hide, either. He's blocking me from my spot.

Pasting on a cheerful smile, I force my feet to move in his direction.

He beams at me. "Erin! What are you doing here?"

Getting food, asshole. "My mom sent me on a mission to hunt down missing ingredients."

Matt nods. "That's what we're up to. Lily forgot half the ingredients for her famous gingerbread cake."

I glance at her, skeptical that she even knows what cake is. She's wearing a low-cut sweater. I can literally see the ribs sticking out below her collarbones. I pull my gaze up, studying the face of my replacement. Dark hair, a wide mouth. Pretty, as much as I hate to admit it.

She pretends to frown. "I didn't forget, Matthew. You didn't tell me how much you liked it."

Matt tickles her and she squeaks.

Gross. Double gross.

"I'm glad we ran into you, though." He turns back to me. "I wanted to introduce Lily last time, but didn't get a chance. Lily, this is my friend, Erin."

I guess that's one way to describe someone you dated for five years. Judging by the glittering look in Lily's eye, she knows exactly who I am.

I can't understand why he's so determined to introduce me to her. Does he need my approval? Is he trying to rub it in?

He always was a little petty, but this seems like a low blow, even for him.

And I really don't have the energy for it. I can usually soldier on without thinking about my dad all the time. But the holidays are full of reminders. Land mines bundled up in gift wrap.

I can't go two feet without missing him and I'm just exhausted. And here I am in the grocery store, when all I really want to be is in front of the Christmas tree in Silver Bend, watching Trace's face when he opens the monster truck he wanted so badly.

"Hey, are you okay?" Matt asks, genuine concern on his face. "You don't look so good."

"Hmm?" I didn't realize it, but I've got my arms around my middle and I'm almost hunching over. Worst of all, tears lurk at the corners of my eyes.

I'm not crying because of this asshole. Good riddance to him. I'm crying over all the Christmases I'll never have. The things I want but can't have.

And then someone is putting their arm around me, spinning me around. His familiar scent fills my nose as his arms wrap around me protectively. His voice is a low growl, it rumbles in his chest. "What did you say to her?"

Matt's stuttering. "Nothing. I'm not sure."

"Then why is she crying?"

I have no idea where Josh came from—if he just sensed that I needed him, but I'm thankful he's here.

"Oh, my god." I bury my face in Josh's flannel shirt. "Please tell me this isn't happening."

Josh cranes his head, peering down at me. "Are you okay?"

I sniff, laughing at myself. "I guess that's relative. Ignore me. Please. I'm just missing my dad. It just sort of hit me all the sudden."

I just came in here for groceries. I didn't bargain for this little circus side show. Everything about this encounter is awful. Except Josh.

His presence is shoring me up.

As much as I want to melt into the floor from pure embarrassment, I force myself to turn back to Lily and Matt. They look almost as mortified as I feel.

54.

Josh

I left Trace and Maven with Erin's mom. Not by choice, but when they met Donnita's dog, I couldn't pry them away. She sent me to the store to surprise Erin.

For the record, I am extremely uncomfortable with this plan. Even more uncomfortable with the fact that I'm the one who has to execute it.

Surprise. Your work followed you home.

The whole thing has me squirming, but for Trace, I'd do pretty much anything.

And he's not the only one who wants to see her.

I've been missing her since the moment she slid her coat on and announced she was leaving.

It isn't hard to find Erin in the grocery store. That coppery hair is a dead giveaway. When I first spot her, she's talking to some friends, so I hold back, not wanting to interrupt.

But the more I look at the guy she's talking to, the more familiar he starts to look. Then I remember where I've seen that dough boy before.

Erin's ex.

Smiling and hanging all over another woman. Right in front of her.

What an asshole.

She needs back-up. But before I can get to her, she starts shrinking in on herself. Almost like her stomach hurts. I can't tell, but think she might be crying.

I'm not sure if I'm going to grab her or punch him in the face.

Fortunately for all parties involved, I grab her first. There's a brief moment of uncertainty when I wonder if this is a good surprise or a bad surprise for her. But she turns into me, accepting my presence like she knew I'd come all along.

I have every intention of scooping her under my arm and helping her escape, but she turns back to look at the fucker that made her cry.

She's blushing underneath all those tears, and yet she faces him with a brave smile.

I'm proud of her.

But I'm still not going to let go. I keep my arm around her waist, glaring down at this mediocre shit head, wondering what she saw in him.

"This is incredibly embarrassing," she laughs, swiping her sweater sleeve across both cheeks. "You all look so freaked out. Really, I'm fine."

Matt is staring at me with open curiosity.

Matching my stance, he slips his arm around his girl and puts his hand out. "I'm Matt. Erin's ex-boyfriend."

I let his hand hang for a few beats, just bordering on hostile, before giving him a little shake. A bone-crunching handshake.

"Josh."

"Are you… how do you…"

He's trying to ask how we know each other. I glance down at Erin, and she looks up at me. The pain in her eyes is still fresh. I've never had the experience, but I can't imagine seeing an ex of five years with a new partner is a good feeling.

I slide my hand up and down her side. Matt doesn't miss the movement.

"We met a few months ago." I say, squeezing her into me. "Your mom is going to think we got lost. We better get a move on."

"Oh. Yeah. You're right." She glances at Matt and his new girlfriend. "Nice seeing you, Matt."

We turn away, walking towards the shopping carts. With a little wink, I lean down to kiss her.

I did it for Matt's benefit, but also for my own. I've been wanting to kiss those lips since I first spotted her.

Am I being petty?

Fuck, yes, I am.

But I'm also enjoying myself.

When we're well out of hearing range, she leans on the cart and peers up at me. "Okay, are you going to tell me where you came from?"

"Surprise." I say with weak enthusiasm.

"Is everyone okay?"

"Yes." I tip my head. "I mean, Trace was losing his ever-loving mind this morning, but aside from that… we're all good."

"In a good way or a bad way?"

"In a Trace freaked out this morning, so here we are, sort of way."

She winces. "Because of me?"

"Yeah. He was really upset that you weren't there. Like... really upset. I haven't seen him like that in a long time. I didn't know what to do. I'm sorry to crash your Christmas like this. Between Trace and your mom, I got outvoted."

"I should have said goodbye. I didn't really explain what the plan was." She pauses. "Wait, you've been talking to my mom?"

"She answered the phone while you were in the shower."

"That sneaky little devil." She laughs. "Now I understand why we're making actual food for dinner."

"This is your holiday break. I really don't want us to be a burden. Trace just would not calm down and I thought we'd just make a quick trip to see you and then let you have your day for yourself."

"He missed me that much?"

"Well... yeah. He's gotten pretty attached. We all have." She's got a strange look in her eyes, like she might start crying again. I feel uneasy, knowing that I've said or done any number of things to make her feel that way. "It's completely inappropriate for us to be here. I get that. I'm really sorry..."

But whatever I planned to say next gets cut off when she launches into me, knocking the wind out of me. I wrap my arms around her and press my nose to her hair, breathing her in.

It feels good to be standing here with her.

Really good.

55.

Erin

Josh opens the sliding door, stepping out onto the patio. His boots crunch in the crusted snow as he crosses the yard to join me. He passes me a mug of coffee, wrapping both hands around his.

I sip it, tasting mom's comforting take on Irish coffee. Brown sugar. Whiskey. Cream.

Josh grins at me. "You have no idea how excited I am about this."

A large silver pot sits on the propane burner, bubbling and boiling merrily. It looks innocent, but that thing is full of liquid fire. So many things can go wrong when you deep fry a big bird, but my dad taught me well. I can almost hear him telling me not to overfill the pot with oil. To lower the bird in carefully.

So many of my memories of him are tangled up with food. Every meal was a celebration. It brought him so much joy, and yet, it took his life in the end. I still haven't figured out how to separate the good from the bad, but I'm trying.

Josh holds out his mug, and I clink my cup against it. "Where are the kids?"

"Playing with your old toys and Marvin. I swear to God, that dog can see into my soul."

I laugh. "He can read your mind, too. So look out."

"Thanks again for letting us crash your Christmas. You really didn't have to feed us."

"Honesty, it's a relief to have you here. I think it was cropping up to be a pretty depressing affair. Trace saved the day."

"I've never seen him like that." Josh studies the surface of his coffee. "I mean, he's four, so he's thrown fits before, but this was different."

"You couldn't distract him with presents?"

"We never opened them."

I look at him, surprised. "Really?"

He shrugs. "We didn't get that far. He was just convinced something bad happened to you and wouldn't calm down until he saw you."

"Does he ever get that way with Lisa?"

"No, but I think that's different in his mind. She's grandma." He rubs the back of his neck. "I told him you'd be back after your vacation, but he was worried you wouldn't come back. He said..." Josh stumbles over his words. "He said his last mommy never came back."

"Oh." My cheeks color.

He glances at me, dark eyes studying my reaction. "Yeah. Oh."

I adjust the propane tank, trying to buy time to gather my thoughts. "He knows I'm a nanny, right?"

"Yes. But I don't know if he knows what that means. He doesn't realize it's your job."

"So, maybe he thinks nanny is another word for mom?"

He winces. "I think that's possible."

It's so unbelievably sweet that Trace has picked me to be his mommy, but the misunderstanding is kind of heartbreaking. "Guess we better have a talk with him."

"Yeah." Josh is quiet for a few moments. "I didn't think he remembered much about how Ana got sick, but obviously, he's got that engraved on his little mind."

"He's getting to an age where he's going to notice the differences between his family and the kids in school."

"Yeah. And he's going to realize he's missing something important. Even so, I don't think it would do him any good to misunderstand our relationship. Building up expectations around the two of us."

"I don't want him to get hurt, either." I say. It's painful to admit it, but this has always been the inevitable outcome. "We should stop."

His gaze jerks over to me. "That's not at all what I was getting at."

"It's not?"

He's so tall. And sexy as fuck. Sometimes, it's hard to look at him, because I start feeling agonizingly bashful. He's studying my face and all I want to do is hide, but I force myself to hold his gaze.

He looks away, suddenly very interested in the clouds sailing overhead. "I almost told your ex that I was your boyfriend."

I laugh. "You should have. His reaction would have been priceless."

"I wanted to. But I wasn't sure how you would feel about it." He pauses, fiddling with his coffee mug. "Aw, hell, Erin. I'm not good at saying how I feel. But I guess the point is, I want to be that person for you. I don't want anyone else to know you the way I do. The idea of you being with one of my friends, or anyone else, makes me want to pull my hair out."

"I'm not interested in them." I wait until he's looking at me. "I'm just interested in you."

A smile tugs at his lips. "Yeah?"

I laugh, despite myself. "Yes."

His smile fades. "I guess it's probably obvious, but I'm damaged goods."

"Don't say that."

"Well, it's true. I don't know how to do this. Or if I'm even capable."

He's warning me right out of the gate. He's telling me I'll never claim his whole heart.

Breaking up with Matt was hard, but being with Josh is showing me how love should feel. It makes me realize that what I had with Matt might have been a convenience and comfort thing.

This thing between Josh and me, it's taking me higher than I ever thought possible.

Something tells me the fall from these heights would shatter me.

If I was smart, I'd run the other way.

So, what's with the damn butterflies?

He meets my gaze. "It's not much of an offer."

I smile. "You've got to work on your sales pitch. But I guess… I want to see what happens next."

"Me too."

"How do we navigate that without the kids getting caught up in it?"

"Think we can keep it under wraps while we figure things out?"

An uneasy feeling settles in my stomach. "From everyone?"

He tips his head. "You've met my family. And my friends. They have no filter. If they knew... I just don't want to put the two of us under a microscope."

I expected him to say he wanted to keep it a secret from the kids—saying he wants to keep it a secret from everyone else comes as a surprise.

It makes sense. His family does take an almost proprietorial interest in Josh's well-being.

I can understand where he's coming from.

But still, it doesn't feel great.

56.

Josh

Farmers don't get Christmas vacation.

Not this farmer, anyway.

Now that dad's retired, my load has doubled. There's equipment to power wash and put away. That old planter needs some maintenance before Spring.

And then, there's the cattle.

It's calving season.

Which means those old girls need constant supervision.

Cattle did not evolve to live on these plains. They're not exactly smart about winter. Bison are built for the snow. They know how to handle harsh Midwestern weather.

Cattle? Not so much.

If bison weren't so damn dangerous to handle, I'd switch in a heartbeat. But unless I decide I'm fine with being gored by a bison horn, I'll stick to cattle for the time being.

My mom pinch hits for Erin while she takes a few days off. Erin planned to spend time with her friends back in Lincoln. She's got a whole life outside of us, but it's hard to picture.

And when she's gone, there's an obvious absence.

We fall back into old routines. The kids adjust to having grandma back, but are quick to point out that she's not doing things right.

Cuts the sandwiches the wrong way.

Puts socks on right side out when Erin knows to put them on inside out so they don't bother Trace's toes.

A few days seem like eons, and we're all thankful when she comes back on New Year's Eve.

With the cornfields shorn from harvest, I can see for miles in any direction. I spot her car making its way down the snow-packed gravel road and head over in the truck to meet her at the house.

My boots crunch in the snow as I walk over to open her car door. She lets me help her out of the car, putting her small hand in my gloved paw.

"You could have spent New Year's Eve with your friends." I say this, but I'm so grateful she didn't.

She shrugs, glancing up at the house. "It's always a let-down."

"Do you usually go out?"

"Every year. My friends think a bar crawl is the only way to go. If I had my way, we'd go to the Karaoke bar and just hunker down."

I pull a face.

She laughs. "Not a fan of karaoke?"

"Not even a little." I shove my hands in the pockets of my canvas jacket. "We're all glad to have you back."

"I was getting a little bored at home. Besides, I overheard Bo and Dusty talking about the big party in Clark. I figured you'd want to go."

"I'd feel guilty partying it up knowing you gave up your holiday so I could go out."

"That's what nannies are for."

"That's what grandmas are for." My mom steps down the front stoop. Trace and Maven barrel out, swathed like the Michelin man in winter coats and scarves. "I'll watch the kids. You should take Erin to the party. She'd have fun."

Mom says it like it's a suggestion, but I can tell from the look in her eye that our fate has already been decided.

I'm sitting on the couch later that night, waiting for Erin to get dressed.

Maven sits on my lap while Trace hangs from my shoulders. They should be in bed, but they wanted to stay up to watch the ball drop. We celebrated London's New Year's Eve and now they're wired.

When Erin steps out of her bedroom, everyone goes stock-still.

"She looks like a movie star." Trace sighs, his little heart racing against my back.

My heart is hammering, too. She's stealing my breath.

Erin's wearing a gold jumpsuit.

To a small-town party where most people treat denim like a second skin.

Her hair is in a high ponytail and she wears dramatic, dangly earrings. Trace isn't wrong to say she looks like a star. She's wildly overdressed and I love it.

Mom stands in the kitchen doorway, wiping her hands on a dish towel. "Oh, Erin. You look beautiful." She turns to scan my clothes. "Josh. You couldn't bother dressing up?"

I look down at my thick flannel shirt and worn-out jeans. "You bought me this shirt."

"For work. Not for going out. At least change into nicer jeans. That pair has holes in it. Good lord. I've raised an animal."

I get up and put on dark wash jeans—the farm boy equivalent of dress pants.

Mom puts the kids in her SUV and Erin and I climb into my truck.

Her scent fills the cab, and she's got my heart racing.

And we're supposed to go to a party and act like we're not together.

That was my idea, but I'm not sure what I was thinking.

The only thing I know for sure… I'm in trouble.

57.

Erin

I'm not a petite girl.

I never have been.

I have a very specific memory of getting cornered by some girls in middle school. They told me I dressed too loudly for a chubby kid.

They thought I should do everyone a favor and just blend in.

Fuck.

That.

Shit.

You only live one life. And you only get one body.

These legs have carried me all around Paris. New York City. London.

These hands have held onto my grandmother's hand on her dying day.

And these lips have kissed Josh Olson.

I'm not ashamed of this body. I'm going to celebrate it.

We step into the bar, and it's immediately apparent that I've overdressed.

But if you ask me, these hayseeds underdressed.

It's New Years Freaking Eve. They can't change out of their jeans for one night?

I have to admit, Josh is looking pretty good in his particular pair, but I'm not supposed to be looking. At least, not in public.

We haven't seen each other since we made our strange little agreement. You'd think talking things through would clear the air. Make life a little simpler. It's done the opposite. We've admitted we're attracted to each other, but all that's done is blown the cover off all the accidental physical interactions. We can't play innocent anymore. If he touches my hand, I know why. If I get caught staring, that's obvious now, too.

He doesn't want everyone knowing we're doing whatever it is we're doing. I can understand why, but that leaves me in a bar full of strangers without a shoulder to lean on.

When I spot Bo and Dusty, relief washes over me. I'm aware I'm drawing a lot of attention. Some of it is good, some of it is not so great. That's just life. Haters gonna hate.

Bo and Dusty are smiling at me, and they're the only friends I'm interested in impressing. I can feel Josh trailing behind me, close enough to feel his warmth, far enough away to appear platonic.

Dusty has no qualms about getting too close. "Holy shit. You look gorgeous."

I let him pull me into a hug, ignoring the flat look on Josh's face. "Thanks. It's not too much?"

"It's just right." Dusty grins. He catches me looking at the stage. "You gonna sing for us later?"

"Karaoke?" I ask, turning to look back at Josh.

His gaze softens. "I thought you might like that."

Dusty smacks Bo. "You two should break the ice."

I glance at Bo. "You sing?"

"Not particularly. I just have less shame than the rest of them."

Dusty laughs. "For the record, I have absolutely no shame. My audience, however, needs a lot more liquor in them before they can tolerate this song bird."

Josh meets my gaze. "You said this was your favorite thing to do on New Year's Eve. You should get up there. Kick it off."

I look at Bo. "Will you go with me?"

He nods, setting his beer aside. "You bet."

We climb up on the stage and I can feel curious eyes following my movement. I haven't sung in front of a crowd since high school, but it's amazing how quickly it all comes back to me.

I don't know a lot of country songs, but Bo and I settle on one I'm familiar with—Whiskey Lullaby. And despite Bo's humility, he has a voice like smoky honey, and he can find the harmonies with no trouble. It's so much fun, we decide to sing another.

I pick another country song I know, "I Hate This" by Tenille Arts. I picked it because it's fun to sing. Bo and I trade off, taking verses, but as I'm singing the lyrics, I'm realizing that the words are a lot more spot on than I intended.

It's a song about a woman who's tired of pretending.

My eyes connect with Josh's part way through and the look on his face almost sets me on fire.

When the song is over, I put the mic down and step away. Leave it to country music to be so easily weaponized.

I'm not really ready to face Josh. I'll have to act like those words didn't mean anything to me, when it's the most honest I've ever been.

58.

Josh

The trouble with taking Erin to a party is that she has absolutely no idea what she looks like.

She could have worn a garbage bag and still had fans.

But she decided to pull out all the stops. I have had more than one person ask me if she's a country star.

Which is kind of funny, because I know country music is not her favorite.

The way she sang that last song, though, she could have a future in it. I don't know if she picked that one on purpose, or if Bo chose it, but it hit me right between the eyes.

I guess I know pretending we're not a couple isn't ideal. It's not fair to her, even if it is in the kids' best interest. But if we were just talking about what Erin deserves, it would be some other man.

Somebody who had a whole heart to give away. All I have to offer is this broken heart.

I'm not sure if it's enough.

It just surprises me that I even have the capacity to care about another woman like this.

After Ana, I just figured everybody only gets one great love in life and I had mine.

It feels selfish to want Erin, too. And it feels like I'm leaving Ana behind.

"You do realize this is a party, right?" Skyler bellies up to the bar.

"When'd you get here?"

"Somewhere between I Hate This and It's Five O'clock somewhere." Skyler laughs. "Who's going to tell Dusty he's completely tone deaf?"

I laugh. "I think he's fully aware and just doesn't give a damn."

"Erin, though." He whistles. "Did you know she had that in her?"

"Yes, actually." I turn to watch Erin. She's talking to a few girls from our graduating class. This girl makes friends wherever she goes. "She's always singing around the house."

"Singing like that?"

I smile fondly. "More or less."

"In that case, I'd say you better nail that down."

I give him a sharp look.

He laughs, swigging his beer. "You're a terrible actor, Josh. I can see right through you. What I don't understand is why you're pretending you're not into her."

"The kids…"

"The kids love her."

I frown at him. "Exactly. What if it doesn't work out? I can't rip another person out of their lives."

Skyler's smile fades. "Life ain't easy, is it?"

"You can say that again."

He turns to watch Erin over my shoulder. "But, meanwhile, if you aren't careful, somebody else might swoop in and take her from you."

I turn, expecting to find that rascal Dusty sniffing around her again, but it's far worse. Tyson Kyle, resident heart breaker, has separated Erin from the pack and appears to be going in for the kill.

"Fuck me." I mutter. "Go over there and break that up."

"Why me?"

"Because I don't want people getting the wrong idea if I go."

Skyler frowns. "Yeah, wouldn't want people thinking you like that woman."

"A little less sarcasm and a little more saving Erin from that walking STD."

"No." He leans against the bar, smiling as he tips his beer back. "You want her? You go get her."

I hesitate, torn between keeping up the charade and stopping whatever Tyson's planning.

When he reaches out to touch her arm, the decision is made.

I push through the crowd, stopping just behind her. I've got a few inches of height on Tyson and plenty of bulk. It's not hard to loom over him.

He looks up at me with a competitive light in his blue eyes. "Josh Olson. How you been, buddy?"

"Doing fine." I say, trying to keep the growl out of my voice. "Erin, Skyler was wanting to talk to you."

She glances over her shoulder, fixing me with a mischievous smile. "I'll find him later."

"She'll find him later, Olson." Tyson gives me a smug smile that says, beat it.

I put my hand on her waist, guiding her away. "She'll talk to him now."

Erin gives Tyson an apologetic shrug, allowing me to tow her back through the crowd by the hand. I pull her in front of me, putting my lips by her ear. "Are you trying to make me jealous?"

I don't miss the shiver that trembles across her shoulders. "That depends, is it working?"

More than she could know.

"Such a naughty little thing." I murmur, letting my fingers brush along the small of her back.

59.

Erin

Josh decides we've had enough partying for one night. That's fine by me. I don't know most of these people and I don't feel compelled to start the new year with them.

The heat in his eyes, though, now that's worth following.

He opens the truck door, helping me up even though I'm perfectly capable of getting in by myself.

Once he's behind the wheel, he starts the truck up. "Clark does a fireworks show every year at midnight. If we drive out to the west 80, we can see it."

"From this far away?"

"It's flat as a pancake out here. You can see for miles." He throws the truck in reverse. "You want to check it out?"

"Yeah. Why not?"

Josh nods, turning the truck down gravel roads.

I prop my elbow on the door, resting my chin on my fist as I peer up at the sky. "You can see so many stars out here. It's beautiful."

"A view like that never gets old."

He pulls down a dirt lane, bumping across rough tractor tracks and snow, before throwing the truck into park. We're sitting over a little pasture. A pond rests at the bottom of the basin, its frozen surface bounces moonlight back like a mirror.

"What'd you think of the party?"

"It was fun."

"You certainly had plenty of admirers."

"Who did? I did?"

"Yes, you." He chuckles. "You couldn't feel all those eyes on you tonight?"

"I felt yours."

I feel them now, the weight of his gaze. The heat.

Even in the dark, I can feel that.

He reaches over, fingers brushing my hips as he unbuckles my seatbelt. Then he's pulling me across the bench until we're thigh to thigh.

"If I didn't say so," He brushes a lock of hair away from my face. "You look beautiful tonight."

He saves me from having to respond, from deflecting, by brushing his lips across mine.

I can smell the hint of whiskey on his breath. I don't like to drink it myself, but on him, it's pretty enticing. My tongue slips across his lips, checking for traces of whatever he was drinking.

His tongue meets mine, caressing mine, sweeping past my lips. He's good at this. He knows how to possess my body, occupy my thoughts.

His hand glides along my neck. Cupping the back of my head, he angles it back, delving deeper. He overpowers me and I am here for it. With a soft groan, he pulls me onto his lap. I'm straddling his thighs, my back pressed up against the steering wheel—caged in.

He breaks our kiss, pulling back to study my body. I want to shrink, but he's holding me up, looking at me with such admiration, I can almost believe what his eyes are telling me.

In this moment, for this night, I feel beautiful.

His fingers trace the neckline of my jumper, roughly pushing the crossover top to either side. My lace bra is exposed and his fingers glide across the curve of my breasts. He bends forward, his breath soft and warm, then he's kissing my skin, breathing me in.

I let my fingers weave through his short hair, fingernails· scratching gently at his scalp.

He charts a path across my breast, along my collarbone and up the slope of my neck. I can feel heat building in my core, buoyed up by the growing bulge in his jeans.

I slip off his lap, dragging the zipper down on his jeans. He lifts his hips so that I can pull his jeans down a bit, before tugging his half-erect cock out of his boxers.

Even like this, it's impressive. I squeeze it, enjoying the way soft flesh slowly hardens under my grip. When I lower my head, taking him between my lips, he lets out a soft hiss. His hands work at my ponytail, gently loosening my hair. He plays with my hair, while I stroke him with my tongue and my hands.

"Fuck, baby." He murmurs. "That mouth is driving me crazy."

I pull back, slowly stroking his shaft. "I can't stop thinking about the last time." My fingers trace the veins on his hard member. "This cock has been haunting my dreams."

"Tell me what you want."

I meet his gaze, hungry and a little wild. "I want you to fuck me silly."

He sucks in a little breath, before half turning, leaning into the back of the truck. With a practiced tug, he flips the back seat upright, unrolling the sleeping bag he keeps in there for winter emergencies.

I guess this would qualify.

And then he's climbing over the seat, taking my hand to help me clamber over the edge. I'm not nearly as graceful as him, tumbling into him with a little laugh.

He catches me easily, wasting no time before sliding my sleeves down my shoulders.

I feel so exposed here, in the middle of a field. Anybody could come along.

And yet, we're completely alone. Just Josh and me and the stars.

He's tugging off his jeans and I'm slipping out of my jumpsuit.

I barely pull the tangled fabric from my ankles, and then he's sweeping me up.

60.

Josh

Sex in the truck is risky.
Kind of public.
And therefore, incredibly hot.
But, also, somewhat limiting.

I want to spread her out and kiss every inch of her skin. But even Erin, all five foot nothing of her, couldn't fully stretch out in the back of the truck, let alone a big fuck like me.

We somehow make it work. I settle back on my haunches, dragging her between my thighs. She feels so soft and warm; I want to press her right into my skin. My cock strains against my boxers, aggressively pushing against her soft belly. Her hand slips between us, stroking me through the soft fabric. I kiss her deeply, letting my tongue delve into her mouth, explore everything there.

But her hand is teasing my cock, and it's going to get me in trouble before we even get started. I slip my hand into her panties, following the curve of her body. My finger slides inside, feeling how wet she is.

Spinning her around, I guide her onto her hands and knees. My cock is throbbing with need, but I have to take a second to just admire the sight before me. Moonlight glows across her skin, highlighting the soft curves of her body. My hands curve over her ass, dragging up that svelte body past her hips, her ribs, to circle around and cup her magnificent tits.

She presses her hips back into mine, forcing my cock against her ass.

Impatient, then.

With a little grin, I push my shorts down and grip myself, running my tip along her center a few times. When my cock is wet and slick, I put the tip at her entrance and slowly, so fucking slowly, slide inside.

She moans, tossing her head back. The sound of her voice does something to me and my hips twitch forward, burying a few more inches inside. She yelps, rolling her hips against mine.

I pause. "Doing okay?"

She laughs. "I might faint."

Concern lances through me.

Bracing her hands against the door, she pushes back, dragging her pussy down the last few inches of my shaft. Her voice is breathless, desperate. "That's your goal, Josh. Fuck me until I pass out."

"You've got such a filthy mouth."

"You like it."

I pull back and thrust in again, earning another moan. "Fuck yeah, I do."

She braces her hands on the passenger seat, the door, and I wrap one arm around her waist, anchoring myself against the console with the other. And then I fuck her.

Hard.

The way I want to.

I'm not holding back and she's crying out for more. It's electrifying. I'm maxing her out with my size and she feels so fucking good on my shaft. Like her body was made for me.

Like I was made for her.

She comes with a lusty groan, pussy squeezing hard on my shaft.

"Ah. Fuck, baby. I'm close."

"Not yet," She pants, riding out the last twinges of her orgasm. Then she's leaning forward, dragging my cock out of her. She flips around, lowering her head over me. Her tongue glides over my shaft and then she's bobbing her head up and down, sucking so hard her cheeks hollow out.

"I'm gonna come." I grunt, but she only takes my cock deeper until the head is sailing over the back of her tongue.

And then I'm seeing fireworks.

Literally.

Every nerve in my body is firing, pleasure radiating out to my toes while Clark, Nebraska starts their annual fireworks show.

Once she's sucked the last drop from my shaft, she sits back, tugging my flannel shirt over her shoulders. I wiggle back into my boxers. Sliding the little window panel open on the back of the truck window, I fish around in the truck bed, retrieving a bottle of chilled champagne.

I grabbed it at the store when she said she'd be spending New Year's with us. I didn't know what we would do, but I knew that I wanted to bring the new year in with her.

Sitting back, I pull her into my lap and wrap the sleeping bag around our bodies.

We pass the bottle back and forth, watching fireworks splash across the sky.

61.

Erin

The new year brings with it more snow and frigid cold.

But with the low temperatures, life surges beneath the surface. Calving season is in full swing and we have four sweet calves to show for it.

Josh has turned into a heifer's midwife, attending births at all hours, in all kinds of weather. Between that and Maven's teething, he's getting worn pretty thin.

I stand at the window by the sink, watching the unfamiliar silver pickup truck plow back down the driveway.

Josh sits at the table, elbows resting on the scratched wooden surface. He has his fingers woven together, pressing his clenched fists into his lips.

"What now?" I ask, setting a cup of coffee in front of him.

He stares in the distance for a bit before focusing on me. His expression is grim. "We keep her comfortable and hope for the best."

"That's it? The vet isn't coming back?"

Josh's drained expression is hurting my heart. "He says she's making progress. Her vitals are good, but…"

"You don't think she can do it?"

His gaze meets mine and slides away. "I get a bad feeling about it. I just don't want her to suffer."

His words dry up and he shakes his head.

"I don't understand. Wasn't Betsy super old? How'd she end up pregnant, anyway?"

"That was my fault. We don't really include her in the herd count, so she snuck in with the other heifers when we put them out to pasture with the bull." He slumps back. "A stupid fuck up."

I want to give him a hug, but he's intentionally keeping himself out of range.

It's almost like he's punishing himself.

Betsy's more or less like the family pet to the Olsons. She's been intermingling with the herd since long before Josh took over. It is true, she is a bovine leader in the herd. They follow her in, calm down when she's around. But the risks of letting her intermingle with the herd are now very clear.

And Josh is the one who gets to carry the blame. He didn't start it, but he let it continue.

This is the way of life on the farm. The cycle of life is brutal.

The Olsons are big-hearted people. I'm not sure how they stand it.

He slips back outside, disappearing into the barn to help Betsy in whatever way he can.

As the hours wile on, I feed the kids and get them ready for bed. Lisa shows up just as I'm reading the kids a bedtime story. She claims she was missing the kids, but I can tell by the way her gaze keeps straying north that she's worried about Josh.

She's not wrong to worry. Josh doesn't even come in for dinner. The barn is heated, but that rickety heater won't be able to compete with these frigid January temperatures.

Once I'm sure the kids are sound asleep, I make up a little basket for Josh. Warm soup. Bread. Coffee.

Throwing the hood up on my parka, I press out into the night. The wind hits me hard, sucking the breath from my lungs. It's so cold it stings my skin, but if I turn my gaze upward, the stars glitter like diamonds. It's frigid and unforgiving and completely breathtakingly beautiful.

Listening to the wind twine through the branches, to the way my boots crunch on the snow, I push into the barn.

Betsy's making low sounds of distress. Josh sits on a stool beside her. His hand sweeps up and down her back. His head is bowed.

"No progress?"

My voice startles him. He jerks around, staring at me with a worried expression. "What are you doing out here?"

Too late, I remember this is how Ana got sick.

Like... exactly how she got sick.

The calving barn.

The cold night.

I hold out the basket, I'm not sure if it's an offering or an apology, but he ignores it. I clear my throat. "I thought you might be hungry."

"It's too cold to be walking around out there."

"I've got my coat on."

He presses his eyes shut, his voice is gruff. "That's not the point." He looks at me, frowning. "What about the kids? You just left them alone in there?"

I feel like a kid getting into trouble with a stern teacher. My hackles go up and I can't help but to feel defensive. How did a kind act turn into a sin? "Your mom came over to spend the night with them. You'd know that if you left the barn. Besides, I have the monitor."

I hold it up and Maven's lullaby playlist faintly echoes back to us on it.

He turns away, putting both hands on Betsy's side. "You shouldn't be out here."

"Okay." I say, not quite keeping the hurt out of my voice. "My bad, Josh."

I want him to turn around. To see a comforting smile on his face, but he won't look at me. It hurts more than if he'd just snap at me some more.

Setting his dinner on the stool, I trudge back into the dark night, feeling empty-hearted.

The cold seeps into my body and I take a shower, hoping to warm the chill from my blood.

But this isn't the type of chill you can warm up with blankets and hot tea. It's a feeling of hurt that goes deeper than my skin. I sleep fitfully and somewhere around two, I hear the door open and close.

Climbing to my feet, I slip into the hall and lean against the doorframe. "How's Betsy?"

He finds me in the dim light from the stove and shakes his head.

He doesn't need to say it. My heart throbs painfully.

Ignoring his prickly exterior, I sweep forward, wrapping my arms around him.

His coat is cold, the zipper is like ice against my chest. He pulls it off and drops it where he stands, kicking his boots off. I watch him wash his hands at the sink. He's not speaking to me and I'm wondering if it would be better for me to give him space, but then he turns around and takes my hand. I follow him into his room.

We've never been in here. Not at the same time.

It smells like him. Like soap and wood and leather. Pulling off his shirt, he kicks off his jeans and falls into bed. He pulls me with him and I let him tug me up against his side. I wrap my arms and legs around him, trying to share my warmth.

He takes a shaky breath, weaving his hands through my hair. "I was a dick, wasn't I?"

Despite myself, my lips pull into a tiny smile. "The biggest."

There's laughter in his voice. "Are you saying I *am* the biggest dick or that I have the biggest dick?"

I grin, burying my face against his chest. "Yes."

62.

Josh

Letting Betsy die was a rookie mistake from start to finish.

It's a humiliating blunder made worse by the fact that everyone was attached to that sweet old girl.

I'm having a hard time filling my dad's shoes. He wasn't just good at his job. He was a master. I can't stack up, not yet, anyway.

But I'm trying.

I was stressed already, and then Erin came out and it was just déjà vu. I could almost see Ana standing there, in the same place, on the same sort of night.

Like seeing double.

Watching Betsy slowly die was putting me in a very dark place. I guess seeing Erin, worrying about her like that, just triggered me.

It's been two years, but the pain and the fear is as fresh as ever. Will I ever outrun these ghosts?

I have to wonder what I've done wrong. What did I do in a previous life, that God or whoever's in charge, would decide to punish me like this? I want to be optimistic, to leave it all behind, but most of the time I feel like I'm just waiting for the other shoe to drop.

When will Erin be taken from us? How?

Maybe she'd be better off if she was nowhere near me. Maybe I'm toxic.

It's superstitious bullshit, I know this. But isn't that the basis of religion?

It gives you hope, but supplies the fear. The sickness and the cure.

Religion can't solve the problems I have.

Call it seasonal affective disorder. Call it PTSD.

Whatever it is makes it pretty hard to see the silver lining.

All I know is that the best I've felt in days was laying there in bed with Erin in my arms. She's warm and comforting and *good*.

Better than I deserve.

At some point in the morning, she must have slipped out of bed. I wake up alone, with the faint sounds of laughter coming from the kitchen. I force my heavy limbs to support my weight, tugging on a pair of sweats.

I stop in the doorway, watching them for a few minutes without being noticed.

My gaze swings to the front window where I can see the empty drive. My mom must have already slipped away. Sneaky little devil. I turn my gaze back to the kitchen.

Erin's making cinnamon rolls again. She knows I like them. And despite the fact that I was 'the biggest dick' to her last night, she's still trying to find ways to comfort me.

I don't fucking deserve this woman.

She's letting both kids help, something Ana probably never would have done.

Ana was very type A. Liked things nice and neat and orderly. Trace has flour all over his shirt. Maven is actively dumping sugar on the floor. And Erin is just taking it all in stride. I appreciate her more than I could ever adequately put into words, but a tiny slice of resentment cuts through me.

It's like she's showing Ana up. The kids' mom. I'd rather keep Ana on her pedestal. She's achieved sainthood in my memories and these perfect little things Erin does draw unfavorable comparisons.

I know I'm being unreasonable.

Sometimes, my moods swing so fast, even I get dizzy. Knowing it's not right, knowing it's hurtful, that doesn't make the feelings go away. It just makes me feel like an asshole on top of everything else.

I've found the best way to deal with these things is in private. That way, there's no collateral damage.

Spinning away before anyone notices me, I walk back to the bathroom.

What I need is a hot shower. I step into the bathroom, cranking the water as hot as possible. While steam slowly fills the room, I notice I'm out of soap. Flinging open the cabinets, I stumble across a purple toiletry bag I don't recognize. Thoughtlessly tugging it open, I come across a little arsenal of skincare products, like little vials of potion. Makeup, too.

Eyeliner.

Red lipstick.

These are Erin's things. She's been living at my place for a few months now and she's still living out of a travel bag like a vagabond.

My gaze is drawn to Ana's half of the sink. Her own collection of products gather dust. I haven't had the heart to touch her things. It's always felt like if I didn't move anything, I could pretend that she never really left us.

But, eventually, I'll need to move on. And in the meantime, I've asked this person to live in my house and I haven't even given her space to call her own.

Guilt suffuses my body and by the time I've stepped out of the shower, I've made up my mind. Dressing methodically, I pull on my boots and slip outside.

I find a box in the garage and carefully store Ana's things away. Maybe one day, Maven will want to see what color of lipstick her mother wore. Trace might want to smell her perfume, jogging long-buried memories. I'll keep them safely tucked away for the kids. I want to protect her memory for them.

But I also want to make room for Erin.

And as much as it all hurts, it feels like maybe I'm finally taking a step forward.

63.

Erin

Flying out of Lincoln is a breeze.

The airport only has one terminal. You really can't mess it up.

But Josh hasn't flown since high school and the kids have never been on an airplane.

I take charge of the boarding passes and navigating security. Josh acts as my pack mule. Somehow, he manages to wrangle three carry-ons and a two-year-old in those massive arms.

We take up an entire row on the plane, but once we're in the air, we condense into three seats. Maven and Trace snuggle up in the window seat, watching Disney movies on their tablet. I glance over at Josh, his enormous frame folded up in the tiny plane seat, and laugh. "How you doing, big guy?"

He gives me a wan smile. "Why are all these seats child-sized?"

I pat his leg. "You can stretch out on this side if you want."

He extends his legs to my side with a grateful sigh. His fingers subtly trace lines on my thigh. "I'm so glad you let us drag you along on this trip."

"Florida in January? Yes, please."

"I would have been a hot mess if I had to wrangle the kids through security by myself."

"They're actually a lot of fun to travel with. Everything's so new to them. Kind of brings the wonder back into it."

"How often do you fly?"

I shrug. "A few times a year."

"Just for fun?"

"Yeah. I like to explore new places. See what's out there."

His foot slips under my leg and I snuggle as close as I can without alerting the kids to our shenanigans.

"You don't travel much?"

He shrugs. "Not much. My parents were never big on vacations when we were little. They didn't start going down to Florida until Charlie was a senior in high school."

"Why didn't you ever go with them?"

"Too busy, I guess."

"Lame." I say, nudging him. "You're never too busy to live life." The words sort of drop off my lips. I've always been someone who believed in sucking the marrow from life, but that feeling has only intensified since my dad's sudden death. But it's a bit insensitive to say to a widower. He's quiet while I squirm internally, regretting opening my big mouth.

"You're right, of course."

I glance at him. "I am?"

He glances at his kids, flying perfectly, like two little jet-set pros. "We always talked about traveling with these two." He clears his throat a few times. "I'm not going to make that mistake again. I'm going to drag these kids all over the place and you're going to help."

"Oh, am I?"

He grins. "Somebody's got to manage the boarding passes."

I laugh. "You literally just put them on your phone."

He shakes his head. "Too much hassle. You put them on your phone, and I'll carry the bags."

"That sounds like a reasonable arrangement. So where do you want to go first?"

He thinks that over. "Florida?"

I wrinkle my nose. "Nah. How about Minneapolis? I hear it's lovely this time of year."

He laughs, nodding. "All that lovely snow."

"So much snow."

As we're stepping into the terminal in Chicago, a woman who sat behind us, taps Josh on the arm. "I just wanted to say you have such a lovely little family."

Josh holds Maven in his arms. "Thank you."

She nods. "You and your wife did such a good job keeping them occupied. It's so nice to see parents who obviously love their kids."

I can feel Josh stiffen at my side, but he smiles and thanks the woman. Trace pulls on my hand. He's spotted the moving walkways and is desperate to try them.

I glance back at Josh. He gives me a conspiratorial smile, but it only goes skin deep. I can see something else in his eyes. It looks a little like guilt. Or pain.

Funny how one innocuous comment, intended as a compliment, can cut so deep.

64.

Josh

Mom and dad's new condo is right on the beach. There's a general commotion when we arrive. Charlie and Parker immediately scoop up the kids to take them out to look at the waves. Mom grabs Erin's arm and leads her through the house. The floors are tiled throughout and the walls are a soft blue. Mom stops in the guest room, going on at length about the closets. I lean down, murmuring in Erin's ear. "So many mermaids."

She tries to hide her smile. "I think they're watching us."

We both glance over at the topless wooden mermaid hanging over the bed. I think the house came furnished, that or mom has a secret affinity for merfolk.

We finish the tour on the patio. A short band of scrubby grass separates us from boundless white sand. The ocean looks incredibly blue from here. "That view is worth a million bucks, mom."

She breathes the salty air into her lungs and lets it out. "I just feel free out here, you know?"

I study her profile, wondering how many of their life choices were dictated by dad and the farm. She certainly does seem more at ease now.

Trace hollers at Erin, and she crosses the sand to hold his hand.

"I'm so glad she agreed to come." Mom says, watching Trace drag Erin towards the water.

"Why is she here?" Charlie asks. Having been replaced by Erin, she's returned to us in all her sulky young adult glory.

"She's the kids' nanny." I say, feeling my ears heat. "I couldn't have navigated the airports without her."

"You're helpless now?" Charlie asks.

"Don't be a bitch." Reese says, coming from one of the back rooms. "Look at how much those kids love her."

Mom's watching the exchange with a worried look on her face.

Charlie tips her chin up. "This is supposed to be a family trip."

"I wanted her here." Mom says, piping up. "I told Josh to bring her."

This is how these arguments usually go. The girls are usually moving at warp speed, while I'm still working on decoding something they said minutes ago. As Erin and Trace return from the beach, the conversation abruptly dries up.

She glances at all the faces. I can see her absorbing the vibe. My sisters aren't as sly as they think they are. Their poker faces suck.

I slip past them, rolling my eyes so that only Erin can see. I nudge her, grabbing Trace's hand. "Come on, bud. Let's see who can find more shells, Erin or dad."

I love my sisters, but they are constantly fighting. It's always something with them. I can usually avoid the fray, but lately, it seems like dear little Charlie has set her sights on me and my family. She's like a vampire, sucking the joy right out of perfectly good moments.

It wasn't exactly a warm welcome for Erin and since she's the odd man out, I feel like it's our obligation to make sure she's comfortable. I stick with her for the rest of the day, in part, to make sure she's having a good time. But also because she's more fun than my bickering family.

Once the kids are finally tucked in bed and sleeping, I find her sitting at the counter, chatting with my mom.

"Where are the girls?" I ask, leaning on the counter next to Erin.

"Charlie and Parker are in their room watching TV and I think Reese is already asleep."

Reese always was the first to go to bed. I glance down at Erin. "How about you?"

Her lips pull into a half grin. "What about me?"

"You want to go for a walk?"

She tilts her head, glancing outside. It's pitch dark. "Now?"

"Yeah. It'll be quiet."

"Okay." Erin says, slowly climbing to her feet.

Mom gives me a secret look. It's too knowing. This woman can see right through me—she's always known what I'm thinking before I do. "Take a blanket, Josh. It gets chilly at night."

We walk down to the beach together and as soon as our feet hit the sand, I take Erin's hand. I was looking forward to taking this trip with her, but I didn't anticipate how crowded the house would be. We've been under a microscope from the moment we arrived and I've had to pretend like my fingers weren't itching to touch her hair. We find a little spot to sit down, and I wrap the blanket around both of our shoulders. She leans into me and I put my arm around her.

The only sound is the constant crash of waves on the beach. There's a full moon and it almost lights up the horizon, spilling silver light across the water.

But no matter how perfect the setting, it doesn't feel complete, unless she's there with me. She feels like the missing piece. I turn, pressing my lips to her hair, breathing her in. I've been wanting to do that all day.

"Why do I get the feeling that your sisters don't like me very much?"

It's not all of my sisters, just the one. "They like you."

"Hmm."

"You just need to spend more time with them."

"I do?" She sounds very unenthusiastic.

"Yes." I let my fingers slide up her side. "For my sake."

She sighs. "It's a good thing you're cute."

"Just cute?" I ask, nuzzling her neck until she's laughing, squirming in my arms.

65.

The strange thing about being attached to Josh is that it gives me automatic big sister status, when I'm actually between Reese and Parker in age.

They're all still in college and I think they assume, because I'm already working, that I'm older than them.

We drive into the nearest beach town, finding the little shopping district Lisa told us about. I end up driving us, even though that may not have been anyone's best choice.

Charlie scours reviews before deciding which coffee shop we should stop at. Half of my travels revolve around finding the best local dives and Charlie does not disappoint. She finds a little hole-in-the-wall Cuban place. Reese and Parker seem somewhat indifferent, but I have a cortado that knocks my socks off.

The girls launch into a rapid fire gossip session that's almost hard to keep up with. They're trading stories about their classmates. Occasionally, some of these stories involve Bo, Dusty, or Skyler. It's almost conveyed in a different language. They share a connection that allows them to speak in half sentences or partial stories.

I feel a little left out, but as an only child, I'm mostly just enthralled by their relationship. I've only really seen them bickering, but this is giving me insight into how close they really are.

It makes me a tad jealous.

It's a beautiful day and I just let their laughter and gossip wash over me. We step into a little boutique and Charlie stops by a rack of seashell earrings. The smile slides off her face. "Ana would have loved these."

A hush falls over the girls. The light that usually glitters in Reese's eyes fades and it occurs to me that Ana and Reese would have gone through most of high school together. I find myself wondering if they traveled in the same circles. When Josh's wife died, did the girls lose a friend?

And then, all at once, it hits me why Charlie doesn't like me. "How long did you know her?"

Charlie picks up some earrings, running her fingers over them. "Pretty much our whole lives."

Reese tries to smile. "She was actually in my grade. We were friends before Josh and Ana ever started dating. I used to say he stole her from me."

Charlie turns away, sniffing quietly.

"What was she like?"

Reese gives me a watery smile. "She was such a tomboy."

"Sweet, though." Parker says, piping up for the first time. She shrinks when everyone turns to look at her. "She always noticed if someone was being left out."

"Competitive and really fucking smart." Charlie says, rubbing at her eyes like she has something stuck in them. Her gaze lands on me, skewering me. "She's not somebody who could ever be replaced."

It feels particularly pointed. I want to say I'm not trying to replace anyone, but is that true? I've been afraid to look too closely at those feelings, afraid that if I exposed them to the air, they'd wither and die.

Parker turns away, snagging a hanger from a rack. She holds up a Spanish-style sundress. "You should try this on."

I look around, realizing belatedly that she's looking at me. "You want me to try that on?"

She nods.

I don't really want to play dress up. Especially not in the middle of a conversation about Ana. But this is hands down the longest sentence Parker has ever uttered directly to me. I'm afraid to say no. Taking the dress from her, I step into the dressing room and put it on.

It's actually a two piece that exposes a slice of tummy. I'm self-conscious about my stomach, so I would never have picked it myself. But the beautiful pattern is calling my name.

"How's it look?" Reese calls out from the other side of the dressing room. "Let us see."

I step out, and they go very quiet.

"What do you think?" Reese asks.

I turn, looking at my curves in the mirror. "I think I kind of love it?"

Parker's face breaks into a huge grin. She's always pretty, but when she smiles, she's stunning. "You should wear it now."

I grin. "Only if the rest of you pick out a dress to wear, too."

The girls smile at each other, turning to look at Charlie who is lurking a few feet away. She runs her hand down the fabric of a green sundress. Looking at them, she rolls her eyes theatrically. "Sure. Why not?"

66.

Josh

I hear the girls before I see them.

Mom and I sit on the patio drinking mimosas when we hear a chorus of Olson girl laughter from the front of the condo.

I know that laugh. That laugh spells trouble.

It means they're having a joke, usually at my expense. I can't decide if it's better for them to be fighting or getting along. When they're getting along, they're usually colluding against me.

One by one, they filter onto the patio.

"Oh, what a pretty dress." Mom says, running her fingers along the green skirt of Charlie's new dress.

"It was a successful shopping trip." Reese says, swishing her yellow skirt. She's even got a little yellow flower behind her ear. Sometimes, I forget how pretty my sisters are. The guys their age never forget and that's why being a big brother is a stressful job.

"Where are the kids?" Charlie asks, sitting on the edge of mom's chair.

Mom puts her arm around Charlie. "With grandpa. He took them down to the bait shop."

Parker and Erin arrive last. The first thing I notice is that Parker, quiet and reserved Parker, has her hands wrapped around Erin's arm.

This is a small miracle by itself, but then I get a good look at the dress Erin is wearing and that's an entirely different kind of miracle. Tension immediately fills my body.

It's two pieces. The top cuts off right below her chest, exposing a tempting inch of skin. The skirt sits right on the small of her waist, the exact place where I like to put my hands. She told me this morning that the Florida humidity is turning her hair into a frizz ball, but I think it makes her curls look like a soft cloud.

Judging by the devious looks on my sisters' faces and the way they're staring right at me, this dress was for my benefit. They are laughing at me, of course, and maybe I should be annoyed or embarrassed, but all I can think about is how badly I want to run my fingers along Erin's exposed skin.

"What do you think of Erin's dress?" Parker asks.

She doesn't speak up very often, so when she does, I give her my full attention. I look her in the eyes and smile. "It's beautiful."

She grins. "I picked it out."

"You did a great job."

"Blech." Charlie says, to no one in particular. She picks up mom's drink and sniffs it. "What are you drinking?"

Mom grabs it out of her hands. "Nothing you can have. You're still a minor."

"Are those mimosas?" Reese asks.

Mom nods. "Champagne's in the kitchen."

When Charlie sneaks in with Reese and Parker, mom narrows her eyes and hops up to follow them.

Capitalizing on the fact that we're alone, I reach out and snag Erin's wrist, tugging her closer. "You look gorgeous."

She blushes a little—a fascinating flush of pink warms her cheeks. "I wouldn't normally show this much skin."

Throwing caution to the wind, I pull her down onto my lap. My thumb glides along the skin exposed on her back. "Why not? You're not usually afraid to take risks with fashion."

She pretends to frown at me. "Not sure if that's a compliment or an insult."

I laugh. "I like the way you dress. And I *really* like this."

I slip my fingers under the back of her shirt. She casts a nervous glance towards the kitchen, but the girls are out of sight and thoroughly distracted. We can hear Charlie making a case for why she needs a real mimosa.

She leans forward, brushing her lips against mine. I brace my hand on her back, fingers stretching out over her soft skin.

Lust ripples through me. I'm nearly overcome with the heady, hazy pull of desire. If it weren't for my family being just feet away, I would happily throw her down on the table and fuck her right there on the patio.

I have never felt a hunger this strong in all of my life.

The blaze of desire is like a comet, but it comes with a tail. Guilt.

Ana and I had a sweet relationship. We were two clumsy, horny teenage kids. But our love life never really developed past that. And while I loved her, so fucking much, I never *wanted* her the way I want Erin right now.

And that makes me feel… like I'm cheating.

You can't cheat on someone who isn't here anymore, but that's how I feel.

It's enough to put a bit of a drag on my lust. Which is a good thing. It was well on its way to getting me into a very awkward situation.

Charlie can be heard singing the cha-cha, which would insinuate she got her way. Erin pulls out of my arms and is sitting across the table with a very serene expression on her face by the time my sisters return.

Reese hands her a glass. "Get your suit on, darling. We're going swimming."

67.

Erin

Nothing will challenge a woman's confidence faster than being forced to wear a swim suit in front of a bunch of sleek and skinny beauties.

I love my body. My big boobs. My ass.

But I wouldn't have complained if God had made me just a little skinnier.

I've done the whole diet thing. The whole hate what the good lord gave me thing.

I'm done with that. This is the body that I was born with. I'm healthy and happy and that's what counts.

But tell that to the ribs I can count on Parker's sides. Charlie's hips are literally concave.

Only Reese has any meat on her bones and she's still stunning.

I am having serious regrets about packing a bikini. What the actual fuck was I thinking? Luckily, I also packed a cover up. I pull the oversized linen shirt around my body and follow the girls down to the beach. Josh easily catches up to us and then I'm sweating all over again.

I have seen this man naked.

I have seen *all* of him naked. And yet, seeing him with those red Baywatch-esque trunks hanging low on his hips is sending butterflies through my tummy. A whole boatload of out-of-control butterflies.

The girls stake a spot out on the sand, setting out their towels, putting up an umbrella, before scampering down to the water. I'm hoping Josh will follow them so I can wither up into a husk of insecurities all by myself, but he stays right next to me. "Aren't you coming?"

I turn, spreading out my towel. "You go ahead. I'll be down in a bit."

He comes up behind me, tugging at the back of my cover-up. "Take this off."

His voice is low and husky. It sends a fizzy feeling down my spine. Putting his hand on my waist, he guides me back around until I'm facing him. Blushing, I let the linen fabric slide down my shoulders.

He steps incrementally closer. "You're blushing… everywhere."

Sure enough, my boobs are flushed pink, just like my neck and cheeks. I look up at his face and I'm almost knocked over by the desire I see there.

Some of that insecurity, the parts that were freezing me up, just sort of melt. I don't need him to know that I'm a beautiful woman. But I do need him to remind me now and then. And right now, I'm remembering the countless times he's told me that I'm pretty and I'm thinking maybe it's time I start believing that he means it.

"Beautiful." He murmurs. His fingers skate over my bare waist. "You're going to get me into trouble."

The soft break in his voice, the low rumble of his words, send my thoughts into a tailspin. I can't think of an adequate response that doesn't sound like utter gibberish, so I just start towards the water. "Race you there."

He catches me easily. Hooking an arm around my waist, he spins me behind him and takes off at a full sprint.

I can't remember the last time I played in the water. My friends and I aren't exactly lake people. And with this pale skin, I tend to burn.

As much fun as I'm having with the Olson siblings, I have an internal clock that is reminding me that my sun exposure limit is up.

Josh and the girls are playing some sort of twist on Marco Polo that I don't completely understand. It involves shouting Mark Bolo, a name that they all find absurdly funny. More inside jokes amongst siblings. I'm not in on the joke, but their humor is contagious. Smiling to myself, I wade out of the water and make my way across the beach to sit under the umbrella.

I reapply sun block and dig out my phone to catch up on the book I was reading. It's literally a romantic beach read and with the sound of the waves crashing against the sand and the smell of salt in the air, I am happy as a clam.

Trace and Maven come barreling down a few minutes later, followed by their grandma and grandpa. I let them pull me back down to the water, where the two of them chase waves, shrieking with joy as the water comes foaming up to meet them.

Josh wades out to join the kids, pretending to be a sea monster, to their utter delight. Keith makes his way down to the water, taking over as sea monster.

Josh comes to stand next to me. He's standing a safe distance away, not blowing our cover, but close enough that

I can almost feel the warmth from his body. "You look like a sugar cookie."

"Hmm?"

He pretends to stretch, but glances pointedly at my ass. "Covered in sugar."

I brush my hands over my behind, finding it covered in sand.

He grins, biting his lip. "I like it. Very tempting."

"You're incorrigible." I pretend to glare at him, but secretly, I like it, too.

I like the way he looks at me.

68.

Josh

Everyone else decides to camp out by the water. Dad brings a cooler down and the girls content themselves between day drinking and wading in the water.

Trace and Maven, on the other hand, have worn themselves out. I don't want them napping out here for fear of getting too much sun.

For that matter, Erin has been hiding under the umbrella like she's part vampire.

We carry the kids back up to the house and by the time we step into the living room, they're both conked out.

Laying Maven on my bed, Erin tiptoes out. I disentangle Trace's arms from my shoulder, carefully setting him down, before following that perfect ass out of the room.

I've been desperate to pull her into my arms all afternoon and we finally have some time to ourselves. But Erin has disappeared. I stop, scanning the living room. Mom is standing in the kitchen pouring a glass of wine. "I thought I'd come up here in case the kids wake up, just in case you and Erin wanted to… take a nap."

She turns, taking a big gulp of her wine, but she doesn't quite hide the ornery look on her face. "I'll just be sitting on the patio."

Judas. Who is this free spirit and what happened to my ultra-conservative mother?

Acting like I have no idea what she's getting at, I nod and turn back.

Heading towards the bedrooms, I hear the shower start up.

I pass through Erin's room, knocking lightly on the door. A little shiver goes through me when she opens the door.

I step inside, locking the door behind me.

She stands in the middle of the bathroom, a hint of a smile on her lips. That swimsuit has been driving me wild all day. I step closer, twisting a lock of her hair around my finger. She tilts her head up to look at me. She looks almost shy, but I recognize the heat kindling behind those beautiful eyes. My thumb grazes her lower lip. I cradle the back of her head in my hand and lean down to kiss her. My lips claim hers, just as my hand finds the small of her back. I tug her into me, pressing my hips into hers, letting her feel how much I want her.

She curls her fingers around the waistband of my trunks and walks backwards toward the shower. She turns away, stepping in ahead of me. I step in behind her, pulling her body against mine. She feels so smooth against my body. Water cascades down her chest, mixing with sunblock, and my fingers glide along her slick skin. I squeeze her breasts, rolling her nipples through her bikini top. She arches against my body, muffling a sigh in her throat. I push my trunks down my legs and step out of them. My cock presses against her back, sliding across her wet skin.

I feel like a bundle of loose wires. Trembling, crackling with electricity. I need her so badly it's almost overwhelming. Guilt snaps at my ankles, but it can't hold a candle to the flame tearing through my body.

Pulling her hair aside, my lips graze her skin. Her hand reaches over her head, hooking around the back of my neck. I push her bikini bottoms over her hips; they catch around her ankles and she steps out of them. My fingers slide up the slope of her shoulder, loosen the strings at her neck. Slipping my hands between us, I loosen the loop at her back. The top falls away and my hands slide across her curves. There's nothing between us now and I'm almost shaking with the need to be inside her. I back her up against the shower wall. There's a built in shelf behind her. I push the row of shampoo bottles to the ground and lift her up to the ledge.

It's just a few inches, not enough to fully sit on, but she doesn't need to. I've got her. She braces her hands on the ledge and I wrap my arms around her thighs, pinning her in place with my hips.

My cock is caught between us, pressing against our bellies as I lean in to kiss her. She slides her hand up and down my shaft, moaning softly into my mouth.

I pull my hips back enough for her to position the head at her entrance and slowly push it in. We both watch as it delves deep inside, disappearing into her perfect body.

The showerhead rains hot water down on us as I thrust in and out, carefully, slowly. Her mouth is almost cool in comparison to the shower. I don't think I could ever get tired of that sweet, velvety tongue.

She's got her hands around my neck, trusting me to hold her, and that fills my heart up. I love that she's trusting me with her body, with her heart.

My lips chart a path up her shoulder, focusing on the spot at the crook of her neck that treads the line between feeling good and feeling ticklish.

It makes her smile, and that's why I go for it every time. Because this woman is a God-damn joy. She's sunshine in a bottle and I want to borrow some of that.

I want to hold her to me and never let go.

She comes around my cock with a sweet, shaky little sigh. I watch her face the entire time, loving the expression of surprise with heady, hazy satisfaction.

I'm nowhere near done. If I had my way, I'd fuck her until the sun goes down.

But we don't have that much time. The clock is ticking.

She slips out of my arms, lowering herself down to the shower floor. She wraps her hands around my shaft. Her fingers can't close around me, but her grip is firm and when she lowers her lips over the head, it all feels perfect.

She feels perfect.

69.

Erin

After our shower, we sneak back out of the bathroom. No one has a clue.

Except maybe Lisa.

I feel like Lisa always knows what's going on with everybody. Everywhere. It's her superpower.

Josh is almost giving us away with how languid and smiley he's being. I suppose I probably have the same look on my face though. I can certainly feel a pleasant ache, a sweet imprint he left inside me.

It's kind of fun to hold on to the little secret, while the girls whirl and chatter around us.

I've seen the way the Olson kids interact with each other, and their parents, in only short stints. Being on vacation with them is the marathon version. As an only child, the dynamics are fascinating. And a little overwhelming.

I'm actually looking forward to bedtime so that I can unplug from the constant onslaught, but the girls decide we're going to have an after-party bonfire after the parents go to sleep.

Grabbing the baby monitor, I reluctantly allow them to drag me down to the beach.

Their afterparty consists of drinking around a fire, trading stories and waxing philosophical. When they slip into old stories about high school, I lean back into the chair I'm sitting on, letting their words and their laughter wash over me.

Josh sits in the sand right at my feet. I have a blanket spread over my legs and in the shadow of the flickering fire, his hand roves up and down my calves. It's a comforting feeling, something I'd much rather focus on than keeping up with the girls' rapid-fire verbal sparring.

Their conversation turns to their college exploits. In an attempt to include me, Reese asks where I went to college.

"I went to Southeast."

"Community college?" Reese asks.

"Yeah. I studied early childhood there."

Charlie peers at me from across the fire. "Why didn't you go to a real college?"

My cheeks redden, and I sit up a little. "I mean, Southeast is a real college."

"No, I mean, why didn't you go to a four-year school?"

Reese frowns. "Charlie."

Charlie shrugs. "What? She seems really smart. I just want to know why she didn't go all the way."

Josh tosses a stick into the fire. "Erin's got me beat. I didn't go at all."

"Yeah. And you should have." Charlie says. "You had a full ride to Chadron, and you decided to stay home and farm instead."

He stiffens. "College isn't the end all be all, Charlie."

She tilts her head. "I guess you wouldn't know."

Maven chooses that moment to insert herself into the conversation. Her sleepy protests squawk out from the baby monitor at my hip. "I better go check on her."

Before anyone can stop me, I climb to my feet and march towards the house. Josh jogs to catch up to me. "I can check on her."

I slow down, but keep walking. "Just let me do my job." My voice comes out harsher than I intended. I try to soften my tone. "I'm tired, anyway. Go back with your sisters. You guys are due for some quality time."

He makes a face. "Is that what we're calling that?"

I laugh. "Have fun."

I'm smiling, keeping my tone light, but inside I'm feeling pretty low.

Charlie isn't wrong when she asks why I didn't go all the way. I ask myself that all the time. I did pretty well in high school. It's not like I couldn't get into the bigger schools. I even had a few scholarships. But I knew what I wanted to do, and I just wanted to get started.

I don't personally regret the decisions I made, but every once and a while, I can't help but to feel a little inadequate.

The Olson siblings have that effect on me. They're all just so fucking... shiny.

Beautiful.

Smart.

Successful.

I feel outgunned when I'm around them.

Josh makes a damn good big brother. He's patient. Easy going. And protective.

But those girls are protective of him, too, even if he doesn't realize it.

I have to wonder if they'll ever think I'm good enough for him.

Seems somewhat unlikely, considering I'm not even sure I'm up to his standards.

I step quietly into Josh's bedroom where the kids are supposed to be sleeping. Trace is laying at a ninety-degree angle, snoring lightly. But Maven is sitting upright crying. I climb in beside her and she crawls into my arms.

Settling back, I lay my head on the pillow and she snuggles into my side.

Life is complicated. Grown-ups are complicated.

The love from a sweet little thing like Maven is pure and simple.

70.

Josh

"Well, way to go, Chuck." Reese flops back on her seat, toasting Charlie with her beer bottle.

Charlie lets her hands flop. "Oh, here we go."

Parker pulls a blanket around her body. "You were kind of rough on her."

"I was just trying to get to know her. Jesus. I can't win with you people. I'm either being too much or too little. Make up your minds."

I hesitate on the perimeter of the light cast by the bonfire. I'm still thinking about turning around. When these girls get going, it can be knockdown, drag out and I'm not in the mood for that kind of thing.

I never really am.

Charlie tilts her chin. "I didn't say anything to Erin that I didn't say to Joshy."

"Yeah, and it was rude when you said it to him, too." Reese says.

"Don't drag me into this." I say, flopping down on the chair Erin vacated.

I don't hold Charlie to the same standards as I would other people. She's not mean, she's just immature. And she's still navigating the distance between cheeky and rude.

Charlie pulls her legs up under her. "Some people just can't handle a little honesty."

Reese huffs a dry laugh. "Next time you decide to serve up a little truth bomb, ask yourself three questions. Does this need to be said? Does this need to be said *by me*? Does this need to be said by me *right now*?"

"That's beautiful." Charlie says. "Did you read that on Facebook?"

Reese shrugs. "I did, as a matter of fact."

"Guys. Please." I say, interrupting further discussion.

Charlie sits back, crossing her arms. "Everybody's always painting me as the bitch. But the truth is, I really like her." She looks directly at me. "No, I didn't kiss her feet at first like everyone else, but I wanted to be loyal to Ana."

Parker fidgets with her beer bottle. "We all miss Ana, Charlie."

"I know, I know. It's just I saw her as a big sister and if someone's going to replace her, I just wanted to make sure she was worthy of the shoes she's going to be filling."

I break out in a cold sweat despite the fire. "Who said anything about replacing Ana?"

All three girls look at me. I can't stand their matching expressions, a mix of pity and sadness. It makes me feel like a broken thing. It makes me feel weak.

"You're obviously in love." Parker says.

I swing my gaze around to her and she shrinks back under its intensity. I try to soften my expression and my voice. "Ana is always going to be the kids' mother. I'm not trying to replace her."

"So, what?" Charlie asks. "You're just going to stay single the rest of your life?"

My heart twists painfully.

This.

This right here is why I don't open up to these girls. They viciously cut right to the heart of the issue.

And my heart isn't fit for the light of day.

Reese tilts her head, studying my face. "You love her, don't you, Josh?"

I shrug, deeply regretting sitting down with them in the first place.

"I have something that needs to be said by me right now." Charlie skewers me with her dark eyes. "You're afraid to move on."

"If by that you mean I'm afraid of hurting the kids while I try to figure things out, then yeah, I'm afraid to move on."

"Bullshit." Charlie says. "Stop hiding behind those kids."

"Excuse me?"

"You're afraid something's going to happen to her."

She's right. And I hate how spot on she is.

"There's more to it than that. It's complicated. Ana was the love of my life. You don't just get over that."

"We all loved Ana." Parker says. "But you never looked at her the way you look at Erin."

I glance at her, wondering where this little truth sayer came from. "And what way is that?"

Parker holds my gaze, not flinching this time. "Like you're head over heels."

Guilt trickles down my shoulders, settling in my stomach like poison.

"Well, sounds like you ladies have me all figured out." I climb to my feet. "Why don't you just propose to her while you're at it? Send me an invitation when you've got it all figured out."

I turn away, unable to look at them anymore.

I don't want them to see what broken down looks like.

It's like a cog is stuck in my brain. My thoughts stutter and fail to form. My feet automatically carry me to my room, and I stop in my tracks. Erin is curled up around Maven. Trace has his feet propped up on her hip and Maven has a handful of Erin's curls in her hand. It's like they're claiming her, even in their sleep.

I can feel my heart shattering, reforming, only to break again.

I loved Ana. We grew up together. That history bound us in a way that you just can't replicate.

But Erin is making me realize that love comes in all kinds of forms. I did love Ana, but in the way you love your favorite song. Or the way my grandma's house smelled on Christmas morning.

Erin, though…

She's got this laugh that sparkles.

When she's embarrassed, I want to wrap that blush around my shoulders.

She is a blaze that melts my heart and builds it back up again.

I didn't know what love was. What it could be.

And it's breaking my heart.

71.

Erin

Maven stirs against me, and my eyes crack open. It takes a few seconds to orientate myself.

Sunlight pours against the far wall in bright bars. I'm at Lisa and Keith's Florida home.

That's Maven nestled against my chest. Trace's feet woven through my calves.

And those are Josh's arms wrapped around my middle. One arm rests behind my head, curling around Maven's back.

His other hand rests on my hip. "Rise and shine." He murmurs against my neck.

"I'm sorry—Maven was fussy when I came in. I must have fallen asleep with her."

"I like having you here."

His hand slips over my hip, flattening against my tummy.

I twist my head back, trying to look at his expression. He lifts himself up high enough to give me a soft kiss before settling into the pillow, tugging me closer.

His entire body is relaxed against mine, languid and content.

I, however, am a mess of tangled, racing thoughts. They sprint ahead, tripping over each other, only to double back.

Shouldn't we be keeping the PDA to a minimum? What if the kids wake up and notice?

As though nudged awake by the thought, Maven stirs and stretches against me.

She opens her dark eyes, staring up at me with a cute little grin. Her hand rests against my cheek. "Hi, mommy."

It's like Josh is pricked with a pin. His arm snakes away from my body and he pushes himself upright. "That's not mommy, Maven. That's Erin."

Maven snuggles closer, glaring over my shoulder at him. "My mommy."

I can feel the tension rolling off him. I'm almost afraid to turn around, but I force myself to. It's a morbid compulsion to see his face. To watch whatever fragile thing we had between us crumble and fall apart.

Josh sees something in my expression, something that pokes and prods him. "You're not."

"Yeah, Josh. I'm aware." I sit upright, lowering my voice. "But she's two."

Anguish twists his features, and he slips away, stepping into the living room.

I turn back to Maven. "Can you stay here for a minute, my dear?"

Maven settles back, propping her feet up on her brother's stomach. Blissfully unaware of the havoc she's sewn with one little word.

I follow Josh into the living room. It's blessedly empty. He's pacing by the patio door.

"What the hell, Josh?" I whisper, moving closer.

He nods at the patio. "Not here."

I follow him outside and we leave the door open a crack in case Maven wanders out looking for us.

He faces the ocean, bare shoulders stiff against the morning chill.

"What Maven said… that doesn't need to be a big deal."

"It is a big deal. It's a big damn deal, Erin." He turns to look at me. "You're not her mother. You can't replace her."

I stand there, poleaxed. Of course, I've let my mind wander down the path that might lie ahead for us. I've thought about what it would be like to raise another woman's children.

I figured I would hear these words, eventually. Maybe from Trace. Or Maven. Just not from him.

"So, that's how it is?" I ask, feeling my pain harden into something sharp and thick.

"I care about you, Erin. More than you can know. But Ana was there first. She's always going to be the first."

"I don't even know what to say to that."

"You don't have to say anything."

I study his face, the look in his eye, and it becomes crystal clear.

He's not going to let me in. He was never going to let me in.

I think I knew that.

But my dumb ass fell in love with him, anyway.

I've been denying how I felt, hiding behind feelings of inadequacy to keep a buffer. But it wasn't enough. It didn't stop me from getting hurt.

And for the first time in a long time, I do something I never do.

I decide to stand up for myself.

"I'll stay for the rest of the trip. Let me know what you need from me. But consider this my two-week notice."

The air goes out of him in a sharp exhale. "Erin…"

The sliding door rolls open and I turn to see a very sleepy Parker being towed by Trace. "Aunt Parker is going to teach me how to surf."

Maven is hot on their heels, sashaying outside in her cute little bunny jammies. Parker shoots me a look of long suffering. I give her what I hope is a smile. "I'll go with you."

72.

Josh

She can't be serious.
She doesn't mean it.
Does she?

I sink to one of the chairs and watch Erin walk down to the water hand in hand in with Maven.

I wanted to keep Erin at arm's length. Far away enough to shield my heart. Close enough that I could still reach out and touch her.

She wasn't supposed to leave.

That was sort of the point. If we didn't complicate things, we could just keep them where they were. Balancing on a knife's edge.

I bury my hands in my hair, staring down at the table.

The sliding door opens, and a pair of feet enter my line of sight. "Considering the meaning of life?" Charlie's voice is filled with too much humor for this early in the morning.

"Fuck off, Charlene."

"Damn, pulling out the Christian names. Still not a morning person, I see."

I want her to go away.

So naturally, she sits down.

"Is it safe to assume this bad mood has to do with a certain redheaded bombshell?"

I sit upright, scrubbing my hair back, trying to look disinterested. My gaze lands on the redhead in question, and that just makes my stomach twist. I turn my gaze upward, studying the dark clouds scudding across the sky.

"Don't worry, Joshy Poo. You two will get it figured out. There's no rush."

I huff a sharp laugh. "She just gave me her two weeks."

"What?" Charlie yelps. "What did you do to her?"

"Nothing."

She gives me a long, skeptical look. "Well, fucking fix it, Josh."

"I can't force her to stay with us if she doesn't want to."

"You can fight for her, dumb ass. You love her, don't you?"

"Yes!" I snap. My eyes start to burn and I look away. "Apparently, it's obvious."

Sunlight breaks through the patchy clouds in brilliant bars of light.

Charlie's tone softens. "So, what's the issue?"

"The timing is all wrong."

"Two years is long enough."

"A lifetime isn't long enough."

She sucks in a deep breath and sits back, letting it out in a whoosh. "Loving someone else doesn't mean you stop loving her. That's the thing about the heart. It can stretch. You can make room."

"I don't know if I'm capable of that."

"Well, you'll never know if you don't try." Charlie scoots back in her chair, climbing to her feet. "You're a lot of things, Joshy. But I never took you to be a coward."

I watch Charlie stomp down the beach, passing in and out of patches of sunlight.

She's joining Erin, siding with her.

I was certain Charlie had it out for Erin. Turns out, I'm the only one who's still confused.

The kids love her. They've claimed her.

I don't know why I can't seem to move on.

I want to.

I want to be whole and unbroken.

I want a time machine.

A fresh start.

"I'm trying, Ana." I whisper. "I just can't carry the weight. I don't know what to do."

A cool breeze passes through the scrubby sea grass.

A drop of rain lands on my hand. The soft sound of rain surrounds me. The sun shines down in thick bars of light, but rain falls in a fine sheet, painting the sand, pattering against the roof of the house.

Ana called them fox weddings. Rain falling when the sun is shining.

She said they were signs.

Signs of something good.

But that's when I hear the first scream.

73.

Erin

A breeze rolls off the ocean, tugging at my t-shirt, going right through my joggers. Charlie stomps down the beach, joining Maven and me. She looks the way I feel.

Grumpy.

I offer her a wan smile and we both turn to watch Trace and Parker chase waves. The ocean is choppy this morning, sending foamy licks racing up the beach. Trace runs away, squealing, only to chase the receding waves deeper and deeper into the surf.

"He's getting soaked." Charlie comments.

I look out to sea, a pit opening up in my stomach when I see a big wave speeding towards the beach. Parker and Trace are oblivious.

"Parker!" I shout. "He's too close to the water."

She turns to look at me just as the wave crashes into both of them. She goes down in a tangle of limbs and when she comes back up sputtering sea water, she's alone.

My hearing sort of goes out. All I can hear is a dull tone. It rings in my ears, filling my head with intense pressure.

I never make the conscious decision; my feet just carry me towards them. My gaze never leaves the water, searching for a little head. Waiting for it, hoping for it to pop back up.

The water is warmer than I expected. It swirls around my thighs, tugging at my shirt as I wade deeper. Charlie tries to follow me, but the waves just force her back. My gaze is locked on the waves, searching. I spot a flash of red fabric. His pajama shirt.

I dive under the next wave, struggling against the pulling, sucking sensation. I don't catch him, so much as collide with him. My fingers scrabble at his body, snagging his shirt. I tug him to my chest and curl around him as another wave batters over us. And then I'm pushing off the ocean floor, forcing our heads above the water's surface.

The next wave carries us closer to the beach. Charlie and Parker are wading closer. Another wave slams into my back and I feel the sand under foot give out from under me. I'm slipping. Their fingers connect with mine and I pass Trace off. Another wave hits me, I'm already off balance, so it easily clobbers me, sucking me under.

I go head over heels, getting dizzy. Disorientated. I can't really tell which way is up anymore.

This is where my life is supposed to flash before my eyes.

But all I can think about is whether the girls managed to get Trace back to shore.

Maybe they're out here with me.

God, let them be safe.

Something clamps around my arm.

Strong hands.

I'm pushed above the water's surface just as another wave crashes over my head. Water fills my nose, my mouth, and I'm choking.

"I've got you. I've got you." His voice is in my ear, his arm is around my waist.

My entire body is exhausted.

I'm dead weight. I'll drag us both down.

"I'm sorry." I hear myself say.

"I'm sorry." I say again.

I'm sorry for everything that happened to him.

I'm sorry I couldn't be enough.

I'm sorry I wasn't brave enough to stay and fight for him.

He gave me the excuse to leave, and I took it.

It felt easier than putting myself through a gauntlet that might not have an end point.

But now it all seems so petty.

What was that fight even about?

I'm vaguely aware that I'm being carried. Gently laid on the sand.

Bodies crowd around, blocking out the light, until Josh barks at them to give me space.

Space for what?

I don't want more space. I want him closer.

I want to feel his skin against mine.

The beat of his broken heart.

74.

Josh

My heart is racing a million miles an hour. I can't stop thinking about how I almost lost her and all she can do is mutter *I'm sorry* again and again.

I'm shushing her, hugging her to me, but she's going into shock and she doesn't hear me.

I do the only thing I can think of, I press my lips against hers, swallowing up those words.

They belong on my tongue, anyway.

I'm the one who should say it.

She calms down, arms reaching for me. I pull her into my arms, trying to will my warmth into her chilly skin. But we're both wet and shivering.

"Trace?"

"He's okay." I say. "You saved his life."

She heaves a shuddering breath. "Oh, thank God. Thank God."

Someone passes me a handful of towels and I take them, wrapping them around her body.

Trace starts wailing, and she looks around, clear-eyed for the first time since she went under the waves. She holds her hands out to him and he pulls out of mom's grasp, barreling into us. "I drowned you."

"No, Trace." She smiles, hugging him close. "I'm right here. I'm fine."

Maven weasels in between Trace and Erin. She puts her hand on Erin's chest, right above her heart. She looks over her shoulder, focusing those big, brown eyes on me. "Mommy's okay?"

A muffled sob escapes my lips. "Yes, baby. Mommy's okay. Everybody's okay." I glance up at my mom and dad, who are hovering nearby. "But let's take them to Urgent Care just to be sure."

"I'm fine." Erin protests, attempting to squirm out of my arms. Dad extracts Maven and mom coaxes Trace away.

"I'm sure you are." I say, climbing to my feet. "But just humor me, okay?"

I pull her to her feet, but her legs are still a bit shaky. Sweeping her into my arms, I start carrying her up the beach.

"So much for subtlety." She mutters.

"Oh, we're way past that."

"We are?"

I smile down at her. "That ship has fucking sailed."

"I'm sorry."

My arms tighten around her body. "Stop saying that. You have nothing to apologize for."

"I was going to run away."

"You're not going to anymore?"

She smiles. "Doesn't seem like it."

"I'm sorry for being such a big dick."

She buries her head into the crook of my neck. "The biggest."

The urgent care in the sleepy little town nearby wasn't prepared for the Midwestern storm that descended upon it. The Olson family can be pretty assertive when need be. Once we got a clean bill of health for Parker, Trace, and Erin, we made our way home.

If it wasn't clear before, Erin had already made a place for herself in our family.

I guess I was just the last one to realize that.

I had the most to lose.

But the most to gain.

We sit on the couch, snuggled under layers of soft blankets, while my sisters play board games with Trace and Maven.

I've got Erin pinned against my side. My arm fits perfectly around her waist. Under the blankets, our fingers twine and untwine, a silent conversation. When she yawns, I offer to take her to bed, but she shakes her head. She doesn't want to be alone. So I tuck her head under my jaw and hold her until she falls asleep. The sound of my family softly chattering with each other forms the perfect white noise.

It feels good to hold her in my arms without worrying about who's looking.

She has the softest skin.

Her curves fit me like they were made for me.

And I was made for her.

She is sunlight on a rainy day.

75.

We trade sand for drywall dust.

The very next day after we got back from our Florida trip, Josh went over to the house and started tearing walls out. Every night and day is filled with a long list of items to check off before we can move.

He says now is the time, because come Spring, the farm will get busy again.

He has a point, but I can't help but notice how much he's changed since the accident on the beach. I worry that the near-drowning triggered him in some way, because ever since we got back, he's been extra protective. If it was up to him, I would be with him every minute of the day.

I should be watching over Maven, but her grandma has her today while Trace is at school.

The guys and I are over at the big house, racing to get it ready to move into by February.

It's a big job. The house has five bedrooms. There's the room downstairs I famously dashed into when I was trying to hide from a very handsy Josh.

Upstairs, there's Bo's old room, which will belong to Trace. Reese was thrilled to pass her room on to Maven. I planned on taking Parker's old room, but Josh made it very clear he and I would be in the same room.

It's a little weird to think about sharing a bedroom with another person. I was an only child and never had the roommate experience. It's even weirder to think that this was the room where all four Olson kids were conceived. My answer to that small nightmare was to completely rearrange the room. New light fixtures, new furniture. I tore the wallpaper down and have slowly worked my way around the room, repainting the jewel-toned walls to a bright, crisp white.

"Erin!"

My paint roller pauses midway up the wall and I cock my head, listening. Was that Bo?

"Erin!" Now it's Bo and Dusty.

I hesitate, thinking about the boy who cried wolf.

If it was Skyler who yelled, or Josh, I would have come running. But you never know with Bo and Dusty. Half the time they're up to no good.

I set the paintbrush back in my pan and wipe my fingers off on some rags. I will come when summoned, but in my own damn time.

I'm just passing through the dining room when all four of the guys shout my name.

"What?" I shout back, feeling grumpy.

They all laugh.

Even Josh.

He's happy. And it's good to see him lighten up for someone other than me and the kids. He nods over his shoulder like a kid showing off his art project. "Look."

I suck in a breath. "Oh." I sigh, coming closer. "The fireplace! It's so pretty."

The boxy drywall has been cleared away and the original fireplace sits untouched below.

"See?" Dusty says, glaring at the guys. He gives me a long-suffering look. "I said it was pretty, and they all mocked me."

I step up to the fireplace, admiring the floor to ceiling brickwork, the subtle arch over the hearth. "It is pretty."

"And look." Josh takes my hand and pulls me around to the kitchen. "It has two sides."

"That is so unbelievably cool."

He tugs me up against his side. "Right?"

The guys head outside to trim lumber and Josh takes the opportunity to pull me up against his hips. His hand skirts along my jaw and cups the back of my head. His kiss is soft and sweet with a hint of a promise. Lisa is keeping the kids all night, so we don't have to worry about little ones barging in.

Flicking his tongue across the seam of my lips, he pulls back and runs his thumb up and down my jaw. "Skyler's dad made us matching mantels, one for each side. And I went to the hardware store and got a bunch of hooks."

I'm distracted by the way his hard body feels pinned against mine. "Hooks for what?"

"Christmas stockings."

I groan. "You're thinking about Christmas already? We have eleven months to go."

"I'm thinking about future Christmases. And Easters. And birthdays. I'm thinking about kids running around upstairs and you and me drinking coffee together in this kitchen morning after morning."

I press my cheek against his chest. "That sounds pretty damn good."

"Mom had something made for us when she heard Skyler's dad was making the fireplace mantel."

I laugh. "Your mama does not like being shown up."

Josh chuckles. "No, she does not."

I follow his gaze towards the box on the table. Flipping the lid open, I pull out the first stocking. *Maven* is embroidered in shining gold thread. There's a darling ballerina on the sock itself. Trace got a fire truck on his. I pull out Josh's *Dad* stocking and smile at the cow stitched across its fabric.

My fingers falter over the last stocking and I almost don't pull it out.

Mom.

It's got a big green four-leaf clover on it.

My heart starts racing. "Why a shamrock?"

He chuckles softly. "She is obsessed with your hair. And the whole Irish thing."

My family is barely Irish.

Genetically speaking, we're very Irish. Both of my parents did a genetics kit. But our family tree is more of a family stump. Neither of my parents know much about their ancestors.

He watches me lift the stocking out of the box.

"I literally had to talk her out of the leprechaun."

I laugh. "Seems mildly offensive."

"That's what I said." He puts his arms around me, reaching over my arm to touch the stocking. "I told her to go with a clover."

I lean back into his chest. "Yeah?"

"Because it's a good luck charm. Just like you."

My gaze traces the word.

There are only three letters and yet, it seems like the biggest word I've ever seen. Suddenly my eyes are burning and my throat feels thick.

76.

Josh

She sniffs and I turn her around so that I can study her face.

Her eyes are glassy with unshed tears. My heart dips. Maybe we misjudged the shamrock thing.

Damn it. I knew we should have picked the song bird. "Are you crying?"

She sniffs, giving me a watery smile. "I'm not crying. You're crying."

"Come here." I reel her in, holding her in a tight, fierce hug. "I'm sorry for what I said in Florida. I can be a little dense at times. Maven recognized you right away for who you are to our family. I wish I could take back what I said."

She leans her forehead against my chest. "You weren't wrong."

"Yes, I was." Putting a finger under her chin, I tilt her face towards me. "Family isn't finite. It's what you make of it. There's a place for you right here in Silver Bend. And if you can put up with two rowdy kids, a bunch of cattle, and a grumpy-ass farmer, I'll spend every day making it worth your time."

Her lips part and she stares at me, ominously short of words.

The front door clangs open and two sets of little feet come pelting in. She pulls away from me, glancing up.

I let her create some space, but keep one hand on the small of her back. "They aren't staying. I just promised to let them come look at the fireplace."

Trace and Maven burst into the kitchen, pink-cheeked and grinning.

With smiles that wide, they're going to give us away.

I can hear mom talking quietly with the guys in the other room.

Trace pelts over to the table. "Are these the stockings?" He looks at each one. "T! T for Trace. This one's mine. Look, Mavey. You got a ballerina."

"Ballernina!" Maven chirps, yanking her stocking from Trace's outstretched hand.

"Hey." Trace digs into his. "There's something in this one."

Erin pulls away, kneeling down beside him. "What did you find?"

He thrusts it into her hands. "I can't get it."

She takes the stocking and fishes around, pulling a shining ring studded with a fine line of diamonds and sapphires. Trace's birthstone.

"Mine!" Maven thrusts her stocking into Erin's hand before she can recover from the odd discovery in Trace's. She turns Maven's upside down and another ring tumbles onto her open palm. Diamonds and aquamarines. Maven's birthstone.

Maven snags the ring from Erin's hand and gets down on one knee. She wobbles there, holding the ring up in both hands.

She's going off script. Trace takes his ring back and follows suit. Both kids look up at me with impatience. "I think there's something in yours, too, Erin."

With shaking hands, she reaches into her stocking and finds the diamond ring waiting for her. I get down on one knee.

"Marry us!" Maven shouts, impatient with the pageantry.

Trace frowns, clicking his tongue. "Mavey! You were supposed to say will you be my mommy?"

Maven looks unphased. She turns back to Erin. "My mommy."

Erin is watching the entire exchange with wide eyes. She's white as a sheet and looks like she might faint. I'm realizing, a bit late, that involving the kids might have been a big gamble.

What if she wants to say no?

Shakey nerves crawl up my spine the longer she leaves us hanging. Her gaze travels from Trace to Maven, back up to me. Our gazes connect and the pain in my chest eases.

I know what she's going to say before she even says it.

But I still want to hear the word, anyway. "Erin?"

She shakes herself. "Yes. Yes, I will. Yes!"

Relief and joy and something bigger than love floods my chest and I'm on my feet, sweeping her into a hug. The kids dance at our feet, hollering about their new mom.

That's when Erin notices we had an audience.

My mom insisted Erin would want the moment on video. I think she just wanted to watch. She's got her phone in one hand and tears rolling down her cheeks. And the three guys, lurking in the background, look a little weepy themselves.

I kiss Erin and taste salt and realize I'm crying, too.

There's been a lot of tears over the last few years.

Sad tears.

And angry ones.

But these tears, they are the best possible kind.

77.

Erin

I pick my way across the living room, stepping around sleeping bags and sprawling bodies. I stop in the kitchen doorway, glancing back. Maven lays with her feet tucked up against Lisa's stomach. I grin, shaking my head. The home place, as we now call it, has plenty of guest bedrooms, but they choose to sleep in front of the fireplace.

Lisa's a marvel. I don't know very many grandmas that would have a slumber party with their grandkids on the living room floor. My back hurts just looking at them.

Selecting one of Josh's heavy canvas coats from the hook by the back door, I pull it on and slip into the cold night.

Frigid December air surrounds me, needling my skin, seeking out the gaps between my coat and my neck. I shove my hands deep in the pockets and trudge through the snow.

Warm light seeps out from the barn, sparkling across the fresh snow.

I can hear the music before I step inside.

Aretha Franklin's voice is a smooth ribbon of sound, beckoning me in. I've convinced Josh that the girls like a little R&B while they're calving.

It's so warm inside I can slip my coat off. This barn is newer and about a thousand times nicer for calving. Instead of one rickety old heater, it has a few industrial units. Josh looks over at me and I feel a little kick in my tummy.

I don't think I'll ever get used to those brown eyes, that sexy smile.

I hold up the thermos of coffee in my hand. "I come bearing gifts. How are the girls doing?"

"See for yourself."

He steps to the side, and I see the next addition to our little herd. Still damp, with bits of straw clinging to its little frame. The calf is already trying to stand while its mother looks on.

I stop next to him, sliding an arm around his waist. "Beautiful."

"Yeah." He says, but he's not looking at the new little calf.

He's looking at me.

He kisses me before pulling back to look at me. His hand slips over the rounded curve of my tummy. She kicks, responding to his touch.

"Already a daddy's girl." I murmur.

His smile is so big. It's contagious.

He wraps his arms around me, and we dance to the music as best we can, considering there's a gigantic baby bump between us.

"You make a pretty good midwife." I say. "Maybe I should hire you when it's time."

He turns me in his arms so that my back is flush with his stomach. "We'll let the doctors take on that job."

"We can't have a home barn birth?"

"Fuck no." He laughs, running his hands over my stomach. "We're going to have the best doctors in the state."

"Okay."

"And I'll call in the National Guard to keep watch over the hospital."

"That's a bit much, but if you insist."

"I do."

I rest my head against his chest. "Where will you be?"

"I'll be right by your side."

"Promise?"

"I swear. That's where I'll be. From here until eternity."

♥

Thank you for reading *This Broken Heart*. If you enjoyed this story, please consider leaving a review.

I'm an independent author. Every review and rating matters.

Cheers!

JT

Thanks for visiting Silver Bend, y'all come back now!

Follow the Heartland Boys into the next book with Bo Thompson.

He let her go once and he's not going to make that mistake again.

Readers are saying…

"revenge, betrayal and a small town where everyone knows your business"

"the rumor mill is alive and well in Silver Bend"

"I loved this story from the first page to the very end"

Sneak Peek of **The Second Dance**…

1.

Bo

Tia slides a piece of chocolate cake in front of me. "Happy birthday, Bo."

"Thanks, Tia." I smile up at her. Keeping the smile pasted in place, I wait until she's out of hearing range to mutter through gritted teeth. "I'm intensely uncomfortable."

Cody is sitting with his arms crossed, leaning on the table, a goofy grin on his face.

He always did enjoy watching me suffer.

Dad whips out a bowling alley matchbook, and we both watch transfixed as he tears one off and shoves it in the center of my cake.

"No." I mutter. "For the love, dad."

I glance around the bar. No one is paying attention. Yet.

But Cody is grinning and when dad strikes a match, lighting the first one, Cody starts cracking up. He's dying with laughter.

Dad has never minded a little attention. He's used to it. The thing about being a star quarterback in a small town? You get to live out your glory days for the rest of your life.

Just so long as you never move.

"Your mother would have made you a cake." Dad gestures at the smoking match. "Make a wish, kid."

"I wish this wasn't happening." I blow the match out and dunk it in my water. "Are we done here?"

Dad leans back, stretching. Mariah Nelson snags his gaze. She's a Sunday school teacher at our church. She's got big tits and a smile that says dad better say his prayers. Dad nods, but he's not even looking at us. "Yeah. We checked the boxes, right?"

He's standing before I can respond. Cody and I watch him strut up to Mariah, the same woman who used to lead VBS story time for us as kids. She was in college then, but that still puts my dad well out of her age range. He's never been one to let an obstacle stand in his way. He leans against the bar, shining his megawatt smile on Mariah. I glance back at Cody's face, but it's completely blank. He either doesn't care that dad's flaunting the divorce, or he's doing a damn good job of hiding it.

Cody's spotted a few of his classmates from high school. "You want me to hang around or…"

"You're good, man. Go catch up with your friends."

I stand up, leaving a generous tip for Tia. She's been a stalwart supporter through dad and mom's divorce. Neither of us guys know how to cook, so we've been eating Tia's food almost daily. She's got the patience of a saint to put up with my dad.

Pushing the chair in, I make my way through the bar. I nod at people here and there. It's pretty crowded for a Thursday night.

Dusty and Skyler wait for me at the end with three shots lined up in front of them. Dusty plants a wet kiss on my cheek. "For the birthday boy."

Dusty is probably the one man in Thorne County who could get away with kissing another man in public without risking his manhood in the process. We do not live in a progressive part of the country. It's exhausting, but guarding one's masculinity is a requirement.

Unless you look like Dusty.

He knows he's a looker. The ladies *really* know he's a looker. Gray eyes. Dirty blonde hair. He can take his pick. And has.

"Those better not all be for me." I say, eying the line of tequila shots.

"Just getting started, baby." Dusty says, tipping one of the shots back.

Skyler and I do okay with the ladies. We inherited our dads' football legacy; and in a small town, that's currency. We're cousins, but we could almost be brothers. I look more like Skyler than I do my own brother, Cody.

I've got a few inches on Skyler, and he keeps his dark beard a little thicker than I do. My mom used to say the pair of us were born at the top of the Thomas family tree and hit every branch on the way down.

We're two sides of the same coin, but occasionally, like tonight, he wears glasses instead of his contacts and really leans into the whole stormy intellect thing.

Skyler puts a shot in my hand. "Catch up, my friend. He's already made me do a round with him."

"Prospecting?" I say, watching Dusty saunter across the bar to chat up a trio of pretty girls.

"Looks like it." Skyler says, but he's got his eye on my dad.

I glance at my dad and, with great effort, try to be reasonable. He's young in the grand scheme of things. He still has his good looks. His life shouldn't be over just because mom took a torch to it.

Still. It's hard to watch.

I look away, knocking back my shot and motioning for Tia to bring another round. "Kind of shits on your view of marriage, am I right?"

Skyler huffs a short laugh of agreement, but mercifully changes the topic. "How's Cody doing in school?"

"He fucking loves it. Joined that damn frat, though."

"Phi Beta Phi?"

I nod.

Skyler shakes his head. "Has it changed since we were at UNL?"

"No. It has not. They're all still spectacular douche bags."

"I guess it's good to know some things never change."

"I guess so. I met some of them when I was moving Cody in. Typical Greek assholes. But that was dad's house when he went to UNL. So, of course, he's over the God damn moon about it."

Dusty cuts the conversation short by turning up with three pretty traveling nurses.

It's kind of intriguing to flirt with complete strangers. Plus, they won't stick around for the next thirty years to haunt me with memories.

Dusty leans in, murmuring in my ear. "The blonde's name is Peyton. Happy Birthday, bud."

He knows my type. Short and curvy.

I've dated other girls, other types, but I always come back to the same well.

You never forget your first love.

And mine rewired my God-damned brain.

2.

It's a little chilly for March, but that's Nebraska. The temperatures swing so fast it can make you dizzy.

I smooth my skirt, push my sleeves up, and march into the restaurant with a professional coolness that only goes skin deep.

Inside, I am a tangled ball of nerves.

"Don't fuck this up, Andy." I whisper to myself before waving cheerily at my mark.

The donor.

A bitter, freshly divorced millionaire.

She sits alone at the bar. Elegant and long-limbed.

It's hard to gauge exactly how old she is because while her face is pretty and youthful, that cardigan set and those jeans are decidedly geriatric.

She catches sight of me, turning those magnetic brown eyes on me, and reels me in.

She holds out her hand. "I'm Heather. And you must be Andy?"

I nod, putting my hand in hers. She's got one of those faces that instantly pulls you in and makes you feel like you've known her your whole life. She wraps her cool fingers around mine and guides me to the stool next to her.

She waves her long fingers at the bartender, a young guy with wavy blonde hair. "Two millionaires for Andy and me."

She glances at me, winking, like we're in on the same joke.

I feel a little off kilter. She knows I'm after her money then.

Crap.

The bartender delivers two *large* chocolate martinis, gaze lingering on Heather, before moving away. She's oblivious to the attention she's getting. She tilts her head, studying my face. "You are just the prettiest thing."

I've never liked when people comment on my looks. It always feels like they're only supplying half of the sentence.

You're pretty, but you're chubby.

She sips her drink. "I love your outfit. What is this style?"

I look down at my thick cardigan and pleated skirt. "Granny chic."

Heather laughs. "Is that a thing?"

I grin despite myself. "Yes, actually. It's called cottagecore."

She nods, smiling ear to ear. "You're doing grandma chic and I'm doing early pre-menopausal chic."

I sip my martini, avoiding the cookie straw. "I spend way too much time deep-diving fashion trends."

"Is this your favorite?"

I shake my head. "No. I usually do fairycore." I grin at her expression. "Think ultra girly. Silk and tulle. Puffy sleeves. Crocheted stuff."

"Can you show me?"

"Sure." I pull out my phone and show her some pictures from the music festival my friends and I went to over the summer.

"I love that." She says. "I need to go shopping. Apparently, I'm going to have to start upping my efforts. Maybe I'll drag you with me."

She's smiling, but there's a tightness around her eyes. I don't know much about her, but Ed gave me the gist. Recently divorced. New to the city. Blew in like a hayseed from a small town.

Not just any small town—the one I grew up in.

That's why Ed is trusting me with a big fish like this when normally, he barely allows me to use the stapler. But he thinks I'll have an in with this Silver Bend expat.

I could tell you every last fact about the kids who were in my class. Where they sat during lunch. Who dated who. But as for my dad's generation? I tune him out when he talks about them. I'm seriously regretting that as I struggle to place Heather. She's noticeable. Beautiful. Surely, I would have seen her around. She's a Thomas. Maybe a cousin to someone?

Heather takes another sip of her martini. "So, why songbirds, Andy? Did you study ornithology?"

"No, not at all. I was a journalism major." I let my finger draw along the stem of my drink. "I kind of lucked into the job, to be honest. My grandma was an avid birdwatcher, though. She passed that love onto my mom and me. Working for the Songbird Foundation feels like I'm carrying on her legacy."

Heather nods. "It must help you feel close to her."

"It really does." I glance at her. "I should ask you the same question. What drew you to the Songbird Foundation?"

"I've always been a bird watcher, too. I don't know their names or anything, but I've always loved watching them. They're so... free."

I came into this meeting with a lot of expectations. Rich white ladies. They carry a reputation.

I didn't expect to be drawn to this woman the way that I am. And I did not expect the sorrow on that face to hit me so hard.

Heather glances at me and laughs. "Girl, look at you. Cheer up. We should be celebrating."

"Celebrating what?"

She leans in, grinning like a kid with a big secret. "Celebrating the eighty acres of Thorne county dirt I'm about to dedicate to the Songbird Foundation."

I blanch.

My dad is an accountant in Thorne county. I know exactly how much one acre of land is worth in that black-dirt, water-rich county.

I came in here hoping to walk away with a check for ten thousand. Maybe twenty-five.

Eighty acres. I do the math in my head.

That's almost 1.1 million dollars.

Heather laughs at my expression. "This is in honor of my husband, who is a magnificent piece of shit."

She holds her drink up until I belatedly lift mine, clinking the rim of my glass against hers.

She laughs to herself. "This will drive him crazy."

3.

Bo

"Son of a bitch."

My dad has always been known to swear, but there's a heat to those words this time that catches my attention.

I set the coffeepot back down, holding my mug in both hands.

He's standing in the kitchen doorway, holding a letter in his hands.

"Fuck. Fuck it all." He tosses the letter down. I watch him pace like a caged lion before he turns and grabs his empty coffee mug. He reels back, momentarily looking like a quarterback again, before throwing it with a beautiful spiral.

It shatters against the cabinets.

Well, fuck me. I survey the damage before glancing back at him. "I'm not cleaning that up."

He huffs, somewhat deflated. Turning back to the counter, he grabs the letter and hands it to me.

It comes on legal letterhead. I skim the contents, looking up at him with pure confusion on my face. "What the fuck is the Songbird Foundation and why did you commit eighty acres?"

He gives me a sour smile. "*I* didn't. That's the Warton eighty.*"

My stomach drops. Of all the acres we own, that little patch of ground is hands down my favorite. Ever since I was twelve years old, I've occupied my mind by imagining the house I'm going to build out there one day. The pond I'm going to stock with bluegill.

"What's this mean? Did we sell it?"

"No. Your mother committed it to the Foundation."

"So, let's uncommit it."

"We can't. That's legally binding. She owns that land, Bo. She got it in the divorce."

My hands feel sweaty. I haven't had the heart to look at the divorce settlement. I knew my mom took a healthy chunk of land with her, but we were going to keep farming it for her. To be honest, just having her leave us was hard enough. Seeing how our family heritage got chopped up was too much to face.

Dad leans against the counter. "We can either go with it or give up the rental rights."

"Rental rights? We can't farm ground that's a dedicated wildlife habitat."

Guys will occasionally work with wildlife foundations and the county to dedicate ground to the squirrels and crows. Usually, it's some dry ass corner of untenable land.

The Warton eighty is irrigated ground. We just put a well out there five years back. Eighty thousand down the drain.

Maybe she doesn't know which field she donated. I know she's pissed at dad, but this feels almost aimed at me. "I'm going to call her."

"Good luck, bud."

Leaving dad to sweep up his temper tantrum, I step into the front sitting room and dial her number.

I haven't spoken to her in weeks. It's been too hard.

She picks up on the second ring. "Bo."

That one word packs a punch. I miss the melodic sound of her voice. I hate the sadness I hear there.

I wish my parents could just get over whatever shit is between them and fix it. They might not have been happy before, but they're sure as shit not happy now.

"We got your letter."

"My letter?" She pauses. "The Songbird Foundation?"

"Did you realize you dedicated the Warton eighty? That's the one east of town with the little pond…"

"I know exactly where it is."

The hardness in her voice scrapes against me, grinding against an open wound. "Then you know that's the piece of ground I always planned to build on."

She's quiet.

I hoped for a denial.

Hoped that once she realized she was hurting me too, she'd back off.

"I know, baby. But you'll find another place to build."

"Can't you pick another spot?"

"No."

"Why not?"

She sighs. "Ask your dad."

My mind is reeling. She was always the picture of patience with us Thomas boys, my dad included. This hard woman is in direct contrast to the big softy I grew up with.

I get off the phone and find my dad pouring himself whiskey.

He scans my face, shaking his head. "Won't budge?"

"She says you'd know why it's got to be the Warton eighty."

He laughs at that, knocking back a gulp of alcohol. "How's your buddy? The one with the new baby."

I run my hand through my hair, irritated. "Josh? They're doing good."

"What'd they have?"

"A girl."

Dad smiles fondly. "I always wanted a daughter. Maybe I'll get a granddaughter. That's assuming one of my boys can figure out how to get married."

I've been feeling the growing pressure to find a woman. It seems like everyone around me is either getting married or having kids. I figured I'd start looking one of these days.

He's not exactly painting a rosy picture for marriage at the moment.

Dad finishes his whiskey and sets the glass in the sink.

"That's where I proposed to your mother."

"The Warton eighty?"

He nods.

"She's making a point, then."

He turns, not quite hiding the pain in his gray eyes. "You got it."

4.

I don't really go to church anymore.

Just Christmas.

Easter.

And funerals.

I stare at the front of the church, looking at the spot where *her* casket sat. The casket is gone, but the memory just won't fade.

Tearing my gaze away, I scan the church, counting up the number of classmates that still live in Silver Bend.

There's Josh Olson. Big as an ox sitting next to a redhead I don't recognize.

Skyler Thomas sits in the same place his family has sat for the last twenty years. Probably longer than that.

I scan the pews to the right, knowing who I'll see, hoping I won't.

Bo Thomas. Skyler's cousin.

They were both in my grade. We grew up together. I knew them when they wore Velcro shoes and they knew me when I had a tendency to get carsick on the school bus.

I know them better than that, but some of the memories I'd rather not revisit.

Bo suddenly stands, cupping a perfect little bundle to his chest.

That sweet little newborn baby girl looks perfect in his arms, snuggled up against his chest. He paces the aisle on the side, bouncing that baby with a natural ease that seems impossible for such a big guy. Nobody seems particularly interested in his movements. Must be a regular occurrence.

An irrational stab of jealousy cuts through me.

I don't know who his wife is, but I already hate her.

She's probably thin as a rail and beautiful.

I take a deep breath, reminding myself that I hate this guy. There is absolutely nothing to be jealous of. Let that other woman have him.

But damn if he hasn't filled out since high school.

He was always fit. Quarterbacks tend to be in pretty good shape. But back then he was lanky and leggy. He's put on a lot of muscle since then, his shoulders seem wider. He even has a short beard.

It looks irritatingly good on his square jaw.

He's transformed from a heartbreakingly cute high school kid to breathtakingly handsome *man*. It just proves the point—Mother Nature plays favorites.

His hands pat gentle circles on the little baby's back and he lifts his eyes, catching me staring.

Aw, fuck.

Instant embarrassment.

I slouch a little, leaning closer to my dad.

For the rest of the sermon, I make a pointed effort not to look at Bo.

And when people start filing out, I hide behind my dad, hoping Bo won't notice me.

He does.

I blush, hoping he won't stop to talk to me.

He does.

"Andy Reed. I haven't seen you in years."

His wife must have the baby, because those hands rest easily at his sides. Long fingers with a dark tan despite the chill in the air.

"Yeah. Crazy." I say, trying to follow dad out. Like a traitor, dad stops over to talk to an old classmate about fishing, leaving me alone with Bo.

He shoves a hand in his pocket. "How long has it been?"

I stare up at him. Was he always this tall? He has at least a foot on me. "Since graduation? Eight years."

"Damn." He sighs. Wincing, he glances back at the cross behind the altar. "Darn."

I grin, and he catches me, matching my smile with a blinding grin of his own.

"You have a baby." I blurt, trying to keep the conversation rolling so that we can *end* it and I can move on.

"Belle? No. She's not mine." He grins, rubbing the back of his neck. "She's Josh and Erin's little girl."

"Erin?"

"He remarried… after Ana…"

Every time I remember Ana passed away, it's a fresh surprise. Unnerving and heartbreaking. She was in the grade below us, so I didn't know her that well, but she always stood out.

She was an athlete. So dogged and strong. It seems impossible. How can someone so vibrant and young just pass away like that?

I glance over, finding Josh standing with his arm around his new wife. She's a curvy little thing.

"He seems happy."

Bo nods. "Yeah. He is. I'm happy for him. He deserved something good after all that." He looks back at me, compassion thick in those dark eyes. "I'm sorry about your mom."

"Oh. Yeah. That was…" Words dry up. My gaze slides back to the front of the church, where her pure white coffin sat under a cascade of flowers.

"I felt bad about missing the funeral. Skyler and I were overseas when we heard about it."

I tilt my head, staring up at him. Why would the Thomas boys feel compelled to go to my mom's funeral? Sure, we were classmates. But her car crash had nothing to do with them. Just a deer and icy roads. The wrong place at the wrong time.

"She was the most reluctant Sunday school teacher we ever had. And both of our favorite. Hands down."

"Oh, right."

"That accent." He chuckles softly.

My mother was born and raised in Germany. I mimic her voice. "Ich zahl jetzt bis drei!"

"That's the one. Skyler and I heard it all the time. What was she saying, anyway?"

I smile. "She was counting to three."

He grins with a familiarity that I find infuriating.

He doesn't have a right to look at me like that.

After all these years, he shouldn't still have an effect on me.

My dad finally breaks away from his buddy. I give Bo what I hope passes for a smile. "Well. It was nice catching up with you." It wasn't. "I'll see you around."

When hell freezes over.

Want free books?

Go to https://linktr.ee/jordantrygg to sign up for Jordan's newsletter.

AUTHOR JORDAN TRYGG

Jordan just wants a PSL and an HEA.

Jordan Trygg is a romance author who loves dreaming up steamy love stories her characters. Farm-raised, Jordan lives in the big city now with her family.

You can take the girl out of the country, but you can't take the country out of the girl.

Follow Jordan on Facebook :

https://www.facebook.com/JordanTryggAuthor